BETWEEN
THE
BLADE
AND THE
HEART

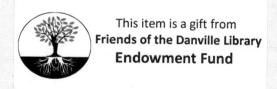

ALSO BY AMANDA HOCKING

Switched

Torn

Ascend

Wake

Lullaby

Tidal

Elegy

Frostfire

Ice Kissed

Crystal Kingdom

Freeks

BETWEEN
THE
BLADE
AND THE
HEART

AMANDA HOCKING

WEDNESDAY BOOKS
NEW YORK

BETWEEN THE BLADE AND THE HEART. Copyright © 2017 by Amanda Hocking. All rights reserved. Printed in the United States of America. For information, address St. Martin's Press, 175 Fifth Avenue, New York, N.Y. 10010.

www.stmartins.com

Designed by Devan Norman

The Library of Congress Cataloging-in-Publication Data is available upon request.

ISBN 978-1-250-08479-8 (trade paperback)
ISBN 978-1-250-08481-1 (ebook)

Our books may be purchased in bulk for promotional, educational, or business use. Please contact your local bookseller or the Macmillan Corporate and Premium Sales Department at 1-800-221-7945, extension 5442, or by email at MacmillanSpecialMarkets@macmillan.com.

First Edition: January 2018

10 9 8 7 6 5 4 3 2 1

For Mike & Gavin—for all your love and support

ACKNOWLEDGMENTS

———————— ◆ ————————

This will be the twenty-second book I've published, and while the process of writing books has gotten easier for me, writing acknowledgments is always hard. It's not because I'm not grateful or because I don't have people to thank—rather, it's the opposite. I worry that I can't properly express my gratitude, but I want to try, so here goes.

As always, first and foremost, I need to thank the readers. I am constantly moved and amazed by the responses I get from all of you—whether it be a message, a tweet, or an Instagram pic. I still can't believe that so many of you choose to spend your time with my imaginary friends, and that you love them just as much as I do. (Some of you, I think, maybe love them even more than I do.)

I still see the occasional article about me, referencing my start in self-publishing years ago, and they usually mention how I did it all on my own. But I didn't do any of this on my own. Without the amazing support from my friends, family, and readers like you propelling me forward, I would not be here writing these words today.

I want to thank my husband, Mike, and my stepson, Gavin, for understanding my long and sometimes frantic work hours, indulging all my odd obsessions, and lifting me up when I am down. Mike, in particular, does the hard work of reminding me that I'm capable of so much more than I think I am. I have a propensity to catastrophize and dramatize everything, but Mike and Gavin are both such literal people, they've made me so much more grounded and responsible. Without them both, I would be a much less happy and much less productive person, and they make even my worst days better.

My mom remains one of my strongest supporters, as does my aunt Cindy (who may be my biggest fan). My whole family in general is insanely wonderful and supportive, and I could write a whole book thanking them all. I want you to know that I love each and every one of you, and I'm so grateful for all of you.

My acknowledgments and my life would not be complete without thanking my best friend/cheerleader/former assistant, Eric. He may not work for me anymore, but he remains in my Top 5 Favorite People Ever. He's still always there to listen, offer advice on my life and my books, and make me laugh when I need it.

Of course, I have to thank all my friends who still remain unbelievably wonderful and loving, despite the fact that adult life has gotten in the way of all of us seeing each other as much as we'd like. Thank you to Fifi, Valerie, Gregg, Pete, Matthew, Josh, Gels, Mark, Lucas, Amelia, and now Baby Isabelle, Sofia, and Oliver.

I also want to give a special thank-you to my longtime editor, Rose Hilliard. She's worked with me the entire time I've been with St. Martin's, and together we've worked on twelve books and five short stories. I am a better writer now than I was five years ago, and that's in large part because of her encouragement and criticisms. She has now moved on to a different path, so this is the last book she worked on with me, but she has left an indelible mark on my life and my writing.

I want to thank the entire team at St. Martin's/Wednesday Books, including my new editor, Eileen Rothschild. Everyone there does an amazing job making my books so much better than I could do on my own, and the team always creates ridiculously beautiful covers. I am grateful to have all of them championing my books.

And finally, I have to thank my dogs, Isley and Sawyer. They are by my side constantly, which means that on days when I spend long hours in my office, they're in here, too. (As I write this, Isley is snoring softly as she sleeps by my feet, while Sawyer chews on a bone two feet away.) They might not work hard, but they make my days much happier, which definitely makes my job easier.

Valkyrie: *noun /val-ˈkir-ē/ from Old Norse valkyrja, literally "chooser of the slain," referring to any of the maidens of Odin who choose the immortals to be slain and conduct them to the afterlife.*

IN THE TIME BEFORE . . .

———◆———

In the vast emptiness of space, the gods grew restless, and so they created the heavens above and the worlds below. They filled the earth with every creature imaginable, from the smallest fish in the sea to the largest dragon in the sky.

Their creations fell into two groups:

Immortals, which could be divine beings such as angels and fairies, or impious humanoids like demons and vampires, and even beasts like dragons or centaurs. They could roam the earth forever if nothing stood in their way, and rarely were mortals able to. But with the gift was one sharp restriction: They did as they were made. Evil begat evil, and good begat good, and they all acted accordingly.

Mortals, which were either humans who lacked the gifts of the gods, or animals like birds and rabbits. Their life spans were short, over in the blink of a god's eye, but unlike the immortals, they had free will. They could act as good or evil as they chose.

While many of the immortals thought of themselves as gods and goddesses and often donned the title, the only real true gods were known as the Vanir gods—a council of supreme immortal beings that ruled over the cosmos. Unlike the immortals, the Vanir gods did not live on earth, and they had no power to create or destroy life at will.

The Vanir gods had agreed to watch from above and not interfere with the squabbles among the beings, but Odin could not be swayed by the pledge he'd made to the other Vanir gods. Despite his best intentions, he'd grown very fond of the humans.

Their joys, their determination, their unwavering belief in their own prestige—Odin relished it all. But he saw they were small and frail compared to the immortal creatures that stomped over them, trampling the humans despite their conviction of their own greatness. Angel and demon alike had taken over, claiming the world for their own, and soon the humans would be all but extinct.

To protect the fragile humans he'd grown so fond of, Odin created the Valkyries. They were mortal women he bestowed with supernatural powers and weapons, passed on from mother to daughter, and they were able to slay the immortals, keeping their powers in check.

The other gods cried out, saying that Odin was playing favorites if the humans could kill the immortals at will. So an intermediary was put in place—the Eralim, angelic beings who would take orders from the gods about what immortal should be slain and when. The Eralim would give the orders to the Valkyries, so that the humans never interacted directly with the gods.

A balance descended on the world, where the supernatural lived alongside the humans. For several millennia, this balance helped create an uneasy peace, one that the Valkyries would do anything to protect.

But one misstep, even the smallest lapse in duty, could send it all into a tailspin. . . .

That is not dead which can eternal lie.
And with strange aeons even death may die.

—H. P. LOVECRAFT

ONE

————◆————

The air reeked of fermented fish and rotten fruit, thanks to the overflowing dumpster from the restaurant behind us. The polluted alley felt narrow and claustrophobic, sandwiched between skyscrapers.

In the city, it was never quiet or peaceful, even at three in the morning. There were more than thirty million humans and supernatural beings coexisting, living on top of each other. It was the only life I'd ever really known, but the noise of the congestion grated on me tonight.

My eyes were locked on the flickering neon lights of the gambling parlor across the street. The *u* in *Shibuya* had gone out, so the sign flashed Shib ya at me.

The sword sheathed at my side felt heavy, and my body felt restless and electric. I couldn't keep from fidgeting and cracked my knuckles.

"He'll be here soon," my mother, Marlow, assured me. She leaned back against the brick wall beside me, casually eating large jackfruit seeds from a brown paper sack. *Always bring a snack on a stakeout* was one of her first lessons, but I was far too nervous and excited to eat.

The thick cowl of her frayed black sweater had been pulled up like a hood, covering her cropped blond hair from the icy mist that fell on us. Her tall leather boots only went to her calf, thanks to her long legs. Her style tended to be monochromatic—black on black on black—aside from the shock of dark red lipstick.

My mother was only a few years shy of her fiftieth birthday, with almost thirty years of experience working as a Valkyrie, and she was still as strong and vital as ever. On her hip, her sword Mördare glowed a dull red through its sheath.

The sword of the Valkyries was one that appeared as if it had been broken in half—its blade only a foot long before stopping at a sharp angle. Mördare's blade was several thousand years old, forged in fires to look like red glass that would glow when the time was nigh.

My sword was called Sigrún, a present on my eighteenth birthday from Marlow. It was a bit shorter than Mördare, with a thicker blade, so it appeared stubby and fat. The handle was black utilitarian, a replacement that my mom had had custom-made from an army supply store, to match her own.

The ancient blade appeared almost black, but as it grew closer to its target, it would glow a vibrant purple. For the past hour that we'd been waiting on our stakeout, Sigrún had been glowing dully on my hip.

The mist grew heavier, soaking my long black hair. I kept the left side of my head shaved, parting my hair over to the right, and my scalp should've been freezing from the cold, but I didn't feel it. I didn't feel anything.

It had begun—the instinct of the Valkyrie, pushing aside my humanity to become a weapon. When the Valkyrie in me took over, I was little more than a scythe for the Grim Reaper of the gods.

"He's coming," Marlow said behind me, but I already knew.

The world fell into hyperfocus, and I could see every droplet of rain as it splashed toward the ground. Every sound echoed through me, from the bird flapping its wings a block away, to the club door as it groaned open.

Eleazar Bélanger stumbled out, his heavy feet clomping in the puddles. He was chubby and short, barely over four feet tall, and he would've appeared to be an average middle-aged man if it wasn't for the two knobby horns that stuck out on either side of his forehead. Graying tufts of black hair stuck out from under a bright red cap, and as he walked ahead, he had a noticeable limp favoring his right leg.

He was a Trasgu, a troublemaking goblin, and his appearance belied the strength and cunning that lurked within him. He was over three hundred years old, and today would be the day he died.

I waited in the shadows of the alley for him to cross the street. A coughing fit caused him to double over, and he braced himself against the brick wall.

I approached him quietly—this all went easier when they didn't have time to prepare. He took off his hat to use it to wipe the snot from his nose, and when he looked up at me, his green eyes flashed with understanding.

"It's you," Eleazar said in a weak, craggy voice. We'd never met, and I doubt he'd ever seen me before, but he recognized me, the way they all did when their time was up.

"Eleazar Bélanger, you have been chosen to die," I said, reciting my script, the words automatic and cold on my lips. "It is my duty to return you to the darkness from whence you came."

"No, wait!" He held up his pudgy hands at me. "I have money. I can pay you. We can work this out."

"This is not my decision to make," I said as I pulled the sword from my sheath.

His eyes widened as he realized I couldn't be bargained with. For a moment I thought he might just accept his fate, but they rarely did. He bowed his head and ran at me like a goat. He was stronger than he looked and caused me to stumble back a step, but he didn't have anywhere to go.

My mother stood blocking the mouth of the alley, in case I needed her. Eleazar tried to run toward the other end, but his leg slowed him, and I easily overtook him. Using the handle of my sword, I cracked him on the back of the skull, and he fell to the ground on his knees.

Sigrún glowed brightly, with light shining out from it and causing the air to glow purple around us. Eleazar mumbled a prayer to the Vanir gods. I held the sword with both hands, and I struck it across his neck, decapitating him.

And then, finally, the electricity that had filled my body, making my muscles quiver and my bones ache, left me, and I breathed in deeply. The corpse of an immortal goblin lay in a puddle at my feet, and I felt nothing but relief.

"It was a good return," my mother said, and put her hand on my shoulder. "You did well, Malin."

TWO

———— ◆ ————

The crimson of the early morning sun glittered off the windows of the skyscrapers that towered above, making the glass look like fragmented rubies. In the heart of the city, dwarfed by all the buildings around it, sat the Evig Riksdag—the eternal parliament. Colloquially referred to as the Riks by Valkyries, it was where we all reported and got our orders from the Eralim.

The building's design made it similar to a concrete mushroom, with the lower twenty floors narrow and almost windowless, while the top ten floors extended far past the base, held up by metal beams. It was a feat of engineering that the top-heavy building didn't topple over. The austere appearance lent itself more to a government prison than to a place of celestial intervention.

A small computer screen was posted next to the front door, and I placed my hand on it. A beam of light flashed hotly over my hand, analyzing it, then the screen flashed green. The thick steel doors slowly slid open, and Marlow and I walked inside.

The lobby was deserted, save for the half dozen armed guards that were posted around the doors. Their black uniforms all had the same insignia on their shoulders—an eagle with the three horns of Odin. It was the symbol of the Vörðr, the powerful police force of the Evig Riksdag, mostly made up of sons of Valkyries.

The solid concrete walls enclosing the lobby gave the room a bunkerlike feel, but the black marble floors swirling with copper added a touch of elegance. Two bronze statues—men brandishing long swords, hunched under the shroud of their massive wings—were the only décor in the entire space.

But the Riksdag wasn't the kind of place that encouraged loitering or visitors of any kind. Security was of the highest priority. There had been many attacks by immortals against the Riks, some that resulted in deaths of the Eralim and Valkyries that ran it, which was why the Vörðr needed to be the most elite police force in the world.

Many immortals took umbrage with the idea of being "returned," which was the vernacular the Riks used for killing. We weren't murderers—we were simply returning the immortals back to a world where they belonged.

Marlow and I took the elevator to the twenty-ninth floor, where we were greeted with a retinal scan before we could exit. A long corridor stretched out before us—more black marble floors and copper walls closing in on us. At the very end was a massive bronze door, and on either side stood Samael's personal bodyguards.

Godfrey Wright was the larger of the two, but both were hulking. Godfrey stood well over seven feet tall, with bulging arms and a shaved cranium. But what people usually noticed first was that he was a cyclops, with a solitary large eye above his nose.

The smaller and younger guard was Atlas Malosi. With light brown skin and cropped black hair, he had an open face and glittering dark eyes that made him appear much too friendly to be a guard.

He was the son of a Valkyrie, so he had the strength and height of one, but none of the supernatural ability that would make it possible for him to slay immortals. Only daughters could wield such power.

"How are you ladies doing this lovely morning?" Atlas asked, with a broad grin to match his broad shoulders.

"Just finished the job," I replied.

"I assume that it all went well for you." Atlas continued grinning.

"Is Samael in?" Marlow asked, cutting Atlas's chatter.

The smile finally fell from Atlas's face. "You know Samael. He's always in."

Godfrey was a man of few words, so he merely let out a grunt of agreement and gestured toward the door.

"Thank you." I smiled politely at the guards, but Marlow was already opening the door and heading into Samael's spacious office.

Samael had been assigned as my Eralim, because he'd been my mother's before me. His office was sparsely furnished—a large desk in front of the glass wall that overlooked the city, a few art deco chairs and a sofa, and objets d'art he'd collected over the centuries displayed on the shelves that lined the walls.

Samael himself was sprawled out on the black velvet sofa, absently reading something on his electronic tablet, but he broke out in a smile when he spotted us. While Samael was well over three hundred years old, he didn't look a day over twenty-five.

Lounging in black slacks and a dress shirt with the sleeves rolled up, he looked more like a college kid playing at grown-up than an experienced supervisor. Adding to that, he was incredibly handsome, with warm umber skin, bright aqua eyes beneath a strong brow, and a mass of shoulder-length chestnut curls with natural blond highlights coursing through.

His full lips always seemed on the edge of a smirk, one that even my stoic mother couldn't resist. As he walked over to greet us, Marlow pushed down her cowled hood and smiled brazenly at him.

"How is it that you always manage to look so beautiful, even this early in the morning?" Samael mused, his eyes locked on my mother.

I rolled my eyes and sat in one of the several uncomfortable three-legged armchairs. I leaned back, propping my black moto boots up on the glass table to wait out Marlow and Samael's flirtation.

"You know work always brings out the best in me." Marlow smiled demurely at Samael, then turned and sauntered away from him, toward his desk.

He kept a crystal bowl on his desk, perpetually filled with treats like red bean paste covered in gold leaf or baby scorpions dipped in chocolate. As Samael turned his attention to me, Marlow grabbed a handful of whatever delicacy he had today, and as he spoke, she absently munched on it.

"So, Malin, how did it go?" Samael asked me.

I looked past him to my mother, searching her expression for clues as to how she thought it went, but she just stared down impassively at the morsels in her hand.

"He's dead, so I think it went about as well as it could have," I said finally.

"*Returned*," Samael corrected me, then cast his eyes toward the ceiling, as if someone upstairs cared enough to eavesdrop on us. "He's returned, not dead."

The immortals weren't killed—they merely shed their mortal coil in a way that meant they could never walk the earth again.

That was one of the basic tenets of the world we lived in, and one of the first things we were taught in grade school. The gods had given us dominion over the earth, where humans, animals, and supernatural beings were all supposed to live in harmony as much as we could.

Valkyries were instated to return immortals to another realm— to an underworld called Kurnugia—and they could not come back.

Mortals couldn't return from the dead, either, but that was mostly because we had no afterworld.

That was how things were kept "fair." Immortals returned to Kurnugia, but mortals could not. When we died, we were left to rot in the dirt.

The dead must stay dead. That which is dead cannot rise.

"If you're going to be a Valkyrie, you'll have to get the lingo down," Samael went on.

"I *am* a Valkyrie," I replied pointedly.

"It may be in your blood, but it's not your job title yet," Samael said, sitting back down on the sofa across from me. "You know how the folks upstairs love paperwork and procedure."

"That they do," Marlow snorted in agreement, but I already had plenty of experience with the bureaucracy of the Evig Riksdag.

My training in their protocol had begun shortly after my eighteenth birthday, with classes at Ravenswood Academy, and it had still taken almost a year before I was able to start apprenticing alongside my mother. Then it had been another six months of testing and training and red tape before I had finally gotten a permit and been allowed to make kills, as long as it was under the close supervision of Marlow.

Since then I had killed—or, rather, *returned*—four immortals. Eleazar Bélanger had been my fifth.

"How are you taking to it, then?" Samael leaned forward, resting his arms on his knees, and something in the softness of his voice led me to believe what he was really asking was how I was coping.

There had been an entire course at Ravenswood Academy called Guilt and How to Handle It, and we discussed how some Valkyries couldn't deal with it. The responsibility of being an executioner was too much.

But I'd never felt guilt. I'd never felt anything but purpose. My

body was made to do this, and when there was too much time between jobs, I began to *crave* it. The way the electricity felt coursing
through me, the buzzing around my heart, the way the pressure
felt growing inside of me that wouldn't stop until I completed my
mission.

It was all relief and release.

"I can't imagine doing anything else," I admitted.

Samael looked back over his shoulder at my mother. "You think
she's doing well enough to go on her own soon?"

"She's ready to go now." Marlow absently brushed at the crumbs
on her black pants. "I know the Riksdag wants her to have seven
returns under her belt, so I'll be happy to shadow for the next two,
but she doesn't need me."

Samael looked back at me, grinning. "Well, it sounds like you'll
be a Valkyrie *very* soon."

My mother looked up, pride flashing momentarily in her dark
gray eyes. "She was born for it."

THREE

———◆———

The city had outgrown the land, and a century or so ago it had expanded out onto the lake. I'm sure the engineer behind the New Edgewater development had visions of romantic architecture with canal streets, like Venice or St. Petersburg, but the reality had become something much different.

The water had become polluted, and it smelled of gasoline and dead fish, and the wealthy elites had fled. The condominiums and apartments that towered around me, scraping the clouds overhead, had become run-down and decrepit. Broken windows and rusty fire escapes, with clotheslines running from building to building.

Vehicles sped by on the canals, splashing filthy water onto the sidewalks. It was all old yellow taxis, hovercrafts, and luftfahrrads—motorcycles that hovered a few inches above the surface of the water.

Somewhere a baby was crying. In New Edgewater, there was always a baby crying somewhere within earshot. There was a large population of pontianaks here, and they lured victims with the sound of a crying infant.

It was getting late, but I walked slowly down the crowded sidewalks away from my apartment. As much as I loved working as a Valkyrie, it always took something out of me, and I crashed for hours after.

The garage would be closed by the time I got there, but the stack of silvery blue bills in my pocket would open the doors. Samael always paid me with freshly minted money, and I often wondered what became of the old worn dollars. Did the Riks shred them and constantly print their own money?

Above me, the overcast sky rumbled ominously. The lights from the city made the clouds glow orange and red, and I quickened my pace. I had only a block left to go when the sky opened up with angry, cold raindrops.

Galel's Garage was right on the edge of where dry land met the lake, and I jogged over to it. The plate-glass window proudly proclaimed that Galel's Garage had been serving the New Edgewater community for over 125 years, but that kind of thing was easier to do when you were immortal.

"We're closed!" a voice boomed from the garage as I stepped into the front lobby.

"I thought you might make an exception for your favorite customer," I said hopefully, and a few moments later Jude Locklear came in through the garage door, bowing his head slightly so his horns wouldn't hit the frame, as he dried his hands on a frayed towel.

His oil-stained overalls were rolled down to his hips, and his white tank top stretched taut over his chest and stood out sharply against his dark olive skin. Jude towered over me, with broad shoulders and biceps the size of tree trunks. His black hair fell in waves that landed just above his shoulders, and his dark eyebrows were always perfectly arched in a look of suggestive amusement.

At first glance, he looked like an ordinary guy—albeit a very muscular and very tall guy—in his early twenties. It was only the two massive ram's horns that curled out from the side of his head that revealed his true heritage as a Cambion, the son of a demon.

His father, Galel, was an incubus, to be precise, and someday his name might show up on Samael's orders to me. But Jude's never would, since he was mortal like his mother. Jude had only inherited his horns and his undeniable sex appeal from his father.

Well, that and his ability to fix nearly any vehicle in a short amount of time for a reasonable price.

"You're late." Jude grinned slowly at me, and there was an irresistible sparkle in his dark brown eyes every time he smiled.

"I overslept, and then I got caught in the rain." I motioned to the rain pounding against the glass behind me.

His eyes flitted over my body, at the clothes sticking wet to my skin, and I arched my back slightly, pushing out my chest. He smiled approvingly before tossing the towel at me.

"Dry yourself off, then I'll show you what I did with your luft." He turned, and I followed him into the garage as I ran the towel through my hair.

My luftfahrrad was a Frankenstein of a hoverbike, with parts from all kinds of old bikes and vehicles pieced together to somehow make a working luft, including a chrome skull between the handlebars. Jude himself had been the one to do most of the work, following my requests to get it done as cheaply as possible. It was actually a credit to his skill that the damned thing ever ran.

"You know, I don't mind seeing you every few weeks to duct-tape some new problem you have," Jude said as he finished explaining all the new adjustments he'd made to keep it afloat. "But I'd be a shitty mechanic if I didn't point out that it would be cheaper just to buy a new luft than to keep getting this one fixed up."

I pulled my cash out of my pocket and ignored his suggestion, the way I did every time he made it. "How much do I owe you this time?"

He rubbed the back of his neck and glanced over at the clock hanging on the wall. "It's getting late. Why don't we go out and get a drink, and we can settle up later?"

I smiled. "If that's what you want, it sounds fun to me."

"Just let me change, and we'll get out of here."

FOUR

————◆————

On the chipped-paint sign above the door, the name CARPE NOCTEM was barely legible. The brick façade was cracked and crumbling, and the large front window had been boarded up, with *yes, we're open* spray-painted across it.

Everything about the exterior looked ancient, except for the sign on the door, declaring that they served liliplum here. And even that had faded to lavender from bright purple, since it had been five years since liliplum was legalized.

Barstools were held together with duct tape, and broken glass littered the sticky floor. Despite the subpar décor and angry thumping of music through the stereo, the bar was always packed.

The clientele were mostly regulars, or at least it seemed to me that I always saw the same folks when I came here with Jude. Mostly big, burly, and male, wearing tattered leather and denim. Some were obviously craven, with horns and fangs and monstrous appendages, but others were just regular humans looking to escape the monotony of the nearby slums.

A place like this one might expect to smell like cheap beer and body odor—and it did, but only slightly, buried deep beneath the sweet floral and clove scent of the liliplum. In the corner of the bar, behind a curtain of beads, was the hookah bar, where patrons smoked the liliplum, and its dark violet smoke filled the room.

Jude found two open seats at the bar, and a waitress with large raven's wings growing from her back and a septum piercing came over to glare at us. He gruffly ordered a bottle of the cheapest beer, and when she set her angry-bird eyes on me, I ordered the same.

"How is work?" Jude asked, after the waitress had rolled her eyes and left us to retrieve our beer.

"It's good," I replied carefully.

Jude knew what I did, and he claimed he didn't care. But many others didn't think so highly of Valkyries, particularly immortal cravens like the kind that frequented this bar. After all, someday in the future, I might be the one to kill them.

"That'll be fifteen bucks," the waitress said, sounding both bored and pissed off as she set two lukewarm bottles of Dante's Lager in front of us. I put a twenty down on the bar, but the waitress had already sauntered off to be irritated by some other customer.

Jude took a long drink of his beer, grimacing as he swallowed it down. I followed suit, drinking down the tepid alcohol. It tasted like old socks but with a heat at the end that made my eyes water. Jude laughed and patted me heartily on the back, his massive hand feeling warm and powerful even through my jacket.

"Dante's Lager is an acquired taste," Jude admitted.

I wiped my mouth with the back of my arm. "Well, it is not a taste I wish to acquire." He laughed again, a warm rumble that seemed to permeate everything.

Jude motioned to the crisp twenty-dollar bill that the waitress had yet to collect. "I take it that you were working last night?"

I nodded, and despite the burning in my throat, I ventured taking another drink, gulping it down quickly.

"Anyone I know?" Jude asked. He was smiling, but there was a twisting at the corner of his lips and his eyes were downcast.

When people found out I was a Valkyrie, they usually reacted in three ways: anger, disgust, or curiosity. Sometimes it started out as one, then turned into another.

But I was already used to hearing the same questions over and over again.

Have you killed anyone?

What's it like to kill?

Don't you feel bad about it?

And then: *Would you kill me?*

So I tried to avoid the questions as much as possible, because nobody ever liked the answer to each.

Yes.

Like sex, only better.

No.

Yes, I would. And I will, if your name shows up on my orders.

"You know I don't like talking about work," I reminded Jude. We'd been friendly for a while, so this wasn't the first time it had come up.

Jude held his hand up in a gesture of peace. "Hey, I'm not one to judge. I don't care how people live their lives and make their money."

"I don't do it for the money," I replied quickly, maybe too quickly.

I was no mercenary, and I hated that people made that assumption. Yes, I got paid for my services, but it wasn't enough to make my rent, and most Valkyries had to have a second job. The paycheck just offset some of our costs, but the truth was that we'd all do it whether we got paid or not.

We were compelled to do it. We needed to do it the same way we needed to breathe.

"My old man always said that if you love what you do, you'll never work a day in your life," Jude said, breaking the uncomfortable silence that had settled over us. "But then again, my dad's also an incubus who works on the side banging women to steal their souls and valuables."

"It sounds like he's got life figured out, then," I muttered.

Jude chugged the last of his beer, then slammed the empty bottle on the bar. "That was shite. Wanna get some liliplum?"

He'd barely gotten the words out before I was already hopping off the barstool and chirping, "Yes, please."

Jude laughed and followed me back through the beaded curtains into the cloud of purple. People were sitting around on overstuffed couches, with the hookahs on tables in the center. The hookahs looked like tall, slender vases, with two hoses coming out of the glass base of each, and everyone was talking and laughing between drags on the hoses.

There wasn't a lot of room, and Jude took up a lot of space, so I sat on the arm of the couch beside him. He took a drag first before handing me the hose, and I inhaled deeply. It was like breathing in a campfire and a bouquet of flowers.

And then already I was feeling it and I sank back on the couch. It was like two shots of vodka, without the burning in the throat or the hangover. It was just lightness and calm, and it wrapped itself around me like a warm blanket.

Back here, the anger of the demonic metal band was replaced with something more melodic and velvety: the voice of a woman, sultry and slow, and the way her words went through me, softening the beating of my heart, made me wonder if she was a siren.

"Come on, Malin, you're not usually a lightweight." Jude's voice rumbled in my ear as he chuckled. His horn brushed against me, cold and hard on my temple, and I closed my eyes and leaned against him. His arm wrapped around me, steadying me. "I've seen you drink ogres under the table before."

"The lili hits me harder," I told him honestly. I usually only saved it for special occasions, and maybe tonight felt special because of my work this morning, or maybe I just didn't want to talk to Jude about it anymore, or maybe I just didn't want to talk.

I just wanted to fall into his arms, the way he would let me, and I knew he would carry me back to his place and do the things that only he seemed to know how to do.

I opened my eyes, preparing to yield to the temptation, to invite myself to his place, when the beaded curtains parted in front of us, and *she* walked in.

FIVE

Quinn Evelyn Devane.

A Valkyrie with long hair dyed silver, so it shimmered and danced in the light, except where her roots grew in black. Her mouth was slightly lopsided, and on other people that might look silly or strange, but on her it just looked like she had a wonderful secret and she was daring you to find out what it was.

She was tall, taller than me, even, with powerful legs that went on for days. Across her collarbone ran a dark red scar, and below that she revealed more than a hint of her ample cleavage.

Around her neck she wore a silver amulet inscribed with the Vegvisir—the Norse symbol of protection.

In the very center was a solitary red garnet that seemed to follow me everywhere I looked.

I was hoping she wouldn't see me, as if somehow, even though she was standing right in front of me, I would be able to disappear completely into Jude's arms. But then her eyes landed on me—bright green eyes, like a meadow in spring—and my breath caught in my throat.

"Malin," Quinn said, smiling her asymmetric smile. Her voice was low and husky, but it managed to carry over the music, and she sat down on the table across from me. "I haven't seen you since . . ."

She trailed off, and my heart pounded in my chest. Inside my head I was screaming, *Don't say it. Please don't say it. Please don't say "since we broke up."*

It was not because I was ashamed or I didn't want Jude to know—I didn't really care what he'd think, but I also knew he wouldn't care at all.

I just wasn't ready to talk about it. It had only been six months since we'd broken up, and I still didn't know how I felt about any of that.

"How do you two know each other?" Jude asked, probably since it seemed like I might not say anything ever again. He pulled his arm from around my waist so he could lean forward, and when Quinn crossed her legs, her foot brushed against mine, so I sat up straighter.

"I'm a Valkyrie," Quinn explained, not lowering her voice when she said that, the way I always did when I was in mixed company like this. "I was licensed a few years ago, so I was helping show Malin the ropes."

"Is Malin any good?" Jude asked, teasing.

Quinn's eyes were on me, sparkling underneath the veil of her dark lashes. "She's very good."

"It was nice seeing you, but I think we were just heading out." I stumbled to my feet. The heady intoxication from the liliplum was mixing with the muddled exhilaration I felt whenever I was around Quinn, and I couldn't handle the combination anymore.

Quinn was on her feet in a flash, blocking my path. "I was hoping we could talk."

"Not today." I shook my head. "I can't today."

"When?" she pressed as I walked around her.

"Later," I called back over my shoulder, and I'd taken Jude's hand so I could pull him through the bar and out into the street.

It wasn't until we were outside, in the pouring rain, that I felt like I could breathe again. The cold helped push away some of the haze, sobering me up.

"So what's with you and that Valkyrie back there?" Jude asked. "You were acting like she was a monster or an ex-girlfriend or something."

"She *is* my ex-girlfriend," I muttered.

"Oh. Well, that explains that, then." He stood beside me for a second, not saying anything. "Do you want to get out of this rain and come back to my place?"

"I would be happy to go anywhere with you, as long as it's not here."

Jude laughed as we started walking in the rain toward his apartment over the garage. "That's the kind of thing every guy can't wait to hear."

SIX

My phone pulsated on the nightstand. The table was made out of bones—Jude claimed they were bones from his own ancestors—with a plate of glass on top, and the screen of my phone made the skulls glow blue.

I picked up my phone to see about a dozen text messages from my best friend/roommate Oona Warren.

Are you coming home tonight?

Where are you even?

I'm guessing you're not coming home tonight, so I went ahead and fed Bowie. I'm assuming that you went home with Jude again.

Just so I know you're not murdered or dead in the lake, you should text me and let me know.

Seriously, Mal. It's morning now. What are you doing?

You have class this morning.

Malin. Text me so I can stop worrying.

"Shit." I groaned, and, pushing the fog of sleep and a burgeoning hangover aside, I got out of bed.

In the darkness of Jude's bedroom, I scrambled to pull on my pants. I'd just gotten my bra on when Jude began to rouse in the bed.

"Where are you going so early?" Jude suppressed a yawn.

I sat on the edge of his bed, yanking on my moto boots and brushing back the tangles of long hair from my face. "It's not early. It's a quarter past eight, and I'm gonna be late for class."

"Class?" Jude asked, sounding more alert. "Wait, you aren't in high school, are you?"

"College," I replied, but Ravenswood Academy was much more of a trade school than a university. It was only for kids studying to work for the Evig Riksdag or other government agencies that dealt with the supernatural elements of our world.

I stood up and grabbed my jacket from the floor. "I still have to get my luft out of the shop."

"Just go in and tell my dad that I sent you to get it."

"Thanks." I dug in my jacket pocket and pulled out a small handful of twenties, and I set it on the nightstand. "I'm leaving the money here for you."

"Damn, Malin, you really know how to make a guy feel like a prostitute," Jude said with his rumbling laughter, but I was already on my way out the door, hurriedly texting Oona before she gave herself a heart attack worrying about me.

At the garage, Jude's dad wasn't so keen on letting me just run off with the luft, but after a quick call to Jude, he grudgingly let me go. The luft started hard, grumbling angrily at me, before kicking out a plume of mist and exhaust, and the wheel-like propulsion fans glowed a dull blue beneath the carriage.

Finally, it levitated off the ground, just above the six inches it would need to be street-legal. I throttled it back and flew down the road toward the academy. At this time of day, traffic could get locked up in the Ravenswood District, but with my luft I was able to swerve around a stalled-out bus and go up on the curb.

The sidewalks were crowded with merchants selling their wares, along with patrons and pedestrians just trying to get by. I narrowly slid past a woman selling brightly colored rainbow snakes out of tubs, claiming they were the mystical descendants of the Wagyl.

I managed to hit the brakes just before crashing into a food cart with a man selling sambusa. Sambusa were fried triangular pastry filled with delicious lentils and potatoes, and even though I was running late, my stomach warned me that I needed to eat something.

"I'll take one," I said as I rummaged in my pocket for money.

The man stood there glaring at me for a moment, but finally he took my money and handed me a sambusa, before muttering, "*Sharmoto.*"

"If you're gonna call me names, then give me my tip back." I held my hand out to him.

"You almost killed me, you crazy woman!" He waved his hands wildly at me. "Get out of here with your stupid bike!"

I didn't really have time to argue, and he was right, so maybe I should've tipped him more. I held the sambusa in my mouth, offered the merchant a small wave, then revved up my luft and sped off down the road to Ravenswood.

The whole area around Ravenswood was high-rise low-income apartment complexes, with a few offices and shops on the lower levels. And there was the Ravenswood Academy. It was an Elizabethan Prodigy house—a massive Tudor-style mansion that looked more like it belonged in the English countryside than in the slums of the city.

While the exterior was all the original architecture, meticulously maintained, the interior was more high-tech. Starting with the underground garage, where I had to pass through a blue wall of light to be certain I wasn't carrying any unapproved weapons, and then scan my school ID to get into the garage, and then scan my retinas to get into the building.

The hallway was relatively empty, and despite the high enrollment of the academy it always felt strangely quiet. The flooring was a mosaic inlay of black and white marble, and the walls were stark white with garishly bright crystal light fixtures in the ceiling.

Paintings and artwork adorned the walls, mostly from previous students and alumni, depicting some aspect of life they might be working toward here at Ravenswood, like careers or the beings they might serve.

There were several I always passed on my way up from the parking garage. One was a hanging mobile, looking a bit like a natural chandelier. Birch branches hung down, with horses carved into the white bark. According to the plaque on the wall beneath it, it was created as an offering for Bai-Ülgen.

Another was a large statue made of marble, titled *Ereshkigal of the Netherworld*. It showed a regal woman elegantly perched on a throne made of bones. The bones and the fabric that draped her body were stark white, while her skin was a darker veined gray. Her mouth was curved slightly into a smile, and even though she was made of stone, it felt like her eyes followed me whenever I walked by.

The final picture in the long hall, before I turned off to go toward my class, always made me pause. It depicted a woman in a chain-mail bikini, her body rippling with muscles and strength, and her hands covered in blood. Her hair blew out behind her, and she stared up at the sky with a smile on her face as a single red tear slid down her cheek.

The plaque on the bottom read:

"The Desire of the Valkyrie"
Painted by Marlow Krigare during her senior year

My mother had painted it.

I made it to Intro to Divinity and Immortality only five minutes late, which really didn't seem that bad, considering. Fortunately, I'd had my messenger bag with me when I went to Jude's last night, which had my e-reader with my textbooks in it and my laptop for taking notes.

I opened the door as quietly as possible, but a girl—an alchemy major named Sloane Kothari—still turned to glare at me. As the daughter of a Deva, she took her divine disposition very seriously, and unfortunately I had three courses with her this semester.

The professor, Cashel Wu, paused in his lecture to watch me take my seat at a long stainless steel table in the back. He stood in front of the classroom, with the large screen at the front displaying a huge photo of a hieroglyph.

I mouthed, *Sorry*, and got situated as quickly and quietly as I possibly could. By now plenty of other students had turned to look at me. Most of them were human, but a few obviously had more exotic parentage, with wings and tails and horns.

But even those with more prestigious pedigrees came from some sort of mixed background, for them to be accepted into Ravenswood Academy, with usually one parent being human. Almost all offspring of immortals—even from the commingling of two different types of immortals—were mere mortals, with little or none of their parents' powers.

Ravenswood was designed to educate and train mortals for

careers in handling the supernatural, which made it the go-to school for mortal children who had no hope of following in their immortal parents' more elite footsteps.

Sloane Kothari didn't have any obvious signs of her parentage, other than the cold smile and the contempt in her dark eyes whenever she looked at me.

"As we were discussing last week," Professor Wu began once I was settled in, "immortality doesn't make one divine or superior, the same way that mortality doesn't make one weak or inferior.

"In past societies, those with longer life spans or different appearances than humans were often either revered as gods or feared as monsters and forced into exile," Professor Wu continued, and as he spoke, he clicked through photos on the screen.

The pictures changed to a depiction of men bent forward, worshipping feline-headed Bastet; then to the multi-armed Vishnu, adorned in gold and jewels; to the wolf-humanoid Lobishomen, with massive fangs, being stabbed with bloody spears; and the birdlike witch Baba Yaga, being burned alive as she cried out.

"But now, in our civilized society, that is not the case. We realize immortality is no more divine than having brown eyes or a short stature." He looked back at the screen, his gaze lingering on the intense agony in Baba Yaga's face, and he frowned.

"We will be looking back through history," Professor Wu continued. "Learning the mistakes that our ancestors made when confronted with immortality, so that we don't make the mistakes ourselves."

SEVEN

———— ◆ ————

"Malin Krigare?" Professor Wu called out, stopping me as I attempted to make my escape out of the classroom. "Can I speak to you for a moment?"

The other students continued their shuffle out of the room, and Sloane snickered at me as she walked out. I took a deep breath and trudged toward the front of class, to where Professor Wu was hunched over his desk making a few notes on his tablet.

"Sorry I was late. I missed my alarm, but I hurried as fast as I could," I began my apology.

"I understand that you're close to getting your license," the professor said, finally looking up at me.

Professor Wu appeared to be in his early thirties, and his well-tailored suits made him one of the more dapper members of the teaching staff here. His black hair was cropped short, and his Vandyke goatee added an additional air of nobility.

"Yeah, it should be soon." I picked absently at my chipped indigo nail polish before adding, "Hopefully."

"Actually, I saw that your Eralim sent a glowing message to the headmaster yesterday." Professor Wu leaned back and folded his arms over his chest. "He thinks your performance is absolutely exemplary."

"That's great," I said, smiling a little, but there was something about Wu's tone that made me worry there was a "but" coming.

"*But*," Wu said, and I grimaced inwardly, "you've been late to my class three times, and school's only been in session for a few weeks."

"I know. I've just been having trouble with my luft—"

"There's always public transportation," Wu cut me off. "But that's not even the point. I've seen plenty of good kids like you, excellent students with bright futures ahead of them, who lose sight of the goal."

I shook my head. "I don't think I'm losing sight of anything."

"I checked. Your grades have been slipping this semester," Wu said, and I lowered my eyes. "You know that even if you get your preliminary license now, it will be revoked if you don't graduate."

Sighing, I nodded. "I know."

"And the Valkyrie program isn't like some of the others here at Ravenswood. You need to pass with high marks or you don't pass at all," Wu lectured. "You still have a whole year left of your courses here. I would just hate for you to lose your career over a bout of senioritis."

"You're right," I said, hating that he was. "I'll start applying myself more and taking my attendance more seriously."

Wu smiled. "That's all I ask for as your professor, Malin."

After I left, I spent my next three classes sucking up, since I knew Wu wouldn't be the only one noticing my recent flakiness, and ended up working on an extracurricular project down in the stacks. Somehow, I'd gotten suckered into annotating a book on medieval demigods, but finally a reprieve came in the form of a text from Oona.

Bowie's out of food. That was all she wrote, but the time on my phone flashing 5:47 P.M. meant that I had been at school long enough for one day.

As quickly as I could without literally running, I rushed down to the parking garage—which was now fairly deserted—got on my luft, and raced out onto the street. The sky was overcast, the way it always seemed to be these days, and the air was cold, but nothing ever felt as good as the wind blowing in my hair as I drove through the city.

I pulled into the cramped parking lot outside Dillinger's Corner Market & Apothecary, and my luft dropped unceremoniously to the pavement. Jude hadn't quite gotten the bug out of the dismount yet.

The market's door beeped as I stepped inside, and Oona looked up at me from where she sat behind the counter. An ancient textbook was spread out before her, which was typical for her, since she usually tried to get as much studying done at work as she could.

"So I guess I can call the search off," Oona replied dryly. Her thick brows were arched downward in an attempt to look angry, but her lips were already curving up into a smile.

I offered her an apologetic smile. "Sorry for worrying you."

She shrugged her slender shoulders, and an easy grin lit up her face, making her eyes sparkle. "I just get bored when you're gone for too long." To emphasize her point, she ran her hand through her new haircut.

The last time I'd seen her—which had been yesterday morning—her jet-black hair had been a little longer, but now it had been cut into a jagged pixie cut, with the curls straightened out. Oona always planned to grow her hair out, but inevitably she'd get impatient or bored and cut it all off again.

"It looks good," I said, but her hair always looked good.

Oona may have been just a human—though she took great exception to the word *just*—but she was one of the most beautiful people I'd ever seen. Her flawless complexion was creamy brown, with high cheekbones above full lips, and her eyes were the color of black walnut. Even under the unforgiving cheap fluorescent lighting she was undeniably gorgeous.

"Thanks." She beamed at me, and the light glinted off her piercings. She had two small metal studs—one on either side of her mouth, just above her lips—colloquially known as Angelbites.

We'd been best friends since the fourth grade, when her family moved down the street from me. While we'd never had a ton in common, we always made each other laugh, and I knew that I could count on her no matter what.

Since Oona was just barely over five feet tall, I liked to joke that she'd stopped growing the day we met, so I grew twice as much for her.

"How was school?" Oona asked.

"Same old, same old," I said with a sigh.

I grabbed a basket and began strolling the cramped aisles of the tiny bodega. Despite the colorful addition of *Apothecary* in the name, the market mostly stocked overpriced food and toiletries, but there was a shelf in the back with crystals, amulets, and various enchanted herbs and potions.

"How about you?" I asked, grabbing a bag of carrots for Bowie.

Bowie was my six-year-old wolpertinger, which basically meant that he was a chubby fawn-colored rabbit with large wings and a tiny pair of antlers between his big ears. Some wolpertingers could fly, but Bowie had always been too fat and preferred doing as little as possible.

She groaned. "I had a pop quiz in Laws of Intercession, which I'm fairly certain I bombed."

Oona was a thaumaturgy major with the goal of a being a great sorceress someday. Even though she went to Ravenswood, we didn't have any classes together. Her area of study tended to be more mystical, while mine was more practical.

"So, anyway, you never did tell me where you were last night," Oona reminded me.

"Just with Jude," I replied, and I didn't need to look up to know that her eyebrows were arched suggestively.

Instead, I pretended to be focused on the bag of Ēostre's Lagomorph Chow, which was alleged to be perfectly formulated for the health needs of jackalopes, wolpertingers, rabbits, pikas, and colugos, before dropping it into my basket.

"That makes it twice in a month, doesn't it?" Oona asked.

"I only see him when my luft breaks down, and it just so happens that my luft kinda sucks." I grabbed a couple packets of ramen noodles and an energy drink that claimed to be infused with the elixir of the sun, whatever the hell that meant.

"I just don't see what the big deal is, Mal," Oona said as I made my way toward the counter. "If you like this guy, what's so bad about making him your boyfriend?"

"It's just not like that." I held up the energy drink. "What do you know about this?"

"I know there's this Nephilim chick in my class, and she swears by it, but I think it's mostly mango juice." Oona shrugged. "Don't change the subject, though. I just don't know why you're so opposed to officially dating someone. I mean, Quinn was your girlfriend before."

"Yeah, and you know how that worked out," I muttered. "Valkyries—"

"—don't fall in love," Oona finished for me with a dramatic eye roll and began ringing up my purchases. "Yeah, yeah, yeah, I know. The great Malin is impervious to the desires of us mere mortals. You may have the libido of a teenage boy. . . ."

I scowled at her, which only made her laugh. "Thanks."

"You know, I've heard you say that thing about Valkyries and love at least a hundred times, but I was reading in a textbook about

Valkyries the other day, and it didn't say anything about that," Oona commented.

"Did it say anything about Valkyries' personal lives at all?" I asked.

She frowned. "Well, no. Not really."

The subject wasn't something I'd really encountered in books, either. There was usually a line or two about Valkyries being loners and isolated, since our job didn't exactly make us popular with the supernatural beings. If it was a real in-depth book, it might offer a tip or two on how to handle those that were prejudiced against us, but that was about it.

Because of the nature of our jobs—which involved occasionally killing our neighbors—we tended to be a lonely people and rather nomadic, with few connections and relationships in this world. Not being able to love made it easier on us, and we were more likely to complete our assignments if there wasn't a risk of us getting attached to them.

Or at least that's what my mom had taught me. Over and over again, since I was very young, usually when I was upset about one thing or another, Marlow would lecture me about how I needed to toughen up, and remind me that we were made of something stronger, so we didn't need love. We didn't need anything.

"I think our inability to really love is one of those things that's common knowledge for Valkyries, but it isn't really talked about outside of the circle," I told Oona with a resigned shrug of my shoulders.

As I paid for my stuff and loaded it up into my messenger bag, Oona informed me that she'd be working for another few hours, so I'd have the place to myself, which gave me time to catch up on my schoolwork.

Oona worked at the market because it was only a couple blocks from our place, and I made it to our apartment complex in record time, parking my luft in the narrow gated alleyway. As I was locking up the luft, the dumpster beside me started shaking and snarling.

I waited a beat, reaching for the asp baton I always carried in my bag, and a Dobhar-chú climbed out, with a mouthful of rotten eggs and lettuce. The Dobhar-chú looked like a cross between an otter and salamander, except with patches of scales mixed in with its slick fur and a row of angry-looking fangs in its mouth.

It stared at me with its small round ears lying flat back against its head, and its gills fanned out as it growled, as if I wanted to steal the garbage from it.

"Go on. I won't bother you," I tried to assure the water hound, but it turned tail and ran out to the canal, where it dove in and disappeared.

The Dobhar-chú and other water creatures like it were part of the reason why complexes like mine— once billed as luxury—had fallen into disrepair. The canals brought along too many pests, smells, and corrosion.

The sign across the building that read TANNHAUSER TOWERS had once been shiny gold and lit up, but all the lights had burned out and the metal began to oxidize and rust. When a strong wind blew by, the letters would groan and shake, and it really was only a matter of time before one of them fell off.

The apartment I shared with Oona was on the sixty-seventh floor, and it had once been a penthouse suite before being cut up and converted into six microscopic apartments. Ours was a dingy two-bedroom, with my room being just barely large enough for a bed and a dresser.

The front door opened into the small living room/kitchen combo, with concrete floors covered in a few worn rugs and cold metal walls that we'd attempted to warm up with a couple posters and a wall tapestry. The only really nice thing about the flat was the rather large window that took up an entire wall and overlooked the canal below.

When I came in, I expected Bowie to greet me, the way he usually did when I got home, but instead of him excitedly hopping across the floor toward me, I was met with silence. Eerie and palpable, and my body instinctively tensed.

I hadn't yet turned the light on, but thanks to all the light pollution from advertising and vehicles, the room was fairly well lit, changing from neon blue to red and back again with the billboard across the canal.

"Bowie?" I called, setting down my messenger bag on the small pile of jackets and shoes Oona and I left by the door.

Then finally I spotted him, huddled underneath the kitchen table in the corner. He stomped his foot loudly on the floor, warning me of danger, but really, I hadn't needed it. I stepped toward Bowie, wanting to get to him and protect him from whatever threat was making the hair on the back of my neck stand up.

But by then it was already too late. I saw a flash of movement in the corner of my eye, and then arms were around me, with a hand over my mouth, blocking my screams.

EIGHT

———— ◆ ————

I bucked against my attacker, kicking back and sending him flying across the room. He slammed hard into the metal door of my bedroom, but he was up quickly. When he charged at me, I swung at him, but he grabbed my fist.

I faltered for a moment, caught off guard, and he took that opportunity to pin me to the floor. He held my hands out to either side, his large hands enveloping my wrists, and he straddled me, using his weight to hold me in place.

I could've fought back, but at the moment I was too stunned, trying to figure out how in the hell someone had gotten me on my back so quickly.

Thanks to my Valkyrie blood, I was almost six feet tall and endowed with a preternatural strength. That meant I could best any human I tangled with, be they man or woman, and supernatural beings stood even less of a chance against me.

Not only was I unnaturally strong, but I made immortals *weaker*. My blood was immortal kryptonite.

But this guy, he had stopped my fist like it was no big thing. I could have pushed through, but it would've taken all my strength, and that was alarming.

"What are you?" I asked, staring up at him in the shifting glow from the billboard.

He looked human, at least—black hair cropped short, dark blue eyes, a shadow of beard, a distressed jacket clinging to his broad shoulders.

His eyes narrowed, and his dark eyebrows pinched together. "How old are you?"

"How old am I?" I gaped up at him. "You pinned me to the floor to ask me how old I am?"

"You don't look a day past eighteen," he said, sounding annoyed, as if I had misled him somehow.

"Nineteen," I corrected him. "And what are you? Twenty-one? Why so judgy?" I shot back. "Who are you and what do you want?"

He tilted his head, looking toward the window, and blinked. I'd grown sick of this game, so I lifted my leg and kneed him in the tailbone. He let out a pained groan, but loosened his grip enough that I could easily push him off.

I turned my back to him so I could rush toward the kitchen counter. His footsteps scrambled on the floor behind me, and I kicked back at him. My foot collided firmly with his chest, slamming him back against the wall, just as I grabbed a butcher knife from the counter.

I whirled on him, holding him against the wall and pressing the knife to his throat. Standing like this, I realized I had underestimated him a bit. He may have been human, but he was a few inches taller than me and muscular, with a T-shirt pulled taut over his barrel chest. He could pack a punch.

"Who are you and what do you want?" I demanded.

He pursed his lips before letting out an irritated breath. "I'm looking for the Krigare Valkyrie."

I pushed the knife harder against his throat, as a warning. "That's me."

"No, it's not," he replied, with so much certainty that for a moment I didn't know how to respond.

"Why don't you believe me?" I asked.

"You're too young," he said, but there seemed to be a confused sadness dampening his insistence, and already I felt his body relaxing against me.

"I know my own name," I assured him. "What I don't know is who you are or what the hell you're doing in my apartment."

Finally his shoulders slackened as he relented, and his eyes met mine. The neon lights outside made the blue in his eyes glow, then darkened them red, as he spoke. "My name is Asher Värja. My mother was a Valkyrie."

I relaxed slightly—but only slightly—since I now had an explanation for his strength. He might not have the same kind of abilities I had, but sons of Valkyries had their own strength unique to them.

"Okay," I said finally. "But that doesn't explain why you're here."

He licked his lips and lowered his eyes, looking embarrassed. "Can you lower your knife so we can talk?"

"You're the one that ambushed me, remember?"

"I know. I made a mistake," he said in a voice thick with apology. "I'm sorry. I was just afraid you wouldn't talk to me if I knocked on your door."

"Well, maybe you should try knocking first, and only move on to assault as a last resort."

"I've just been looking for a long time, and I was overzealous," he admitted wearily.

"Fine." I took a step back from him, giving him some space, but I kept the knife in my hand. "You said I was too young, and your mom is a Valkyrie. What does that have to do with me?"

The light outside abruptly changed, as the billboards switched over to brand-new advertisements that glowed blinding white, and the apartment was suddenly flooded with light. In the brightness, I was able to get a better look at this Asher Värja, and I realized that my original assessment of his age may have been off.

He looked around my age, maybe a couple years older, but there was something about him that made him seem so much older. A world-weariness in his face, pulling all the lines down into tired angles.

But mostly it was his dark eyes that seemed to contradict his youthful appearance. He had the eyes of someone who had seen a great deal.

"Your sword came up on a search because it was recently registered," he explained, rubbing at his eyes with the palm of his hand. "I thought you were an older, experienced Valkyrie who was just relicensing it. You're the only M. Krigare I've been able to find, so I just assumed you were who I'd been searching for."

That did explain his confusion over my age, since both my mother and I were listed as M. Krigare in our records. We were assigned numbers that helped differentiate us in our personal files, but for someone just gathering info, it would be easy to mistake Malin for Marlow without more context.

He cleared his throat, looking at me with a desperately hopeful look in his eyes. "Is there any chance that your mother is named M. Krigare?"

"What do you want with her?" I asked carefully, rubbing my

thumb absently on the handle of the knife in my hand. "Is she an old friend of your mom's?"

"Not exactly." He glanced out the window, and hoarsely he replied, "I'm looking for Krigare Valkyrie." Then he turned back to look at me. "Because she killed my mother."

NINE

———◆———

Vengeance was an occupational hazard of being a Valkyrie. Most immortals didn't like the idea of being returned (although a few did welcome it with open arms). Those who resisted us were known for performing preemptive attacks on Valkyries, as if killing one of us would stop another from coming in our place.

And there were reports of loved ones retaliating after a Valkyrie had taken someone out. Just like everyone else, immortals had friends and families that didn't like being left behind.

While unfortunate and problematic, this reaction was normal. It was something we'd been taught to deal with. But vengeance from *another Valkyrie*? That didn't make any sense.

"You must be mistaken," I said after a long silence while I tried to absorb what Asher was saying. He stood in the center of the room, his arms hanging at his sides and his eyes locked on me with an odd expression of defeated determination.

"I'm not mistaken," he replied. His words were soft but blunt, and the deep rumbling of his voice conveyed absolute conviction.

"A Valkyrie *cannot* kill another Valkyrie," I insisted, but my words sounded weak, even to me.

Because that wasn't exactly true. It wasn't impossible—just incredibly difficult, thanks to how evenly matched we were.

"I may have been oversimplifying," Asher admitted, keeping his eyes locked on mine. "Your mother didn't kill my mother herself, but her actions led directly to her death."

A wave of relief washed over me, and I let out a shaky breath. "So you're blaming my mom for some kind of accident?"

I hadn't wanted to believe that Marlow had done what Asher accused her of, but the brutal truth was that I wouldn't have been able to put it past her, either. She was strong-willed and stubborn, and my mother did hold the rather unfortunate belief that violence was the solution to most problems.

"Three years ago my mother Adela was killed. She was left burnt beyond recognition." He spoke slowly and deliberately, as if the words were getting caught in his throat and he had to force them out.

"I'm sorry," I said simply.

Asher shook his head, brushing off my apology. He reached for the front of pocket of his moto jacket, then stopped himself. "Is it all right if I show you something?"

"As long it's not a weapon," I allowed.

"Of course." He gave me a brief, grateful smile before pulling out a small electronic tablet. "Here's an article about it—the *only* article, actually."

He held the screen out toward me, and I stepped closer to get a better look. It opened with a rather disturbing black-and-white photograph of an ashen skeleton. Below followed three quick sentences.

An unidentified woman was found dead in the alley behind a
Huitaca-owned discothèque in Ou'helstad, Panama. Coroners
say the woman died from smoke inhalation. Investigators are
still looking into the incident, and Huitaca's representatives
could not be reached for comment.

"So?" I asked, looking up at Asher, since there didn't seem to be even the slightest connection to me or Marlow.

"This was the only thing that was ever said about it." Asher tapped the screen, and I was about to repeat the word *so* when he added, "When was the last time you remember a Valkyrie getting killed?"

"Ten years ago?" I shrugged, but it suddenly came back to me.

Shortly after my eighth birthday, a Valkyrie was murdered by an angry widower. For weeks after, I was worried something like that would happen to my own mother. I remember begging Marlow not to leave, not to go out on jobs, and I'd thrown such a tantrum once, crying and fighting to get her to stay, that she'd finally locked me in my bedroom to keep me from chasing after her.

"Eleven years ago," I corrected myself.

"It was all over the news," Asher said. "The billboards downtown replayed endless interviews with witnesses and crime scene footage."

Valkyries were notoriously hard to kill, earning us the nickname of "cockroaches" by some of the more colorful immortals. We also provided a sense of order and safety to the world—at least from humankind's perspective. So whenever one was killed, it was a huge story.

"So why wasn't this all over the place?" Asher asked, pointing to the article on his tablet.

"It didn't say anything about her being a Valkyrie," I said. "That's probably why no one picked up on it."

"Exactly!" he said, sounding triumphant that I seemed to be catching on to what he was laying down. "They suppressed it."

"Who's they?" I asked.

"I don't know. The Evig Riksdag, maybe?" He shook his head. "After my mother was killed, my grandma and I started looking—"

Startled, I couldn't help but interrupt him to ask, "You know your grandmother?"

"Yeah, of course I do," Asher replied, giving me an odd look.

I'd never met mine, and Marlow told me that she'd never met hers, either. The only other Valkyrie I knew well in terms of a personal relationship was Quinn Devane, and she all but refused to talk about her family. As far as I knew, no Valkyries had relationships with their extended family.

"Never mind." I brushed it off. "Go on."

"Anyway, my grandma and I went to Ou'helstad and started looking into it, and no one would give us any answers about what happened to my mother," Asher explained. "It didn't seem like any kind of investigation had been done."

"You're telling me that a Valkyrie was killed and no one cared?" I asked.

"No. I'm telling you that a Valkyrie was killed and someone covered it up," Asher corrected me.

"You know you sound super-paranoid, right?" I asked.

"I know how it sounds, but look at the facts." He pointed to the article on his tablet again. "A Valkyrie is killed outside of a club owned by Huitaca, and no one reports on it?"

Huitaca was an immortal known as much for her beauty as she was for her partying. Her reputation for hooking up with celebrities and getting arrested had led to the media crowning her queen Celebutant for the past quarter of a century.

"So you think Huitaca killed your mom?" I asked.

"No, I know who killed her," Asher assured me. "I'm just saying the media covers every scandal Huitaca is involved in, but somehow ignored this one."

He had a point, but I was too distracted by the fact that he claimed he'd already found the murderer, so I asked, "Who killed her?"

"My grandma and I started our own investigation, since no one else seemed to care about my mother's murder," Asher expounded. "It was a lot of knocking on doors, bribery, and threats of violence, but we were finally able to come up with a name: Tamerlane Fayette.

"Everything we found pointed to him," Asher went on. "From what we gathered, Adela had gone to Huitaca's club on orders to return another immortal—a Laka—so it was no big deal."

Lakas were peaceful flower goddesses renowned for being among the easiest to deal with, and they almost always welcomed death and thanked the Valkyrie.

"The Laka even turned herself in to the Evig Riksdag two days later, where she was promptly returned," Asher elaborated. "So she had no reason to kill Adela. But while Adela was there, Tamerlane got a whiff of a Valkyrie in the club, and he lost it. Witnesses saw them arguing until a bouncer made them take it outside, and that's the last time anyone saw Adela."

"So who is this Tamerlane Fayette?" I asked.

"He's a Petro Loa," Asher said.

A Petro Loa was essentially a fiery angel. They were divine, which meant that they usually didn't cause much trouble, but a fiery angel would explain Adela's burnt corpse.

"Great. So you got your guy."

Asher looked at me somberly. "I *never* found him. Every avenue I tried was a total dead end. He'd completely disappeared. And then, a few months ago, I figured out why."

He quickly scrolled through his tablet until he found a screen-shot of a form I knew very well.

PERSONAL DATA	LAST NAME FIRST NAME **FAYETTE TAMERLANE**		IMMORTAL NUMBER **PL87653422**			SOCIAL SECURITY NUMBER			
	SPECIES **PETRO LOA**	BRANCH **DIVINE**		GRADE **7C**	D.O.B.	DATE **08**	MONTH **MAR**	YEAR **03**	
	CITIZEN ☒ YES ☐ NO	PLACE OF BIRTH **CAP-HAÏTIEN HAITI**			D.O.T.	DATE **22**	MONTH **JAN**	YEAR **33**	
DATA	VALKYRIE NUMBER **25 VL MK 91**	ASSIGNED VALKYRIE **M. KRIGARE**			DATE ASSIGNED **20**		MONTH **JAN**	**33**	
TRANSFER OR DISCHARGE DATA	TYPE OF TRANSFER OR DISPATCH **RETURN**		STATION OF ASSIGNMENT **NEW EDGEWATER**						
	AUTHORITY **SAMAEL**			SERVICE DATE					
	MAJOR AUTHORITY		AUTHORITY GRANTED ON THE CONDION OF						

"Where'd you get this?" I asked.

"Like I told you, we used a lot of bribery and threats of violence," he replied vaguely. "But even all that couldn't get me an entirely unredacted version."

"But you can't just get this," I insisted, as a sick feeling grew inside. "The Riksdag won't just hand out this kind of information. These forms are supposed to be top-secret."

"It took me over *two* years to get this," he said.

"Even if I believe this is authentic—and I don't know that I do—it doesn't mean anything," I said. "This says my mom was sent to kill Tamerlane Fayette, so I'm sure she did."

That's what I said, but that's not what I felt. A cold anxious feeling had settled inside me, working its way deep into the pit of my stomach, making my organs twist and my heart race.

Asher tapped the numbers beside the D.O.T.—the date of transfer, which was how the Riks coded returns on forms. "The date she was assigned to kill Tamerlane was over a year before my mother was killed."

"Maybe they put in the wrong date. It's much more likely this was a clerical error than that my mom didn't do her job." I kept asserting this, that none of this meant anything, but my words felt empty and left a metallic taste in my mouth.

He laughed darkly, and the raw pain in it cut through me like a knife. I realized he wasn't lying. He might be wrong about things—maybe even everything—but he *believed* everything he'd told me.

"Your mother failed in her duties and did not kill Tamerlane Fayette, and because of that, my mother is dead," Asher said, looking me directly in the eyes. "And I need to know why. You can help me. I'd like it if you did, actually. But whether you do or not, I'm going to find the truth."

TEN

W̲ith the blinds closed, the only light in the apartment came from my laptop screen. Bowie sat curled up beside me, content now that the threat of Asher had gone. He cooed when he slept, sounding like a sleepy pigeon, and I absently scratched at the soft fur between his antlers.

After Asher had made his request for help, there hadn't been much more to discuss. He had already told me everything he knew, so it was then that I asked him to leave. Just before he did, he offered me his business card, and I took it quickly to hide the embarrassing trembling of my hands.

"In case you change your mind," he'd told me, then he turned and left my apartment.

I didn't plan on changing my mind, but I couldn't seem to stop glancing over at the card where it sat discarded on the arm of the couch beside me.

It was a tiny little screen, no bigger and no thicker than a playing card. It was black now, but when I reached over and touched it,

it slowly faded to white. His name, job title—private investigator—
and his number were in bold, beneath an animation of an eye looking around, a play on the term *private eye*, I assumed.

Once he'd left, I fed Bowie, closed my blinds, double-locked the
door, and then immediately got on my computer. In the time since
Asher had been gone, I'd done nothing but search online, looking
for anything to destroy his story.

Unfortunately, I had yet to find it.

There was very little online about his mother, but that was typical for a Valkyrie. The only thing I could find tagged with her name
was her obituary, which was deliberately sparse. I did manage to
find the article that Asher had shown me with the burnt corpse in
Ou'helstad, and the date of the murder did match up with her obit.

Tamerlane Fayette, on the other hand, had plenty written about
him. After all, he had been alive for 230 years. That was more than
enough time to make the news.

Most of what I found on him seemed positive and in line with
what I knew about Petro Loas. He traveled a lot, working on foun-
dations to help orphaned children. While he'd been born in Haiti,
he spent the last fifty years living exclusively in the States.

Since he'd been here, he'd gotten married to a mortal woman and
had three children. The pictures of his family I found in his sister-
in-law's social media showed a happy family—all bright smiles, like
they were doing an advert for toothpaste.

Then, four years ago, he'd disappeared. There was no trace of
him, other than a few posts online of people inquiring where he
went. According to official posts on the site for the orphanage he
ran, he'd simply stopped showing up to work one day, and after a
few months they'd had no choice but to replace him.

And then, six months later, his entire family was murdered. His
wife and all three children. Well, *murder* wasn't exactly the right

term. The agents investigating the crime were divided on whether it was a criminal act or simply an animal attack. The bodies had been shredded, so many were convinced it was an errant dragon or other wild beast that got them.

Some speculated that he'd show up for the funeral, but there was no sign of him. He'd simply vanished.

That is, of course, until he popped up to kill Adela Värja four months later, assuming that I believed Asher's story.

The locks on the door clicked, and I nearly jumped out of my skin. Bowie'd already had a rough night, so he squawked, flapped his wings, and then dashed under the table to hide. Oona walked into the apartment and flicked on the light.

"Why are you always sitting in the dark like some kind of weirdo, Mal?" Oona asked through a mouthful of food.

She had a small paper sack filled with fat round pastries in her hand. Based on the smell of clove and onion, I guessed it was kibbeh—a deep-fried croquette stuffed with mushrooms, onions, and pine nuts that a friendly marid sold at the street corner near our apartment.

"I'm not a weirdo." I closed my laptop and stood up to stretch. "It's just been a long night."

She held out the kibbeh toward me, offering me some, but I shook my head. I hadn't eaten tonight, but my stomach felt too queasy to put anything in it. My encounter with Asher left everything feeling . . . off.

"Were you working on something for school?" Oona asked as she flopped back on the couch.

Asher's business card had been sitting precariously on the arm, and it fell forward toward Oona, causing the screen to flash on.

"Who's Asher Värja?" Oona asked, picking up the card. "And why is this here?"

I poured myself a big of glass of water and took a deep breath before launching into the long story about Asher and everything he'd told me, and then about everything I'd found online.

"I thought that Draugrs were just urban legends," Oona said once I finished.

"Draugrs?" I asked.

"Yeah. You know, immortals that skip their death by Valkyrie, and become *really* immortal," she elaborated. "They walk the earth long after they're supposed to be gone."

"I've never heard that term in school," I said.

"Maybe that's because they've been trying to convince you that they don't exist, so you don't try to make one yourself," Oona supposed.

"Maybe," I allowed.

"But the rest of the story doesn't make any sense," Oona said.

"I know." I sat on the couch beside her with my legs crossed underneath me. "None of it does."

"Do you believe him?" Oona asked.

"I mean, no." I rubbed my temple and looked at Oona out of the corner of my eye. "Do you think I should?"

"There's parts of his story that seem like they add up, but then there's other parts that I just can't wrap my head around. I know I don't know your mom that well—"

"Join the club," I snorted.

"—but I just can't imagine her letting anyone go," Oona went on. "Not without good reason."

"So you're saying that I should talk to her about it?" I asked with a heavy sigh.

Growing up, I'd thought that Marlow was a pretty good mom. Not that I really had anything to compare her to, but she always made sure I had food, clothes, and a roof over my head. She just wasn't the kind of mom who tucked me in at night or read me bedtime stories or talked about my feelings. Hell, I'd been calling her "Marlow" instead of "mom" since grade school, and she preferred it that way.

In retrospect, she was more like a gruff aunt who really, really believed in self-reliance. And most of the time, that wasn't a bad thing.

But at times like this, I couldn't imagine her reacting well to me asking her if she'd ever failed at the one thing she prided herself on more than anything.

"That would be a start," Oona suggested. "Or if you're afraid of Marlow shutting you out, you could talk to somebody that's an expert on Valkyries. I honestly don't know enough about what you do to know if what Asher is suggesting is even possible."

I laid my head back on the couch and reached over to grab the last kibbeh out of Oona's bag. "First I eat, then I sleep. I can't ever come up with good ideas when I'm hungry and exhausted."

"So you're gonna talk to Marlow?" Oona asked with wide eyes.

"I'm gonna start small. I'll talk to Professor Wu first."

ELEVEN

───────◆───────

Even though I made it to Intro to Divinity and Immortality ten minutes early, there were already a few students in their seats, including a busybody vampire talking to Professor Wu about bringing up his grade.

"So you're saying that if I do a report on an important figure in the netherworld, it will help my grade?" the vampire was asking.

"I'm saying that we're going to be covering Kurnugia in a few weeks, so having a knowledge of important figures would be helpful," Professor Wu replied carefully. "Researching immortals like Ereshkigal, Osiris, and Anguta would definitely be beneficial for you."

Since a moment alone to talk to Wu about Asher's claims was out of the question, I resigned myself to sitting in the back row and using the extra time to bone up on my coursework. I'd only just taken my seat when Sloane Kothari came into the classroom.

Her brown eyes widened, and then she narrowed them and grimaced, as if resenting the fact that I'd gotten here before her. Her perfectly coiled black curls bounced as she stomped to her spot.

"Nice outfit," Sloane sneered, taking her seat in the row in front of me.

Because of my muscular build, most clothes built for the average human woman did not fit me. Thankfully, Oona's mother was a seamstress by trade, and either she or Oona modified a lot of my clothes to make them work. Since we'd moved in together, Oona had even begun taking it upon herself to make me a few pieces herself, in exchange for me kicking in a bit extra when rent was due.

What I wore now was an ombre maxi skirt with a slit down the side—an Oona creation specifically for me—with a cropped black bralette and a frayed smoky open-knit sweater over the top. I actually really liked my outfit, especially in comparison to the prim and proper schoolgirl number that Sloane had on today.

I'd also added a leather garter around my thigh, where I'd sheathed a dagger, because my run-in with Asher last night had made me jumpy. I moved my leg so the slit would fall open and expose the dagger.

"If you wanna compare fashion tips, we can go outside after class and have a little chat," I suggested, deliberately aiming the garter so she'd be able to see it.

She glanced back at me, and when she noticed my dagger, she scoffed. "Must you always be so crude, Malin?"

"You just seem to bring out the worst in me," I admitted.

"So many early birds here today," Professor Wu commented, stopping whatever snide comment Sloane had right on her lips, and she turned back to face him. "Is everyone getting antsy about the midterms?"

"I just like to stay on top of things," Sloane said in her saccharine voice.

Wu sat on the corner of his desk and crossed his arms over his chest. "Well, you all should be a little worried. We had a staff meeting this morning, and I know for a fact that many of your midterm exams are going to be incredibly difficult."

A few of the students groaned, including myself. That's just what I needed on top of everything else right now. Impossibly hard tests.

"Is there anything that any of you have questions about that you'd like me to explore more in depth?" Wu asked.

No one said anything, and the class was still kinda empty, so I took a deep breath and decided to go for it. "What if, um, Valkyries didn't kill—or, *return*—someone?" I asked carefully.

"The biggest problem would be overpopulation," Wu explained. "We're already facing population growths that are causing major problems all over the world, and if you added the hundreds upon hundreds of thousands of immortals that *never* died into the mix, we'd all risk extinction from oversourcing the earth."

"No, I mean, what would happen if just *one* Valkyrie didn't kill *one* immortal?" I asked. "I would never, ever do that, but I was just curious. What would happen exactly?"

"It would be catastrophic," Wu intoned ominously. "The system we have in place is a perfect equation written by the gods and the Eralim. You've heard of the butterfly effect."

"It is the phenomenon whereby a minute localized change in a complex system can have large effects elsewhere," Sloane supplied to a question that Wu hadn't even asked.

"A butterfly flaps its wings in Brazil, and that causes a tsunami in Japan," Wu simplified. "And we don't know how one immortal living longer than he was intended to can affect everything else."

He grabbed a marker and began diagramming on the whiteboard, drawing symbols and numbers until they filled up the entire space.

"This is the basic formula—what's known as the Mortal Equation," Wu explained, gesturing to the board. Supposedly, it was math, but it looked like an alien language to me. "I'm not an expert on this, but essentially it explains every decision the Eralim ever pass down. Are you taking Devil's Abacus: An Advanced Course on Mathematics and Existence with Professor Lovelace?"

"I am," Sloane chirped, but I just shook my head. I was taking basic algebra for my math credit, and I'd barely scored high enough to even get into that class.

Wu waved his hand, attempting to cover up his mild disappointment. "Anyway, Professor Lovelace can explain this all better to you than I ever could, so that's where you should go if you have any more questions about the Mortal Equation.

"But to answer your question, it would be horrific if a Valkyrie failed to kill an immortal," Wu finished. "Our whole world could collapse on itself."

"Thanks," I mumbled, looking down at my tablet.

Which meant that if there was any truth to what Asher Värja had said, we would all be in serious trouble.

TWELVE

———◆———

As soon as my last class of the day had finished, I got on my luft and made the half-hour trek across the city to the Tesla Park borough. When I put my mind to it, I could make the trip in as little as fifteen minutes, but today I was in no hurry.

Marlow lived in a tiny fourth-floor walk-up apartment in a narrow brownstone. Even though I'd shared it with her until I moved out on my own over a year ago, the place never really felt like home. Still, it always felt strange coming back and knocking on my old front door.

It took her nearly five minutes to answer, and when she finally did, she was blurry-eyed and her short bleached-blond hair stuck up at odd angles. Her lips were permanently stained a shade of red from her lipstick, but the rest of her face was pale, other than the dark circles under her eyes.

"Malin?" Marlow asked, squinting at me. "What are you doing here? Did you have a job today?"

"No. I just wanted to visit," I explained lamely and offered a smile that I hoped didn't look as sick as it felt.

Marlow continued to stare at me, blinking a few times, as if the concept of visiting with your child was completely foreign to her, but then she stepped back and motioned me inside. "Come on in, then."

The apartment had always been rather cramped, but since I'd moved out, it seemed that Marlow had become a bit of a hoarder. Empty cardboard boxes were piled up on one wall, blocking the only window into the living room, and her new purchases were stacked on every available surface.

Except for the lumpy old couch, but based on the blankets and pillows on it, I guessed that for some reason Marlow had taken to sleeping on the couch instead of in her bedroom.

"I'm still half asleep. I was working last night," Marlow explained as she walked into her tiny kitchenette. She worked nights at a call center helping people in emergencies.

"It's okay," I said, absently picking up an olive-green bayonet that Mom had stacked on an end table. Glancing around the room, it seemed like most of her new stuff was army surplus. Other than the sealed plastic tubs labeled *brown rice* and *lentils* stacked up beside her TV, which glowed dully with an old black-and-white movie.

Marlow had apparently become some kind of prepper.

"Do you want anything?" Marlow asked, moving aside take-out containers to make herself a cup of coffee.

I shook my head. "No, I'm good."

"Suit yourself." She topped off her mug of coffee with a half-empty bottle of vodka, then she leaned back against the counter and turned to face me. "So, to what do I owe this visit?"

"I just wanted to see how you were doing," I lied.

Marlow took a long drink of her coffee and shrugged. "Well, as you can see, I'm fine."

I barely managed to suppress the scoff in my throat. Marlow did not look *fine*, but I couldn't say that to her. So I just lowered my eyes and pulled out a kitchen chair from the table, one of the only clean spaces in the apartment.

"Now, do you want to tell me what you're really doing here?" Marlow asked, cutting straight through the bullshit. She'd never had time for small talk.

"Actually, I wanted to talk to you about something weird that happened last night." I stared down at my hands, fiddling with the multiple rings I wore. "This guy broke into my apartment."

"Was he trying to rob you?" Marlow asked without a hint of worry.

I suppose she knew that I could handle myself, and she could see that I was fine, but it still would've been nice if she'd feigned a little bit of motherly concern.

"No, he just wanted to talk, and he apparently thought breaking in was the best way to do that," I said, trying to ignore the growing ball of dread in the pit of my stomach. "He told me about his mom, Adela Värja. She was a Valkyrie, and she was killed three years ago."

Marlow furrowed her brow, but didn't show any signs of recognition. "Why did he think you would care about that?"

"Well, he had this whole long story about what happened," I tried to explain as nonchalantly as I could, like I'd never even considered the possibility that he might be right. "He said an immortal had killed Adela because a different Valkyrie had failed to kill that same immortal."

I waited a beat, watching Marlow's blank expression before saying, "The immortal's name was Tamerlane Fayette."

She coughed then, choking on her coffee. She turned her back to me and leaned over the sink, coughing hard for a moment, and I felt like I might throw up.

Even though I knew—I knew the moment she gagged on her coffee—I pushed on ahead. I had to hear her admit it. I had to know her side of the story.

"He said that you were supposed to kill Tamerlane, but that you didn't," I went on. "Did that happen? Did you not follow your orders?"

Marlow leaned with her hands against the sink and her shoulders slumped. "How could you even ask me that?"

"Marlow, I just need to know," I pressed. "I have to know if what he said was true."

She cleared her throat, then wiped her mouth with the back of her arm. "Do you know how many immortals I've killed in my career?"

"No, I—"

"Over seven hundred immortals," she said and turned back to face me. "I've been doing this since I was eighteen years old, so that averages out to twenty-five a year."

"That's an impressive number," I said, since I had no idea what kind of response she was hoping to elicit.

"I have been an excellent Valkyrie," she insisted. "I did what I was told, when I was told, and I killed seven hundred immortals. Some of them fought me. Some of them went out quietly. A few even thanked me.

"But most of them . . ." She took a deep breath and closed her eyes. "Most of them just cried and begged for me to spare their lives. And I would tell them all the same thing: 'It's not my decision.'"

Marlow opened her eyes. "But that was a lie. Do you know that?"

I shook my head emphatically. "It's not *our* decision. It comes down from the Eralim."

"But we have a choice, Malin!" Marlow snapped at me. "We are living, breathing humans. We might have different powers and skills than most other mortals, but we have free will just like the rest of them. We don't have to just follow orders!"

"Right, you can quit!" I shot back. "If you don't want to be a Valkyrie, then don't be one. Valkyries quit or retire all the time. A girl in my class last semester flunked out because she couldn't hack it."

She laughed bitterly. "Oh, Malin, it's not that simple."

"Yes, it is," I persisted. "That's your choice as a human—you can work as a Valkyrie or not. But if you choose to be a Valkyrie, you must follow orders! All of life on earth depends on it!"

Marlow rolled her eyes. "You are so melodramatic sometimes." Then she pulled out a kitchen chair, knocking a stack of boxes to the floor as she did, and sat down across from me. "You want me to tell you about Tamerlane Fayette?"

No. I didn't want to know. It would be so much easier if I never knew the truth, but I couldn't seem to stop myself from saying, "Yes. Please."

"After Samael gave me my assignment, I tracked down Tamerlane and I followed him, the way I always do when I get a job," Marlow explained. "And you know what he did in the days that I stalked him? He bought his wife flowers. He took his kids to school. He raised money for orphans. Once, I saw him rescue a mangy dog on the street."

"He sounds like a real saint, Marlow," I said dryly. "But he can't have been the first saint you killed."

"No, he wasn't," Marlow admitted, barely blinking back tears. "But he was *good*, Malin. He helped so many people! Why would the world be better without him? How could it?"

"Oh, holy hell, Marlow." I bowed my head and rubbed my temples, desperately fighting to keep the bile from rising in my throat. "He was *supposed* to die! Don't you understand what you've done?"

Marlow stood up quickly, pushing her chair back so hard it clattered to the floor. "No, I know what they've told me. But I just couldn't believe it, with him. I went to kill him, but when I looked into his eyes, I only saw his light and goodness. He promised me he'd make the world even better if he lived."

"Well, obviously he lied!" I shouted. "Because he killed a Valkyrie!"

Marlow shook her head. "That's what they told you. Doesn't make it true."

I stood up. "Do you know what happened to Tamerlane's family? They're all dead. They were all brutally killed six months after he was supposed to die."

Her face paled even further. "What? Why?"

"I don't know. Maybe Tamerlane killed them." I shrugged. "Or maybe you're just not supposed to fuck with the order, and now everything is out of balance, and who the hell knows who is going to die next?"

She pressed her lips together tightly, trying to stop them from trembling, and shook her head fiercely. "No. He was good." Her breath caught in her throat, and when she spoke again, her words were barely audible. "I wanted to do something good, for once."

"You *do* do something good!" I yelled in disbelief. "Don't you get it? The world will fall apart without Valkyries."

My phone started ringing in my bag, an impatient demand, and I didn't want to argue anymore, so I turned my back to Marlow and dug it out. Samael's name flashed brightly across the screen.

"It's Samael," I told my mom.

"Go," she said in a blank voice. "Take it. He probably has a job for you, and we don't have anything more to talk about."

I left without saying anything else to her, and I didn't answer the phone. I needed to compose myself before speaking to someone like Samael. I hopped on my luft and sped across the city, fighting back nausea and feeling like I'd just learned that everything I believed in was a lie.

THIRTEEN

———— ◆ ————

Atlas greeted me with a warm smile at the end of the long copper corridor, but Godfrey just stared ahead with his solitary bulbous eye. My footfalls seemed to echo off the marble floors louder than normal, and the distance to Samael's office had never felt farther before.

"You're on your own today, Malin?" Atlas grinned down cheerily as I finally reached him.

I attempted to return his smile, but I couldn't shake the sick feeling I had, so I was sure it came out crooked and tense. "Yeah. Just me."

"I think this is the first time I've seen you here without your mother," Atlas commented. "You must be doing well, then. It won't be much longer until you're licensed to go solo."

"Yeah, something like that." I laughed uneasily and rubbed the back of my neck. "Is Samael ready to see me?"

"He should be," Godfrey muttered in a few gruff syllables.

"Go on in," Atlas said and pushed against the massive bronze door, holding it open for me.

Samael sat behind his desk, studying something intently on his computer monitor. With his curls tucked up in a messy bun paired with the tailored dress shirt he wore, he appeared even more like a college kid playing dress-up.

He lifted his head and smiled at the sound of the door opening. As soon as he realized it was just me, standing alone in his spacious office, his smile fell away.

"Where's Marlow?" Samael asked, slowly getting to his feet.

Behind him, rain pattered against the large window. A flash of lightning glared off the buildings that surrounded us, and the glass trembled for a second.

"She's, uh, she's at home," I replied, gulping back my nerves. "She thought I would be able to handle this on my own."

"Well." He stared off for a moment, drumming his fingers against the dark stone of his desk, and then he cleared his throat. "I'm sure you can." He smiled at me, but it felt flatter than usual.

When I'd finally returned Samael's phone call, he'd told me to come in for another assignment. He hadn't specifically requested that Marlow come with me, but he hadn't needed to. Protocol was that I wasn't supposed to attend meetings or go on any assignments on my own until I was licensed.

But after what Marlow had told me today, I didn't trust myself to act normally around her. It was hard enough acting normal *without* her presence. Besides, it didn't seem like Marlow cared as much about the rules as I once believed she had.

"Anyway." Samael picked up his e-tablet and came around his desk toward me. "I've got another assignment for you."

"So soon?" I asked.

Last year, when I had first started apprenticing with Marlow, she was getting two or maybe three assignments a month, and my own assignments were usually much, much fewer and farther apart. But my last one had been completed early Tuesday morning, and today was just Thursday.

"We've been busier lately," Samael answered vaguely as he scrolled through his tablet and took a seat on the couch.

"I thought it would be more consistent, like a job every two or three weeks," I said and sat down beside him.

"The birth and death rate isn't an exact constant, not for humans or immortals. Right now we must be having a rise in births, which would explain the compensation in the other direction," he explained, but he didn't sound entirely confident in his answer.

He stopped, staring off into space again. There was a subtle twitching at the corner of his eyes, like he was trying to figure something out.

"Samael?" I asked at length, when it felt like he'd been lost in thought too long.

He snapped back to life, offering me an apologetic smile. "Sorry about that." He rubbed the palm of his hand against his eyes. "It's been a long week."

"It's okay," I said, but I was beginning to fear that it actually was not okay. That nothing might be okay ever again.

"Anyway, your new assignment." Samael tilted the tablet toward me so I'd be able to see the screen. "All of this info has been uploaded to your secure Riksdag drop box, just like always, but it's still important for me to go over it with you, especially since you're still new to the job."

The picture showed a beautiful woman onstage for what appeared to be a high-class burlesque show. Her features were so perfect—flawless alabaster skin, flowing black hair, and wide brown eyes.

"Her name is Amaryllis Mori," Samael explained as he scrolled through a few more pictures, before stopping at a screen with all her pertinent info. "She's a Jorogumo. Have you ever dealt with one of those before?"

I shook my head. "No, but I've heard of them."

Samael brushed this off with an easy smile. "They're not too hard to deal with. A little more difficult than a Trasgu, but most things are."

Her profile said that she had been born in Japan 349 years ago. Sometimes, seeing a number on the screen like that, it hit me about all that she'd seen, all that she'd done, and now it was all coming to an end. And there was nothing she could do, even with all her experience and power.

"She's been working at a gentleman's club called Nysa in the Gold Coast District, which thankfully is only about an hour from here," Samael said. He lowered the tablet, then spoke more conversationally. "You know, I've sent Marlow on assignments as far away as Tanzania."

I remembered. When I was ten, I'd spent two weeks with Oona and her mom while Marlow took care of business on the other side of the world. She didn't call or write the entire time she was gone, and I'd had nightmares that she died.

"I went with her that trip. Didn't seem safe for her to go that far alone," Samael explained, but there was something wistful in his eyes. Then he shook his head, clearing it of the memories. "But this business with Amaryllis should be no problem."

"I'm sure it'll be fine," I said, even though I no longer had such confidence in myself or in the job. Marlow's confession had shaken everything I thought I knew.

Samael locked the screen and tilted his body to face me more directly. "So, do you have other questions or concerns?"

In my head, I wanted to tell him about Marlow and Tamerlane Fayette and Adela Värja's death. But I couldn't. While I knew that Samael was fond of my mother, I knew also that if the Evig Riksdag found out what she'd done—or rather, *hadn't* done—it would be very, very bad news for her.

So instead I just forced a smile and said, "Nope. I think I got it."

I stood up, preparing to leave, when Samael stopped me. "Is Marlow okay?"

"Yeah, of course," I replied quickly. "Why wouldn't she be?"

"I've just never known her to miss a meeting like this," Samael said.

"Yeah, um, yeah, I think she was just feeling a bit under the weather, and she thinks that I'm ready for more responsibility," I explained lamely.

Samael stood up slowly. "If Marlow is busy, we could maybe look into getting you a new mentor."

I swallowed back my unease. "I'm not sure what Marlow's schedule is like right now. You'd have to talk to her about that."

"Hmm." He rubbed his chin absently as he thought. "Maybe I could talk to Quinn Devane . . ." He trailed off, glancing back over at the couch behind us.

That's where Quinn had been sitting the first time I met her just over a year ago. Her hair had been dark then, a vibrant midnight-blue that cascaded down over her shoulders, and she'd been wearing a minidress that showed off her long, sinewy legs.

When she smiled at me—her lopsided smile filled with secrets and wishes—time seemed to slow for a moment. I could hear the sound of my heart beating, and the air suddenly felt too thin in the room.

Then she was standing and walking over to me, and my thoughts were scrambling—had I ever seen anyone as beautiful as her before, why did my hands feel so clammy, did I look as dumb as I felt, what would I say to her, and how could I speak?

"You must be Malin Krigare," she said, her eyes fluttering over my body in a way that made my skin flush. "I'm Quinn Devane. Samael thought I could help you."

"Why, uh, why would you do that?" I fumbled over my words, my tongue thick and clumsy. I tried to play it off all cool but I knew everything was coming out wrong.

"Because I'm a Valkyrie." Her smile broadened, looking amused. "I have more experience, so I can show you around."

I couldn't tell if that was an innuendo, or if I was just hoping it was one. The playful look in her green eyes and the mischievous twitch of her slender lips made me question this, and I could feel my cheeks reddening. I'd dated plenty before Quinn, both guys and girls, but I'd never felt so tongue-tied and flustered before.

"That should be very educational," I replied, trying much too hard to seem nonchalant and cool.

"I'm the finest teacher," she assured me.

I lowered my eyes, struggling to calm the racing heart and the growing swirl of butterflies inside me. My gaze happened to land on her chest—just above the crescent of her décolletage a dark red scar ran across, connecting her collarbones.

"An ennedi," Quinn said, startling me into looking back up at her.

"What?" I asked dumbly.

"Well, I assumed you were either staring at my tits or my scar," she said, still smirking playfully at me, but now my cheeks were burning with shame. "If it's my tits, I ought to point out that it's not polite to stare, though I suppose that works for the scar too."

"I didn't—I wasn't—I'm sorry," I stammered.

Quinn ignored my apology and ran her slender fingers across the scar. "It's from the scratch of an ennedi, which is sorta like a saber-toothed tiger. I returned it a few weeks ago, but not before it left me this nice permanent gift to remember him by."

"See? She's already teaching you something," Samael had said brightly and put his hand on Quinn's shoulder, attempting to diffuse the tension, but honestly, I'd forgotten he was there. As soon as Quinn had smiled at me, everything else had fallen away.

Back in the present, Samael cleared his throat and scratched his head. "Though, I suppose it wouldn't be appropriate for you two to work together, given the nature of your relationship."

"Since we've broken up, I would rather not be teamed up with her again," I admitted.

"That's understandable." He walked with me toward the door, seeing me out, with his hands in his pockets. "I'll look into other options for the future. But how is school going? Everything on track?"

"Yeah, it's all going great," I lied. "I'm working on a project for school, and I've been kind of learning about the Mortal Equation."

His blue eyes widened in surprise. "Are you a math major?"

"No, I'm horrible at math, actually, but my professor was talking about it, and I just got kind of curious to know more. Do you know the Mortal Equation?"

"I know some," he allowed, choosing his words carefully. "But I don't work on it myself. That's for the higher-ups." He motioned toward the ceiling. "I just interpret the orders for Valkyries like you."

"That makes sense, but . . ." I paused, trying to figure out how to phrase the question burning on my tongue. "Math can be difficult. I make mistakes all the time, and I know that the bosses upstairs are way smarter than I can even comprehend, but . . . do they ever make mistakes? They forget to carry the two, and the whole equation is off?"

Samael chuckled. "No, they don't make mistakes. That's not how they work. Everyone they send the Valkyries to return was meant to be returned."

"But what does that mean?" I pressed. "How can anyone be 'meant' to die? Unless everything is preordained, and if it's all preordained, then how can we ever veer off course?"

"You can't," Samael said firmly. "But the concepts of free will and predestination are rather lofty. If you're really interested in learning more, I suggest you talk to your professor. I'm certain he'd be able to explain everything far better than I ever could."

"Right, thank you. I will." I forced a smile at him. "I should get going. I have homework and all that."

Samael opened the door for me, telling me to call him if I had any problems. I promised that I would, but I didn't know if I meant it.

FOURTEEN

————— ◆ —————

Oona and I sat in the booth in the back corner of the restaurant. Aprazivel was a dark little hole in the wall that happened to serve some of the tastiest, cheapest Brazilian cuisine in the city, and it also happened to be only a few blocks from our apartment.

"So?" Oona asked. She sat across from me, sipping her cachaça—a liquor distilled from sugarcane—and stared at me expectantly with her big dark eyes. "How did it go with Marlow?"

On the wall behind Oona, the head of a tamanduá chifres had been mounted. The Brazilian great horned anteater. It was huge, roughly the size of a moose, with massive antlers to match and a long gray snout with its slender tongue poking out. Its two black eyes stared down at me, and for a moment I felt almost as if it were looking straight through me.

"I don't know," I said finally.

"You did go see her today, right?" Oona pressed on, undeterred by my apathy. This was the first chance I'd had all day to tell her about my visit with Marlow, but I wasn't ready to just dive into the topic.

As soon as I'd gotten home from meeting with Samael, Oona had demanded that we go out and get something to eat. I'd hardly eaten anything all day, and she claimed I was looking pale. Her solution to most problems in life seemed to involve food.

"Yeah, I saw her," I replied, looking down at the table, and then I noticed her hands. "What's that?"

Her dark skin was covered in elaborate white henna designs from her wrists down to her fingers, stopping just before her long fingernails, which were shaped to a point and painted a matte gray.

"What?" She glanced down, then waved me off dramatically. "It was just something I did for class today. Don't change the subject, Mal."

I gulped down the rest of my beer, then I put my arms on the table and leaned forward. The lighting in Aprazivel was dim and low, and it was crowded enough that the noise from the other customers should keep our conversation private. But still, I felt edgy about someone overhearing, and the unblinking gaze of the tamanduá chifres did nothing to ease my nerves.

"He was right," I whispered.

"What?" Oona leaned forward to hear me better.

"Asher Värja," I said, and it was at that moment the waiter appeared with our food, and I nearly jumped out of my skin.

"For the lovely lady." The waiter smiled, putting a bowl of rice, beans, and curded cheese in front Oona. "And the palmito for you."

Another day, I would've made a comment about his lack of a descriptor for me when he put my plate in front of me, but today I couldn't focus enough to come up with something to say.

"What do you mean?" Oona asked after the waiter had gone.

"I mean . . . she didn't do it," I explained in a hushed voice.

Oona had taken a bite of her food, and she stared at me for a moment, her mouth full, not chewing. Finally, she swallowed and asked, "Marlow didn't do her job?"

"No." I shook my head. "She had one thing to do, and she didn't do it."

"But Marlow loves her job, and it's a *really* important job," Oona said. "Why wouldn't she do it?"

I leaned back in the booth, and the warped plastic seat groaned underneath me. "She said she thought he could do more good alive than he would dead."

Oona put her hand to the side of her face, as if she just couldn't believe what she was hearing. "That's not how your job works, right? The people that are chosen to die are chosen for a reason. Leaving them can only do harm."

"That's pretty much exactly how it works," I said.

"Oh crap." She took a long drink of her cachaça, then motioned to me with her fork. "Eat your food. Starving to death won't help anything."

I sat up straighter and did as she commanded, cutting into my baked heart of palm. It was normally one of my favorite meals, but today it just felt tasteless and empty.

"So what's the plan?" Oona asked.

"What plan?" I shook my head. "Everything is totally messed up, and I don't know how anything can ever be made right."

"For starters, finishing the job that Marlow left undone would be good," Oona suggested.

"But he's already killed someone. Asher only knows about his mother, but that doesn't mean there aren't others," I realized. "He might have a whole trail of dead behind him. The damage is already done."

"The longer he's left alive, the more damage he can do," Oona countered.

"Probably," I conceded. "But I have no idea how to find him. Asher's been looking for him for *years*, and he has no clue."

"But he was looking on his own before," Oona persisted between bites of food. "He didn't have you or the connections you have."

I snorted. "What connections?"

Oona held up her hand, raising her fingers as she went down her list. "Samael. Your professors at school. Other Valkyries."

I shook my head adamantly. "I can't tell any of them what's going on or they'll string up Marlow." I paused as I came to a dark realization. "That's probably what she deserves, but I can't be a party to that. She's still my mom."

Oona's expression softened and her voice was gentler when she spoke. "No one is suggesting that you turn Marlow in. But maybe if you team up with Asher and pool your resources, you two could figure something out. Without dragging the authorities into it."

"Maybe," I admitted grudgingly.

"Look, you can't undo what Marlow did, but you can do what she wouldn't."

I laughed sourly. "That doesn't really make sense."

"No, it does," she insisted. "You're just overthinking it."

"But that Asher guy seemed too unstable," I reminded her.

"Breaking into our apartment was extreme, but just imagine how pissed you'd be if you were him. I mean, when he broke in, he thought you were Marlow," Oona reasoned.

"I *am* pissed at Marlow, and I haven't even lost what he lost," I agreed.

But that wasn't exactly true. My mom hadn't died, but I had lost the idea I had of her.

When I was growing up, she'd been cold at times—well, most of the time—but she was also strong and infallible. I'd always thought of her as a lighthouse, guiding the immortals safely to the end of their journey so they didn't go crashing into the shore.

But that wasn't her. She wasn't a hero or a savior. She had managed to become the villain in her own story.

"He left his business card, right?" Oona asked, drawing me from my thoughts. "You can give him a call tomorrow."

I picked emptily at my food. "Maybe I should wait until Monday. It's the Feast of the Dead this weekend, and it's gonna be crazy."

"Malin," Oona said firmly, causing me to look up at her. "Don't make excuses. You're going to have to deal with this, and it's better sooner rather than later."

"You're right," I said with a heavy sigh. "I'll call him tomorrow."

"Excellent." She beamed at me. "Now eat your food and order another beer."

"I don't see how that will help."

"Alcohol and food may not fix everything, but I've yet to encounter a problem they haven't at least helped with," Oona assured me.

FIFTEEN

———— ◆ ————

Most of the historical texts had been transferred onto digital formats for ease of reading, but not all of them. Ravenswood Academy had a whole wing dedicated to books that weren't permitted to ever be transferred into digital.

Those who oversaw Ravenswood Academy—a joint effort between an elite board of education and the Evig Riksdag—believed that some texts contained information too valuable and dangerous to be distributed en masse to the population, and they feared that digital media was rife for pirating.

The "sacred texts" were all carefully locked up behind secure doors in the Sacrorum Wing. As an added level of security, several Sinaa roamed the halls, guarding the books and chasing out troublemakers. The Sinaa looked just like jaguars, except some of their spots were actually additional eyes, so they could see everything, and they were obsessed with preserving knowledge at all costs.

Two dozen bomb-shelter-like rooms filled the wing, and each had shelves filled floor-to-ceiling with books. Some of the books dated back centuries, worn tomes bound with leather made from human flesh, and others were brand-new, with hardly a crack in the binding.

Once, between classes, Quinn had shown up and taken me down here, under the guise of studying, which for some reason I had believed. Leading me by the hand, she had chosen the room titled PLANTAE VITAM AETERNAM.

As soon as we'd gone in, she'd thrown me up against a bookcase—so hard it nearly toppled it over—and began kissing me roughly on the mouth.

"We shouldn't be doing this," I protested as her hands slid underneath my shirt. "What if someone comes in?"

"These are all books on immortal plants. Nobody wants to read these," she assured me between kisses, but it had only been a few more minutes before a Sinaa caught us.

A dozen tiny dark eyes locked on us, staring up from the spotted camouflage, and the Sinaa let out a low growl. We'd raced out of the room, Quinn laughing all the way as the beast chased us down the hall and out of the sacred library.

What I remember most about that afternoon was the way my heart had been pounding—terrified the Sinaa would maul us if it caught us, and also terrified I might get kicked out of school. Quinn had ignored all my fears, and then, after, once I was certain we were safe, I'd been so exhilarated and relieved. I told Quinn that I never wanted to do that again, but she'd only laughed and silenced me with kisses.

Today I had an hour-long break between my first and second class, so I headed down to the Sacrorum Wing to see what more I could find out about the situation with Marlow and Tamerlane Fayette.

The search took me to a room marked by a plaque above the door that read ET VIRGINES IN MORTE. My Latin wasn't as good as

Oona's, but I deciphered it out to be DEATH AND THE MAIDENS. The Valkyrie room.

Last night, after dinner, Oona and I had proceeded to get drunk on cheap beer, but that hadn't done anything to help the situation. Before I left for class this morning, she'd reminded me to call Asher, but I thought it might be better if I did some research on my own first.

It would be easier for me to be able to just ask my professors or Samael about things, but that would only raise a lot of red flags. I mean, I was a Valkyrie in training, and if I kept asking what happens if a Valkyrie doesn't kill her mark, people were liable to think either I was plotting something or that I had already screwed up.

And I definitely didn't need that added scrutiny.

I'd just sat down, leaning back against a shelf with a small stack of books on my lap, when my phone started ringing in my messenger bag. I scrambled to answer it, before one of the Sinaa came in and chased me out, because the last thing I needed was a supernatural jaguar angry with me.

"Hello?" I whispered into the phone, glancing around to make sure nobody was around.

"Malin, it's Marlow," she said wearily, sounding irritated that I had disrupted her, when she had been the one to call *me*.

"I'm kinda busy—"

"I've been looking into that Värja boy's claims," Marlow interrupted me. "And it seems like something went wrong."

That something being her failure to do her job, but I couldn't say that to her. So I just waited for her to explain what she meant.

"Mistakes were made," Marlow said, still skirting any culpability. "But I want to help make things right. Before things get worse. Do you know how to contact the Värja boy?"

"Yes," I replied cautiously.

"I'd like you to arrange a meeting with him," Marlow instructed me. "Today, if possible. I'm free this afternoon, so that would be best."

"You want to meet him?" I asked, so shocked I forgot to keep my voice down.

"Yes, I feel that we should talk," she elaborated. "There's a nice coffee shop near where I work—Kahvaltı. That should be good. See if you can get him to meet there, and let me know what time."

"Yeah, okay," I said. "I'll see what I can do."

And that was it. She hung up without thanking me or saying goodbye. Which was just as well, because a Sinaa poked his head into the room, his ears back flat, and let out a low rumbling growl before stalking off to quiet someone else.

I sat in a stunned silence for a few minutes, then I decided that I ought to text Asher before I lost my nerve. His business card was in my bag, so I pulled it out and quickly entered it into my phone.

Hi Asher—this is Malin Krigare. I've spoken to my mother, and she wants to meet today to talk to you. Would that be possible?

Roughly twenty seconds later, he replied back with, **Yes. Of course. Where/when?**

I gave him a time and the place, then forwarded his response to Marlow. Then I turned my phone off and shoved it way in the bottom of my bag. I couldn't handle dealing with anyone else.

I finally opened the book on my lap, and then I buried my hands in my hair and stared down blankly at the words. My mind was still reeling and I barely noticed the sound of footsteps until it was too late.

"What are you doing here?" Sloane demanded, like she'd caught me digging through her underwear drawer instead of reading a book in the library.

"What does it look like I'm doing?" I shot back.

She stood over me, glowering down at me with her arms crossed over her chest. Her plaid skirt was short enough that I would've been able to see her underwear, if it weren't for the opaque nylons she wore.

"Sucking up and doing an extra-credit project for History of Supernatural Professions and Their Modern Applications," Sloane said.

"Yes . . . that is what I am doing," I said, since that sounded much better than telling her I was trying to figure out how to save my mother and the world.

Sloane rolled her eyes. "I should've known you'd pick Valkyrie. It's so obvious."

"Why wouldn't I pick something that's relevant to me?" I asked, growing irritated about a fictional problem that I didn't even care about. But if Sloane Kothari was going to accuse me of something, I was damn sure going to defend myself. "Why did you pick it?"

"I'm trying to broaden my horizons and stretch out of my comfort zone." Sloane pursed her lips and shifted her weight from one foot to the other. "My career adviser said it would be good for me."

"Sounds great," I said, hoping that would be the end of that.

She narrowed her eyes at me. "Well, what are you doing? Maybe I can approach it from a different angle."

"I doubt it—" I tried to deflect her, but she was already bent over and lifting up the cover of the book to see the title.

"*Predestination and Divinity*?" Sloane asked, wrinkling her nose. "That doesn't have anything to do with the history of your job."

"Yeah, it does," I insisted, mostly because I didn't want to raise her suspicion. "I've just been thinking, and . . . do you think we have free will?"

She arched an eyebrow and stared down at me over her sharp nose. "What are you going on about?"

"Did I choose to be a Valkyrie, or did it choose me?" I wondered.

"You were born into it," Sloane reminded me. "I can't be a Valkyrie. Ninety percent of the beings on this planet could never be a Valkyrie. So, yeah, I would say it chose you."

"But I could've said no. Lots of people aren't cut out for it," I said.

"Then say no." She shrugged. "Are you rethinking your career? Because I've never really thought you were cut out for it."

"Thanks," I muttered, slamming my book closed, and got to my feet. "I'm looking for help, and you kick me when I'm down. Nice."

I started walking away, but Sloane sighed and called after me. "Sorry. I didn't realize you were actually having a genuine existential crisis."

I stopped to look back at her. "Well, I am."

"All the Valkyries I've ever known have been dumb jocks," Sloane explained, as if that would somehow make me feel better. "I'm working on trying to get over my own prejudices, and it's unfair of me to stereotype you like that."

"Thank you," I replied cautiously.

She took a deep breath, relaxing her stance slightly, and seemed to start over.

"To answer your question about free will . . . I used to believe in it. I still do, to some degree. Or at least, I'd like to believe that *I* chose to wear my hair up today." She pulled at one of her black curls, causing it to bounce back into the ponytail when she let go.

"I know some people find comfort in the idea that gods are watching over every little detail, helping them decide everything from what color underwear to put on to who they're going to marry," Sloane went on. "But I'm not one of those people."

"Neither am I," I agreed.

"I like to believe I make my own decisions. That I'm in control of my own fate. But . . ." She drew in a shaky breath. "My father is a Deva. He's inherently honest and good, because he was born that way. He has a great difficulty lying, which leads to some awkward situations sometimes."

"That can be helpful, too," I piped in.

She narrowed her eyes. "I'm not asking for your approval on my dad," she said in a haughty voice thick with venom, but then she apparently remembered that she was trying to be nice, and she forced a smile. "Sorry. It's just not about my dad."

"Okay. What is it about, then?" I asked.

"He's good, not because he wants to be, but because he was made that way," Sloane explained. "Sure, he still chooses how he likes his coffee or what color tie he's going to wear, and that might seem like free will, but it isn't."

Her expression changed again, slackening a bit. Her mouth turned down in a frown, and sadness darkened her eyes. "And one day, you'll kill him."

"Sloane—" I began, but she held her hand to silence me.

"If not you, then someone like you," she went on. "But his time will come, and that will be that. He didn't choose to be born. He didn't choose to be good in life. And he won't choose his death. Where is the free will in that?"

I let her words sink in, then softly said, "There isn't."

"So that's my answer," she replied.

"But what if he could?" I asked. "What if he changed the way he lived and went rogue and started lying and being bad?"

Sloane laughed. "You show me an angel that breaks bad, and I'll show you a devil in disguise."

"You think we can only be bad because we were made that way?" I asked. "Then we're all just behaving as we were made to, filling our role as good little cogs in the machine, and we can't choose to get off the tracks."

"Exactly. Then something else is the one in control of it all," she said. "If I don't believe in free will, the unfortunate logical conclusion is fate. If we're not choosing things for ourselves, then someone must be choosing it for us. They're the ones deciding our destiny."

Her words hit me like a slap across the face. If Sloane was right—and her theory made sense—there were only two conclusions about what Marlow had done.

The first assumed that Marlow was supposed to kill Tamerlane, and she didn't. That meant she somehow managed to bust free off her preordained track, and the whole thing would break down without her cog there rotating in its place.

The second assumed that this was actually Marlow's destiny the whole time. She did exactly as she was always meant to by shirking her duties in killing Tamerlane. But if she was only running her true course, who was the one plotting her path?

SIXTEEN

———◆———

Marlow sat closest to the window, amber sunlight spilling in through the wooden slats of the blinds. Hot black coffee filled the mugs before us, each rim stained with our own particular shade of lipstick. Hers was a sharper blood-red, while mine was more of a matte merlot—aptly called Velvet Vampire.

A spread of tasting food dubbed the Turkish Delight sat un-touched on the table before us. Bowls of olives and Beyaz peynir cheese, a platter of cucumbers and tomatoes, a basket of katmer flat bread, and several tiny bowls of rose jam and fig marmalade. We had ordered this as a nicety and as a distraction, giving us all some-thing to munch on.

The reason Marlow had chosen Kahvaltı to meet wasn't the food anyway—although the food was fairly good. It was the long, slen-der cigarillo she held between her fingers with its pungent bouquet of smoke hovering over us. Kahvaltı was one of the only places in the city that still allowed smoking tobacco.

"If I'd known he was going to be so late, I would've taken the time to touch up my hair," Marlow said.

Her bleached-blond hair had begun to grow out a bit, leaving a sliver of black roots along her scalp, but it had been styled well, hiding most of that flaw. Marlow had really done herself up today. Her makeup was a bit heavier than normal, with thicker eyeliner and false lashes, and her form-fitting black dress had long sleeves and a short hem.

Marlow exhaled smoke from the corner of her mouth and cast her scrutinizing gaze on me. She reached out, running her fingers through the thick stubble on the shaved side of my head.

"If you're going to insist on this ridiculous haircut, you ought to keep up with the shaving," she chastised. I leaned away from her touch, so she let her hand fall away. "It's getting long."

I dug through my messenger bag, searching for my phone so I could text Asher and find out what the holdup was. He was already twenty minutes late.

We were poised at a table right by the front entrance, and when the door opened, I looked up to see Asher. He'd cleaned up some since I'd seen him last, appearing a little less grizzled and a bit more rested.

I smiled and waved toward him, then realized that might not be the appropriate response for this meeting. His eyes met mine—as hard and dark as the ocean during a storm—and he nodded once, so I let my hand fall awkwardly back to my lap.

He turned, speaking quietly to a woman who had followed him in. Her jumpsuit was perfectly tailored for her tall frame, and a sarong was draped elegantly over her shoulders. With her glacial white hair meticulously styled and oversized black sunglasses covering most of her face, she looked stunningly regal.

Pursing her lips, she lowered her sunglasses to look at Marlow and me, and I could almost feel the daggers she was shooting piercing into me.

"Who is that woman?" Marlow leaned over and asked me.

"I don't know," I whispered, but they were already on the way toward us, and I suddenly felt so nervous that I wasn't sure I could do this.

Marlow set her cigarillo in the ashtray and stood up as they reached our table. "Hello," she said, flashing her most winning smile. "I'm Marlow Krigare."

I realized belatedly that I should've stood, but now my mother was leaning over to shake Asher's hand, and it felt too forced.

"I'm Asher Värja," he said, casting an uneasy glance down at me as he shook Marlow's hand. "This is my grandmother, Teodora Värja."

Marlow extended her hand to Teodora, but she just sniffed and sat down, ignoring Marlow's offering. My mother cleared her throat uncomfortably and took her seat across from Teodora.

"So, my daughter told me that you were looking for me," Marlow said, her eyes bouncing between Asher and his grandmother.

"You could say that," Teodora said with a weary sigh. She took off her sunglasses, and they clacked loudly when she set them on the table. "You really sodded things up, didn't you?"

"Beg pardon?" Marlow asked, and her plaster smile began to waver.

"*Amma*," Asher said, using the old Norse word for *grandmother*. "They invited us here. We should hear them out."

"He's right," I said, desperate to diffuse the growing tension between Teodora and Marlow. "We thought maybe if we could meet and exchange ideas, we might be able to track down Tamerlane."

"We did just want to be of help," Marlow replied, but her words came out stiff and robotic. She held her head and shoulders so high and straight, it looked painful.

"Oh, please." Teodora leaned back in her chair and gave a dry laugh. "How old are you?"

"I don't see what that has to do with anything," Marlow replied tightly.

Teodora rolled her eyes. "Fine, play that game. I turned seventy-five last May. I worked as a Valkyrie for almost fifty years before I retired." She leaned forward, resting her arms on the table and staring directly at my mother. "And do you know how many of my assignments I failed to return?"

I looked helplessly over to Asher, and his panic-stricken expression nearly mirrored my own. We were powerless to get our matriarchs to behave.

Marlow's lips twisted into a bitter smile. "You think I asked you here to listen to this shit? I thought I could help you."

"Yes, you're a real saint, aren't you?" Teodora continued with a nasty smile. "Inviting the family of your victim here to commiserate."

"My *victim*? I never even met your daughter."

"She wouldn't be dead if it weren't for your failed actions," Teodora countered.

"You don't know that," Marlow insisted coolly. "Maybe she was always meant to die. Only the gods know the true plan."

I actually winced when she said that.

"So that's why you called us here?" Teodora asked. "So you could convince yourself that you did nothing wrong?"

"I wanted to try to make things right. I wanted to help you. But now I see that you don't want my help. You just want to spew all your anger and hate out at me, and I won't let you." Marlow pushed her chair back and stood up. "I am not your punching bag."

"We're all emotional," Asher said, his voice taking on the same pained tone as it had when he was in my apartment. "Let's all just calm down for a second."

My mother shook her head as she grabbed her jacket from the

back of her chair. "No. You had your chance. Good luck getting justice for your mother."

"Marlow, please." I reached out, meaning to grasp her hand, but she pulled away from me. "They just—"

"I'm out of here, Malin," she said and slid around me on her way to the door.

"Marlow—" I repeated and started to get up, but Teodora held out her hand to me.

"No, stay. I'll go after her." She sighed as she slowly rose to her feet and grabbed her sunglasses from the table. "I can make nice if it means that I can avenge my Adela."

Asher turned to watch Teodora follow after my mother. Through the window blinds, I could see Marlow standing on the sidewalk, smoking a new cigarillo. When Teodora reached her, she didn't immediately punch her, so that was a good sign.

"I'm sorry about that," I said to Asher once it seemed like Marlow and Teodora were talking.

"No, I'm sorry. My grandmother said she just wanted to come for support. . . ."

"It's a very complicated situation," I said.

I spread jam on the flatbread, mostly so I'd have something to do, and Asher reached for the small butter knife at the same time I was putting it back, so our hands bumped against each other. His skin felt rough brushing against mine.

"Sorry," I said.

"Don't be," he said gently, his dark eyes meeting mine, before he roughly spread the marmalade on his own bread, but like me, he never actually took a bite of it.

After a stretch of silence, Asher cleared his throat and asked, "So, you call your mom by her name?"

I nodded. "Yeah. Marlow told me that most Valkyries call their moms by their first names."

"Well, it's starting to sound like Marlow has a bit of a skewed view on what it means to be a Valkyrie," Asher said, and the truth of his words stung hard—harder than he'd intended them to, based on the apologetic expression on his face.

"It seems that way," I agreed with a heavy sigh.

"Did she tell you why she didn't kill Tamerlane Fayette?" Asher asked directly.

"She did." I paused, trying to figure out how exactly to word it, but the hopeful look in Asher's eyes underneath his gathered eyebrows compelled me to just tell the truth. He deserved to know. "She said that he was good, and she thought the world would be better with him in it."

He laughed darkly. "Yeah, the world is real great with him in it."

"She knows she made a mistake," I hurried to say, defending my mother even though I really knew there was no defense for her actions. "She wants to make it right."

"How?" Asher asked skeptically.

"She wants to kill Tamerlane," I lied, because I wanted it to be true.

Marlow hadn't shared any of her intentions with me or even why she'd wanted to meet with Asher. I had no idea how she planned to try to make this right, or what she even thought the right thing would be anymore.

"Do you think she really will?" Asher asked honestly.

"I don't know," I admitted. "A few days ago I would've said yes, definitely." I took a deep breath. "But it doesn't matter. If she doesn't kill him, then I will."

He smiled then, crookedly because of a scar he had on the left side of his top lip. It was a small gash, like a comma dropping down from the smooth skin of his face to his full lips. But his smile softened his whole face. Even his eyes seemed lighter.

It wasn't until that moment that I fully appreciated how handsome he was. He had this ruggedness about him—unshaven, with slightly disheveled hair, thick eyebrows, leathery hands—and it clashed wonderfully with the beauty of his other features—high cheekbones, full lips that were almost pouty, eyes that were a disarming shade of blue.

He wasn't much older than me, but he had a world-weariness that made him seem older, like he'd been through things I couldn't even imagine. It was in the rumbling tenor of his voice, and he still somehow managed to be soft-spoken.

Everything about him seemed to be a contradiction—weathered but youthful, gruff but gentle, angry but forgiving. Yet it all seemed to work for him.

"I do appreciate you meeting with us," Asher said finally. "I know this all must be very hard for you. The position that you're in."

"Nobody's in a good position. I mean, I can't imagine what this all has been like for you and your grandmother."

"It hasn't been easy," he admitted.

He looked out the window, at the animated conversation between Teodora and Marlow. Both of them were waving their arms and shouting at one another.

"But I do really want to thank you." Asher turned back to me and reached across the table.

He took my hand in his—strong and rough and warm—and I noticed the paracord bracelet around his wrist. It had a small metal plaque imprinted with the three horns of Odin on an eagle. That was the insignia for the Vörðr—the Evig Riksdag police.

Competition to get into the Vörðr was harsh, and the job itself was renowned for being grueling. Recruits had died going through the relentless boot camp, but the Vörðr had to be the best of the best to protect the Riks from vengeful immortals or rogue Valkyries.

I lifted my gaze, letting his eyes meet mine, and I felt heat flush through me as he smiled at me.

Then Teodora came in like a blizzard, her sarong billowing around her, and Asher pulled his hand back from mine. She walked over and sat down heavily in her seat beside Asher.

"We managed to come to an agreement." Teodora motioned vaguely out the window, where Marlow was still standing on the sidewalk. "She's out there waiting for you when you're ready."

"What's the agreement?" Asher asked.

"She's going to work with you to find Tamerlane Fayette," Teodora explained as she poured herself a cup of black coffee. "And then she's going to kill him."

Asher raised an eyebrow and glanced over at me, before asking her, "That's your agreement?"

"Yes." Teodora sipped her coffee. "Well, that and if she doesn't kill Tamerlane, then I'm going to kill her."

SEVENTEEN

———◆———

Marlow was waiting outside for me, just as Teodora had said. But as soon as she saw me, she turned and started walking back toward her brownstone, and I had to jog to catch up with her. I was actually half an inch taller than my mother, but she'd always had these long strides that I had to struggle to match.

"Teodora said you reached an agreement," I said as I caught up with her.

"If you can call it that," Marlow snorted.

We stopped at a crosswalk, and a woman with a small child at her side glared up at Marlow—more specifically, she was glaring at the cigarillo in her hand.

"That's disgusting, and you're polluting the air for everyone around you that has to breathe in that noxious smoke," the woman reprimanded my mother.

Marlow turned to face her, putting her hand on her hip, and

leaned forward, reminding the woman of her size and strength. "Look around, honey. This whole city is nothing but pollution."

She gestured wildly with her cigarillo, and unfortunately she wasn't wrong. Even on a sunny day like today, a thick haze hung in the air. No matter how many attempts were made to be more environmentally friendly, there were just too many beings living too close together.

The light changed, and the woman huffed on ahead. Marlow laughed to herself, but she tossed her half-finished cigarillo into the gutter anyway.

It was late afternoon, and the sidewalks were full. They usually were, but today had the added benefit of being unseasonably warm for autumn. The air was still brisk, and Marlow pulled her coat more tightly around her as she stalked down the street.

Plus, it was the Friday before a holiday weekend. Sparkling black and purple garlands were wrapped around light poles, while images of skeletons and coffins were pinned up everywhere. All the storefront windows had flyers proclaiming their sales and specials for the Feast of the Dead celebrations.

"You know, I got an assignment from Samael last night," I told Marlow, since she seemed to have no interest in discussing her conversation with Teodora.

"He's got you busy, busy, busy," she said, and I swear she picked up her pace again, so I was nearly jogging to stay at her side.

"I was thinking tonight we should stake her out," I said. "She lives in the Gold Coast, which isn't too far."

"Tonight's no good. I've got to work at the call center."

"Tomorrow—"

"Tomorrow's no good," Marlow cut me off. We'd reached her brownstone, so she stopped and turned to face me. "Honestly, this whole weekend is no good because of that damned feast."

I glanced toward the front door, but apparently she wasn't going to invite me up, so we were going to have this conversation on her front stoop.

"But when we get an assignment, we're supposed to make the return within seventy-two hours if at all possible," I said, reciting the rules I'd been taught.

She shrugged. "Well, I'm telling you it's not possible for me to help you this weekend."

"Should I call Samael?" I asked.

"Why don't you take care of it yourself?" Marlow asked.

"I'm not licensed."

She rolled her eyes. "Can you handle it yourself or not?"

"I can," I replied, trying not to sound as uncertain as I felt.

"Then what do you need me for?"

"You're supposed to go with me," I persisted.

"Who cares? You got it covered."

"I know. I would just feel better if—"

"I'll only drag you down." She rummaged through her purse and pulled out her keys as she walked up the steps toward her place. "I just screw things up, Malin. I ruined everything with Tamerlane, and I don't think I'll be any good to you tonight. Go take care of this yourself."

I stood outside her brownstone for several long minutes after she'd gone inside. Some part of me hoped that she would come back out and apologize, explain that she was all worked up about the meeting with the Värjas, and she didn't mean any of it.

But she didn't, and really, I shouldn't have been surprised. In the nineteen years I'd been alive, I'd never known my mother to apologize. Not even once.

Marlow had left me with very limited options.

Samael had been okay with meeting him on my own, but there was no way he'd be cool with me actually going out on the assignment by myself. If I told him that Marlow was too busy to help me, that would most likely result in some kind of reprimand for her, and if there was an inquiry that went along with it, Tamerlane Fayette's name would almost certainly come up. That would lead to termination for her—and I didn't just mean of her career.

The second option was that I could just wait around for the weekend, and hope that Marlow changed her mind come Sunday or Monday. But that was a long shot, and I would most likely end up back where I was. But by then I'd already be extended past my deadline.

And the final option was just to follow Marlow's advice and take care of it myself. Assuming there were no hiccups in the assignment, then everyone would be none the wiser. The target would be killed, and neither Marlow nor myself would be in trouble.

So I headed back to my apartment to do as much prep work as I could. Samael had sent me all the files on Amaryllis Mori in my drop box.

I told Oona of my plan, so she made supper, which freed me up to spend as much time as I could studying everything I could about Amaryllis and the best ways to fight Jorogumos in general. Oona made tofu meat loaf, which I slathered in hot sauce and ate while hunched over my tablet, with Bowie curled up at my side.

Finally, it was time. According to the information Samael had sent me, Amaryllis should be getting off work in a few hours, and I wanted to be sure that I got there with enough time, in case she got out early.

I geared up—my sword Sigrún was sheathed around my waist, my dagger was in my thigh garter, and I had my asp and acidic pepper spray in my messenger bag.

"I still don't think you should do this," Oona told me for the hundredth time as I dropped my messenger bag over my shoulder. She stood in the center of the living room, cradling Bowie in her arms and frowning at me.

"I know, but it has to be done," I insisted. "I can't just let it go, or I'll end up with another Tamerlane situation on my hands. And we've all seen how that turns out."

"What if something happens to you?" she asked.

I walked closer to her and scratched Bowie between his antlers, and he nuzzled up against my hand. "If I die, you get Bowie, and you have to take care of him, because I said, and that will be my deathbed declaration."

She gave me her I'm-not-kidding-around look. "Mal. I can handle Bowie. He's not what I'm worried about."

"I gave you all the info." I motioned to a note I'd tacked up on the fridge.

Oona looked back over her shoulder at it and read it aloud. "*Amaryllis Mori. The Nysa club in Gold Coast.* That's it?"

"That's all you need to know if you decide to send out a search party," I said. "But don't be premature about it. Wait until at least three A.M. before freaking out. If you're worried, text me first."

"But you have to reply to the text, or I'll panic. You know me."

"I do."

"Be careful, Mal. There's a lot of crazies out tonight because of the holiday tomorrow," Oona cautioned. "I'd go with you, but I'm no good in a fight."

I smiled. "That's true, but I appreciate the sentiment." I bent down and kissed Bowie on his forehead. " 'Bye, Bowie. Be good for Oona."

With that, I left, heading out into the city to commit my first independent kill.

EIGHTEEN

———◆———

Hiding out beside the dumpster in the back alley behind the gentlemen's club, I had to appreciate that at least the garbage smelled better in the Gold Coast than it did around Shibuya. It was still dank, and the air held the putrid stench of stale beer, moldy food, and exhaust fumes.

Even a nice establishment like this—and Nysa was arguably the nicest strip club in the whole city—had a familiar stench to it. Whenever the back door to Nysa opened, the scent of cheap buffalo wings and sweat would waft out, along with the thumping bass of whatever music the women danced to.

The building itself had been styled after the Greek architecture that inspired the name, with Parthenonesque pillars surrounding it. They'd added plenty of gold flourishes and neon lights for good measure.

It was getting late, and while I had seen plenty of women coming out after their shifts—all high heels and body glitter—I had yet to see Amaryllis Mori. I was beginning to fear that tonight might be a bust, but then I began to feel it.

My sword felt heavier and grew warmer on my hip. I glanced down and saw that Sigrún had begun glowing a dull purple in its sheath; soon it would be bright enough to light up the entire alley.

The anxious electricity raced through me, and it was difficult to force myself to stand still. My body wanted to move, to run, to chase anything it could. My breathing grew more shallow as a metallic taste filled my mouth. The buzzing around my heart intensified, sending a heat pulsing through me, and the pressure began to build in the base of my stomach.

The hyperfocus kicked in, and I could barely feel my own body. I was aware of every subtle change in the breeze, every tiny sound that happened in the fifty-foot radius around me. The world slowed down, and I saw everything.

Amaryllis finally stepped out of the club, and she was even more beautiful in real life than she was in pictures. Her skin was like porcelain, with her long slender legs stretching below her short skirt to her stiletto heels. A few gold-leaf extensions had been added to her long silken black hair, glinting as she walked.

She took a few steps in the opposite direction from me, going toward the street where she could catch a taxi, but she stopped short. Warily, she turned back to look at me—she was the first to look at me the entire time I'd been staking out Nysa—and her big doe eyes widened even farther.

"No." She shook her head once, slow and deliberate. "It can't be you. It can't be now."

"Amaryllis Mori, you have been chosen to die," I said, as I walked toward her. "It is my duty to return you to the darkness from whence you came."

She smiled then, a bright red slit spreading out across her face. "Not if I send you first."

In the hours leading up to our confrontation, I had read every single thing I could find about the Jorogumos. But I had never seen one in real life before, and there really isn't anything that can prepare you for watching a beautiful young woman transform into a spider.

Her face changed first—her lips peeled back, revealing a mouthful of sharp teeth, including two fanged incisors, and her eyes multiplied, with bright red eyeballs popping out all across her forehead and cheeks.

Her legs went next—the pale satiny skin ripping open with an audible tearing sound. Her two legs quickly became eight spindly spider legs, covered in venom-filled razor-sharp hairs called setae, and her abdomen filled out and expanded to take on the bulbous shape of a black widow.

Her torso remained mostly unchanged, with her slinky dress clinging to her womanly curves, and human arms. Her willowy neck remained attached to her monstrous half-human, half-spider head, and her long black hair swirled around her.

"You think you can kill me, little Valkyrie?" she cried out at me, smiling through her fangs at me. "Kurnugia is more powerful than you'll ever know."

As she stepped closer to me, her pointed feet pattered on the asphalt. I stood my ground, and I felt no fear. The Valkyrie in me had taken over completely, and the only thing I could think about was ending Amaryllis.

"It gives me no pleasure to end you," I told her as I unsheathed Sigrún, but the pressure was building inside me so much, I could hardly stand it.

"Too bad," Amaryllis said, somehow making a *tsk*ing sound with her awful mouth. "Because I am going to *love* killing you."

She swung at me with her leg, and I narrowly ducked out of the way. In her spider form, she was much taller than me, which made it much harder to cut off her head. I jumped at her, but my sword merely nicked her shoulder before she struck me with her leg and sent me flying back into the building.

It didn't hurt, because I couldn't feel anything other than the anticipation of the kill, but for a moment I couldn't breathe. But everything I read had said she shouldn't have been able to throw me like that. Jorogumos were weak compared to Valkyries.

Amaryllis ran at me, and I tried to scramble out of the way. The sharp end of her foot stabbed through my calf like a knife, and she lifted me up off the ground. I dangled upside down, as she held me up by my left leg, and I could hear the sound of my pants and flesh ripping.

"The tables have begun to turn, little Valkyrie," Amaryllis said, holding me up in front of her. "But don't worry. Soon enough, the underworld will come for you."

She cackled then, and I swung out with Sigrún, slicing off the end of her leg. She howled in pain as I fell to the ground, with the end of her leg still embedded in mine.

I lay motionless on my back, letting her charge at me. She stabbed her foot into my right shoulder, pinning me to the ground, and I allowed her to. I waited until she was hovering right above me, her saliva dripping down onto my forehead, and I drove my sword right into her abdomen.

She screamed like a banshee—her voice echoing through everything and sounding like a thousand voices screaming out at once. Her belly opened up, pouring out thick black blood, and she stepped back from me, unpinning me.

As she lost blood, she stumbled and tried futilely to hold it in. While the injury was severe, it wasn't fatal, and I still needed to finish the job.

"No! *No!*" she screamed as I climbed onto her back. "No, you can't do this! It isn't supposed to happen like this!"

I grabbed her by the hair, yanking her head back, and told her, "This isn't my decision to make." Then I pulled my sword across her throat, easily slicing through her neck and decapitating her.

The air around us began glowing bright purple from Sigrún, and a wind came up, out of Amaryllis, and twisted through the alley. Relief began flowing over me in warm waves, and my muscles quivered.

I climbed off the corpse of the Jorogumo, and I fell to my knees on the ground beside her, breathing in deeply.

The sound of wings flapping pulled me from my moment of relieved euphoria, and I looked up to see a massive black raven standing at the end of the alley. It was roughly the size of a bobcat, larger than any raven I'd ever seen before, and its beady eyes were locked right on me.

Even though the purple light from Sigrún had all but gone out, the light somehow seemed to linger on the bird's black feathers. It tilted its head as it watched me, squawking once.

"What do you want?" I demanded, but the raven had no reply. It just flapped its wings and disappeared into the night sky.

NINETEEN

◆

While I was in full Valkyrie mode I may have felt nothing, but now the pain hit me with the intensity of a thousand suns. I doubled over on the ground, writhing in the thick blood spilling out from Amaryllis's body.

"Malin?" a familiar voice called out, sounding panicked, and suddenly Quinn Devane was at my side, kneeling down beside me. "By the gods, Malin, are you all right?"

"Yeah, I'm great," I lied through gritted teeth.

She frowned at me, brushing back her silver hair from her face. "You are not great. You were attacked by a Jorogumo, and you have poison flowing through your veins."

I wanted to argue with her, but there was an agonizing fire inside me that felt like it was burning me from the inside out, so all I could manage was a grimace.

"It shouldn't be hitting you this hard, though," Quinn said, her husky voice tightening with worry. "Valkyries aren't entirely immune, but the pain shouldn't be so severe."

I squeezed my eyes shut and barely managed to say, "Sorry my pain isn't at the correct levels."

"Wait. Just wait," Quinn commanded, and I heard her rummaging through her purse. A few seconds later, she held a cold vial to my lips. "Drink this."

"What is it?" I asked.

"I'm not a stranger trying to roofie you in a bar. I'm your . . ." Quinn trailed off, then quickly added, "Whatever. Just drink it."

I did as I was told, swallowing down the cold bitter liquid. It tasted exactly how gasoline smelled, and I barely gagged it down.

"Oh, hell, that's terrible," I groaned.

"It's not supposed to *taste* good," Quinn said. "It's an antivenom, not a soda pop. It'll stop the pain."

Sure enough, within moments I felt it running through me like ice, putting out all the fire that had been threatening to burn me alive. I blinked a few times, and stared up into her worried emerald eyes.

"Thanks," I said.

"You're not all healed up yet," Quinn warned me. "You'll still need Oona to stitch you up when you get home."

I groaned as a realization hit me. "That's what you're doing here. Oona sent you to check up on me."

"And you're lucky that she did. It's strange that the venom affected you so powerfully. . . ." She trailed off for a moment, thinking, then she shook her head. "But it did, and you could've died, rolling around in pain, if I hadn't gotten to you."

"I would've been fine," I insisted, even if I wasn't sure that was true. "I'm always fine."

Quinn let out an exasperated sigh, a sound I'd heard quite often during our brief relationship. She would always talk about how much she enjoyed being around me, but the thing I seemed to do most was exasperate her.

"Why do you always have to be like this?" Quinn asked. She sat back on her knees, watching me as I struggled to get up. "There's nothing wrong with accepting help."

"There is if I don't need it," I said and then stumbled and nearly fell over.

I would've actually fallen, if Quinn hadn't gotten up and raced to catch me. Her arm around me felt strong, stronger than I remembered her being, and I allowed myself to lean into her.

"I'm walking you home," Quinn said firmly. "And I don't care what you say. I won't be able to live with myself if I don't make sure you get home safe."

"Fine, if it's what you want. . . ." My voice trailed off.

"It is," she said, and we started walking down the alley toward the street. Her arm securely around my waist, me leaning against her as I limped.

My luft was parked three blocks away, but I was in no condition to drive it. I didn't know if Quinn planned on walking me the entire way home, or if she had a car somewhere nearby. But at the moment I didn't care all that much. I was just relishing the way it felt to be touching her again.

Her skin was so soft, and I remembered the way it felt when she ran her hands over my body. My mind flashed to when she had kissed me for the first time. Her mouth had been so hungry and eager, and she tasted like plums. We had been drinking, but the only thing I was drunk on was her.

I had never felt that way before I met her—so light-headed and excited and nervous and wonderfully sick.

"What were you doing anyway?" I asked, trying to distract myself from my own thoughts. "Before Oona called you to come rescue me."

"A Feast of the Dead pre-party," she replied, and that explained her outfit.

It was a skintight sweater dress with thigh-high boots. The dress was low-cut, so when I happened to look down, I could see the edges of her black lace bra barely covering her chest, and her Vegvisir amulet lay between her breasts.

I pulled my gaze away, forcing myself to look at the sidewalk in front of us. "Were you with anyone?"

"So what if I was?" she asked, not unkindly.

"I was just making conversation," I contended.

She waited a beat before asking, "Are you still seeing that guy you were with the other night?"

"I'm not seeing him."

"That's not what it looked like to me."

"He's just my mechanic," I insisted.

Quinn scoffed. "Uh-huh. My mechanic has never looked at me the way he was looking at you."

"Well, maybe you should wear this outfit, then."

"What is that supposed to mean?" she demanded.

I sighed. "I was just trying to say you look amazing tonight."

"Oh." She paused. "Thank you. I'd say that you look good, but honestly, you look like crap."

I laughed. "I wouldn't expect any less from you."

"Why were you out on your own, anyway? You could've gotten yourself killed, and are you even licensed yet?" Quinn asked, and I involuntarily tensed.

Telling Oona about Marlow had been one thing. She'd been my best friend forever, and I pretty much had to tell her everything. But the more people who knew about Marlow's flagrancies, the more likely it would be that a higher-up would find out, and then she would be done for.

"My mother had stuff to do," I answered cagily. "She couldn't be here, and I had a job, so I did it."

"That's not protocol."

"Please, Quinn," I begged. "I've had a long night. Can you not lecture me, for once?"

"Oh, sorry," she said with exaggerated remorse, her words dripping with sarcasm. "I didn't realize that having a conversation was lecturing you."

And then I remembered exactly why I had ended things with her. Quinn was always pushing and pushing, demanding more from me than I was ready to give. Probably even more than I was capable of. I would never be enough for Quinn, no matter how hard she tried to mold me into being who she needed me to be.

When we'd first met, she'd taken my breath away with her beauty and her quick wit. But by the end I was suffocating under her unmet expectations.

I stopped. "You know what? I'll just get a taxi." I pulled away from her, even though putting the full weight on my leg hurt like hell, but I kept my expression stoic, so she wouldn't know how much it hurt to walk away from her.

Her face instantly fell, and she reached out for me, but I just hobbled back from her. "Malin, no. I didn't mean it like that. I can get you home."

"No, a taxi will be fine." I walked to the edge of the sidewalk, raising my hand to flag down the first thing that came by.

"Malin," Quinn repeated, just as a bright yellow hovercar pulled up beside me.

"It's fine, Quinn," I assured her. "Thanks for all your help. I'll see you around."

TWENTY

———◆———

O h, bloody hell!" I cried out, causing Bowie to thump his back foot on the floor in a show of anger.

He'd already taken to hiding under the kitchen table, since I'd been cursing and yelling for the past twenty minutes as Oona attempted to take care of my battle wounds. She had cut off my pants just above the knee so it would be easier to get to my injury.

"Isn't there something you have to make this more painless?" I asked through gritted teeth.

Oona knelt on the floor in front of me, wearing thick vinyl gloves to protect her from the Jorogumo venom inside the setae, and her tackle box of thaumaturgy healing and apothecary tools was open beside her. She'd placed a towel on the floor underneath me to help maintain the mess, since my leg was soaked with blood—red from me and black from the Jorogumo.

"Okay, Mal, you have a giant spider leg jabbed straight through the muscle of your calf," Oona explained as calmly as she could.

"There's only so much I can do to make this painless. You really should go see a doctor."

"No doctors." I shook my head.

While a doctor, with expertise, sterile equipment, and syringes filled with beautiful, beautiful morphine would be ideal, I couldn't risk it. Doctors would ask questions, which could lead to them figuring out that I was working on my own as an unlicensed Valkyrie, and they were legally required to report that to the Evig Riksdag.

So that left Oona as my only option for medical care. And she really wasn't that bad at it. She'd already stitched up the puncture wound in my shoulder that Amaryllis had given me, but pulling a spider leg covered in needlelike hairs out of my leg was a little beyond her usual area of expertise.

"Here." Oona held a thick piece of leather toward me. "I'm gonna pull the leg out now. Bite down on that."

"All right, screw it, let's do this." I took it from her and did as I was told. I bit down as hard as I could and squeezed my eyes shut.

"Here goes nothing," Oona said, more to herself than to me, and pain exploded in my leg.

It already hurt like hell before she even touched it, but now the setae were burrowing deeper into my muscle as she yanked on the spider leg. It felt as if she were trying to pull my leg inside out.

When the pain began to reach the point where I felt I couldn't take it anymore—I screamed against the leather in my mouth as nausea rolled over me, and darkness edged around my thoughts like I was on the verge of blacking out—I heard the wet *thwak* as the spider leg finally came free.

"There!" Oona declared proudly, but I already felt it.

My leg still hurt something fierce, but nowhere near as bad as before. I spit out the leather and relaxed back against the couch, gasping for breath.

"It should be much easier from here on out," Oona assured me. "I'm going to start cleaning it now."

I winced as she started digging around in my leg, getting out any setae that had decided to stay embedded in my muscle, and I stared up at the ceiling.

"This is why you shouldn't have gone alone," Oona said after I cursed under my breath again. "I bet this wouldn't have happened if Marlow was there."

"Maybe not," I allowed. "But it shouldn't have been this bad anyway."

"What do you mean?"

"Valkyries have immunities to this kind of stuff. From everything I know about Jorogumos, their poison should only have a minimal effect on me." I shook my head. "Even Quinn commented on it."

Oona spritzed a pale purple liquid on my leg wound. It stung for a moment, then the pain quickly faded to a dull nothingness. "That should help numb it a bit, and now I'm gonna start stitching you up."

"Thanks for the heads-up." I made sure to keep my eyes on the ceiling so I wouldn't see the needle go in. Oona was right—the spray did numb the pain. I still felt it, the pressure of the needle and thread going through skin, but it wasn't as bad as it could have been.

"Do you think it could be because you're not licensed yet?" Oona asked.

"That's not how it works," I explained. "A piece of paper doesn't give me the antibodies or super-strength. I'm born with it. It's in my blood."

"Could your father have diluted it or something?" she asked.

"No. All Valkyries have mortal fathers, and I've never heard of them having fewer abilities for that reason."

Oona lifted her head and looked up at me. "Who was your father?"

"I don't know. Just some human," I said, then quickly added, "No offense."

She snorted. "None taken."

Valkyries were in an odd place where we weren't immortal, but we weren't exactly human, either. We were a breed all our own, with many of the same weaknesses as humans, like death, aging, and the need for oxygen and sunlight. We were just stronger, more resilient, and had an innate ability to hunt immortals, and while our blood weakened the immortals around us, it had no effect on humans.

"But this is different anyway," I said. "Amaryllis was saying all this weird stuff."

"What do you mean?"

I closed my eyes, trying to remember exactly what Amaryllis had been saying to me through her fangs. "That she was going to kill me, and the underworld is more powerful than I'll know, and the tables are turning."

"That's not normal posturing and threats?"

"Kind of. But it just . . ." I sighed. "I don't know. It didn't feel like an empty threat. It was almost like . . . like she *knew* something."

Oona stopped stitching me for a moment. "I'm doing the best I can with this, but you're still going to need to go to the doctor at some point to make sure this is taken care of for real."

Then I felt the needle going back in, and Oona said very little as she concentrated on finishing the sutures. When she was done, she started washing off my leg and then covered the wound with some kind of anti-infection salve.

"Did Marlow ever get beat up like this?" Oona asked as she wrapped my leg in a bandage.

Marlow had returned with a black eye or a fat lip a dozen or so times. I remember waking up once when she came in late. Her lip was bloody, and her knuckles were all scraped up from punching. She sat in the darkened living room, drinking vodka straight from the bottle, and when I tried to ask her what had happened, she just snapped at me to go back to bed.

But that was probably the worst I'd ever seen her. No broken bones. No puncture wounds. No parts of spiders trapped inside her.

"She came home with a few scrapes and bruises from time to time, but it was never this bad," I admitted.

"So it could be because of your inexperience." Oona had finished bandaging my leg, so she sat back and looked up at me. "Or it could be because something is up." She waited a beat before asking, "Is there any way this could be related to that guy that Marlow didn't kill?"

I groaned, realizing belatedly that it could be. "I don't know."

"You're gonna have to talk to someone, Mal. That's the only way you'll find out what's really going on."

"Who am I gonna talk to?" I asked, sitting up straighter on the couch. "Marlow is stonewalling me, and anyone else I could talk to, like Samael or my teachers, they would just turn me in."

"You could talk to Quinn," Oona proposed.

My heart skipped a beat, as if Oona saying her name would somehow invoke her presence, and I shook my head adamantly. "No, I'm not talking to Quinn."

"She wouldn't turn you in."

"You don't know that, and even if it's true, I can't," I maintained. "It's too complicated."

"First off, I *do* know that," Oona argued. "She cares about you. When I told her what you were doing, she freaked out because she was so worried about you."

I groaned loudly in exasperation.

"And second, I don't even know why you broke up with her," Oona went on, undeterred by my reaction. "You two were crazy about each other, and then you suddenly pulled the Valkyries-can't-fall-in-love card."

I rubbed my hand over my face and regretted ever introducing Oona to Quinn. "I already told you it's complicated."

"Okay, it's not, but let's say that it is," she conceded. "That there's all sorts of complex, unrequited feelings going on between you and Quinn. You know what I say to that? Suck it up, buttercup. If she can help you deal with whatever crap is going on right now, then you need to ask for help. That's the bottom line."

"I know you're right. . . ." My voice trailed off.

"But?" she supplied.

"But the fewer people that know what's going on, the safer it is for both me and Marlow. So let me just try talking to her, and if I can't find out anything, I'll go to Quinn."

"That's all I'm saying," Oona relented finally.

I stood up slowly, careful to not put too much weight on my injured left leg. "Right now I should get some sleep."

Oona scrambled through her thaumaturgy kit, before finding a miniature mason jar. It was filled with tiny ocher crystals, and she dumped out two into the palm of her hand. "Here." She held them out to me. "Take this."

"What is it?" I asked, already taking it from her.

"It's called solamentum, and it's made with ginger and angelic toadstool with just the smallest touch of codeine," she explained. "It should help with the inflammation, pain, and risk of infection."

I threw back my head and tossed them in my mouth, and instantly regretted it. They were tart and acidic, like grapefruit juice mixed with battery acid. "That tastes terrible. Why does everything that's good for me taste so awful?"

"That's just how the world works, Mal."

I smiled down at her. "Thanks again for taking care of me."

"That's what friends are for, right?" Oona smiled back.

"Come on, Bowie." I whistled for him as I hobbled toward my bedroom, and he hopped after me. "Let's hit the sack."

TWENTY-ONE

———◆———

It wasn't even noon yet as I made my way to Marlow's place, and the city was already bursting with Feast of the Dead celebrations. A parade had traffic blocked up all over, and it took my taxi driver an extra thirty minutes just to get me to where I'd left my luft parked in the Gold Coast.

The streets were dripping with decorations, from black streamers to strings of purple lights. Each light post I went past on my way to Marlow's had a different poster of a figure from the underworld, all of them labeled with:

ᕈᎯᏟᏒᎾᕼ ᏚᎯᏆᕼᏆ ᎾF ᏦᏌᏒᕼᏌᏀᏆᎯ

Normally the Feast of the Dead seemed like a fun—albeit obnoxiously traffic-jam-inducing—holiday, but today everything felt strangely unsettling. The patron saints posters—the sage Hades with a thick beard and blue flames rising behind him, the terrifying horned Supay with red eyes and bloody flesh peeling from his body, and the arresting Ereshkigal with lush black skin and an impish grin sitting atop her throne of bones—were particularly unnerving.

Even though they were just pictures on paper—an artist's rendering in exquisite detail—they carried such an imposing presence that I could swear their eyes were following me as I hurried past, making the hair rise on the back of my neck and an icy chill run down my spine.

To get to Marlow's stoop, I had to push my way through a throng of teenage girls and ghouls, all dressed up in couture mourning gowns, several replete with gauzy black veils flowing around them. They all talked and laughed loudly, and if the smell was to be believed, they were already drunk on cheap booze and liliplum.

Marlow hadn't answered her phone when I tried calling this morning, and given the severity of everything that had happened with Amaryllis Mori, I decided I couldn't wait to talk to her, and I was coming over uninvited.

After walking up the four flights of stairs to her apartment, I was really hoping she was home, because I doubted that my leg could handle the trek again. Oona had even given me a couple more of those solamentum crystals to help with the pain, but my wound was still throbbing. I'd smartly worn a flowy skirt with slits down the side, so it wouldn't rub against my leg too much.

I knocked, and though it took a bit for her to answer, I heard Marlow talking inside. The slot for the peephole clanged and she muttered, "Dammit," on the other side of the door. Just what every daughter wants to hear when she visits her mother.

Finally she opened the door a crack. She was wide awake, with hair and makeup properly styled, which was usually a good indicator that she would be less cranky, but based on the irritation in her eyes, I realized that wasn't the case.

"What are you doing here?" Marlow demanded through the gap in the door.

"I just—"

Before I could finish, she shouted back over her shoulder, "Did you tell her you were here?"

"No," Asher said from inside Marlow's apartment. "I didn't talk to her."

"Asher is here?" I asked. "What's going on?"

"Fine, come in." Marlow opened the door all the way and gestured wildly around her. "Let's all just have a big old chat."

The first thing I noticed was that her apartment was significantly less cluttered than it had been when I came over the day before yesterday. All the garbage had been removed from the kitchen, and most of her random military surplus objects seemed to be stowed away somewhere.

The boxes were still stacked up, blocking the only window, and there were still the tubs of rice and lentils, but in general everything felt more orderly and neatly piled up. The only light came from what little spilled around the boxes, several fat candles on the coffee table, and a solitary bulb shining over the sink in the kitchen.

Asher sat on the couch, smiling sheepishly and offering me a small wave as I stepped inside. Marlow had stomped off to the kitchen, pouring herself a cup of coffee with a hefty dash of vodka, so I closed the door behind me.

"Your mother invited me over to discuss things," Asher explained awkwardly, since it seemed like Marlow didn't plan to. "I got here about ten minutes ago."

"Why didn't you tell me?" I asked Marlow.

"Why would I?" She sat down in a slipper chair across from Asher and crossed her long legs, one over the other. She stared up at me with her steel-gray eyes. "This doesn't involve you. This was part of my agreement with Teodora, not you."

"How does this not involve me?" I protested.

"I'm the one that made a mistake, so I'm the one fixing it," she replied coolly. "You don't have anything to do with it."

"Yeah, sure, you're right." I took off my messenger bag from where it hung looped across my chest and walked over to the couch, where I sat down heavily beside Asher. "I almost got killed last night, but you're right. None of this concerns me."

Marlow tilted her head and narrowed her eyes slightly. "What do you mean, you almost got killed?"

"Remember how you were too busy this weekend to help me do a job I'm not ready to do yet?" I clunked my heavy moto boot on her battered coffee table and pulled my skirt to the side to show my leg. Oona had rebandaged it this morning, but it was still bleeding through. My skin above and below it was dark purple from bruising. "Well, I went to take care of it myself, and the Jorogumo almost got the best of me."

My mother looked at my wound and exhaled wearily. "By Odin's ass, Malin, you should've been able to handle that yourself."

I dropped my skirt and tried to ignore the sting I felt in my chest. Asher had gasped when he saw my leg, and he stared at me with wide eyes. Marlow had hardly reacted at all.

I wanted to scream at her, demanding to know how she could take pity on some condemned angel like Tamerlane Fayette but she couldn't manage to care at all about her own daughter.

But I didn't. Instead I just said, "The Jorogumo was stronger than it should've been. The poison wasn't supposed to affect me, but it nearly killed me."

"Are you okay?" Asher asked. His body tilted toward me, and his voice was low with concern.

"Yeah, I'll live." I forced a reassuring smile at him. "Thanks."

"It didn't kill you, and you need to learn to fight better," Marlow interjected.

"No, Marlow, you're not listening. Quinn was there—" I began to argue, but my mother cut me off.

"Quinn Devane?" She snorted. "Since when did she become an expert on all things Valkyrie?"

"At this point, I honestly feel like she knows more than you," I replied defiantly.

Marlow narrowed her eyes. She'd been about to drink from her mug, but she stopped after I mouthed off, her lips hovering a centimeter above her coffee. "Don't even—"

"I mean," I cut her off, "she does know enough to always kill her assignments."

"This is exactly why I didn't invite you over here." Marlow set down her coffee on the stone end table, and opened the wooden humidor resting on it, pulling out a slender cigarillo wrapped in dark brown leaves. "I knew you'd just hold that over me."

"Marlow!" I shouted in exasperation. "I am not browbeating you! I am trying to tell you what's going on and ask for your help."

She scoffed as she lit her cigarillo. Then she took a long drag from it, before licking her lips and eyeing me. "What could you possibly need *my* help with?"

"Figuring out what's going on," I replied simply.

"What's going on is that I need to finish this shit with Tamerlane so he stops wreaking havoc on the world and Asher can get some closure," Marlow said. "That's plenty, isn't it?"

I pursed my lips and nodded. "Yeah, that's plenty."

She cleared her throat. "Now, as I was telling Asher before you interrupted us, I have a contact. She's always made it a point to know everything about everything. I reached out to her last night, and she said she'd be willing to meet with us."

"Does she know anything about Tamerlane Fayette?" Asher asked.

"I didn't ask her anything directly yet," Marlow said. "I didn't want to set off any alarms. But if Tamerlane is still alive somewhere, she'll know about him."

"How can you be so sure?" I pressed.

"It's what she does. She's over six hundred years old, and she's managed to accumulate a lot of knowledge and a lot of friends in that time," she explained.

"Six hundred?" I asked. Most of the assignments had been for immortals that were only a couple hundred years old. I'd never even met anyone over four hundred years old. "Why hasn't she died?"

"She just hasn't been chosen to return yet." Marlow shrugged and cast her annoyed gaze toward her window, which was mostly blocked by her boxes. "Now, with the ridiculous Feast of the Dead today, traffic is going to be murder, so we should get going if we want to meet with her before the sun sets."

"Is that a stipulation?" Asher asked.

"It's what she requested," Marlow replied simply.

"Who is this magical all-knowing person?" I asked.

"Cecily Stavros. She's a gorgon," she replied as if meeting with a gorgon were no big thing, and then she stood up. "Now, if you don't mind, I'm going to go to the bathroom, and then we can head out."

Marlow took her cigarillo with her when she went into the restroom, but the cloud of clove-scented smoke lingered behind. Asher and I sat in the dimly lit living room as silence enveloped us.

He leaned in closer to me, so his knee brushed up against mine, and in a low, conspiratorial tone he said, "I don't want to sound rude, but your mother is kind of a bitch sometimes."

I laughed. "Yeah, she certainly is."

TWENTY-TWO

———◆———

Marlow locked up her car, then started walking. The sidewalk was crowded and cluttered with decorations and garbage, but she kept clomping on ahead, not waiting for either Asher or myself.

"Now, she doesn't know I'm bringing the two of you," Marlow said, once we'd scrambled to catch up to her ridiculous fast pace. "So don't say too much or you'll freak her out. She doesn't like visitors."

"Then how does she find everything out?" I asked.

Marlow waved me off. "It's not my business how she knows her business. I just know that she's helped me track down many of my trickier assignments."

"I thought you hadn't talked to her in a while," Asher said.

"It's been over ten years," Marlow admitted.

"Why has it been so long?" I asked. "If she was so helpful in the past."

"We had a falling-out," Marlow replied vaguely, and then she stopped so short, I almost ran into her. "We're here. Well, she lives down there."

She pointed to the narrow stairwell to her left. It was dark and dank, running so deep underground I thought it might lead us to the sewer. Leaves and trash had piled up at the bottom, blanketing the concrete in front of a keyhole doorway.

"Have either of you ever met a gorgon before?" Marlow asked, turning back to look at Asher and me.

I shook my head, while Asher replied, "I've seen pictures of them."

"She won't turn you to stone," Marlow prepped us. "I mean, she *can* if she wants to, but it doesn't just happen automatically. But don't look directly at the snakes. It's rude."

I was about to ask if there was anything we should know about Cecily Stavros specifically, but Marlow had turned and was already bounding down the steps. Asher and I waited politely in the darkness behind her as she knocked.

It was a few minutes before the door finally creaked open. Her hand on the doorframe was the first thing I saw. Long red fingernails and pale skin with a few iridescent green scales trailing down the back of her hand to underneath her satin dressing gown.

Then her face slowly materialized in the gap from the open door. At first she appeared to be a woman in her sixties—an admittedly attractive woman in her sixties, but on the older side nonetheless. Her skin looked soft and smooth, though wrinkled, with more of the green scales trailing around her hairline and down her neck toward her décolletage.

Her hair was beautiful golden waves, and intertwined with it were five living, breathing snakes. They grew out from her scalp and danced around her head like a halo. The snakes leaned out farther than her, their tongues flitting out, and the light from above the stairwell shimmered off their scales.

"It's been a long time," Cecily said, and her eyes—brilliant green, matching the snakes—were locked on my mother. Her lips twisted into a strange smile.

"It has," Marlow agreed, returning her own uneasy smile.

"You killed my sister," Cecily told my mother.

I sensed Asher's posture grow more rigid, as if readying himself to spring into action if necessary. He was beside me, but he took a half step forward, almost as if to protect me. Which was silly, because I was far more equipped to battle something like a gorgon. Instinctively, I reached for my hip, but I'd left Sigrún at home. The sword was useless when I wasn't on an assignment, anyway, but it gave me comfort just touching it and knowing it was there.

"I did," Marlow admitted calmly. "I was only doing my job. It's not me who decides who lives or who dies."

The peculiar smile remained fixed on Cecily's face as she stared up at Marlow. "Just following orders, were you?" she asked, and Marlow nodded. "I've heard that excuse to explain away all kinds of evil acts in this world."

"I don't expect it to explain away anything I've done," Marlow said. "I'm only telling you that it wasn't personal."

"Well, if you had known Calixta, it would've been personal," Cecily said with a light laugh. "I hated my sister, and I'm glad she's dead." The gorgon stepped back and opened the door wider. "Come on in."

Immediately inside the door was a small foyer that looked about as dark and dank as the stairwell around us, but when Cecily opened the door beyond that, it was a totally different story.

Brightly lit by an opulent chandelier, everything was white marble with gold embellishments and crystals everywhere. Huge mirrors with ornate bronze frames hung on the walls. Every piece of furniture—from the flared bench by the door to the mirrored sideboard cabinet—was all glamorously art deco.

Cecily led the way through the surprisingly spacious apartment, her long blush pink dressing gown flowing on the marble floors behind her, and went down a few steps into her sunken living room. She sat on a sofa near a baby grand piano and gestured widely to the room.

"Please, sit," she said, lounging back on the sofa.

In the center of the room was a large glass coffee table sitting atop a white fur rug, and Marlow sat down on the tufted ottoman beside it. I decided on the velvet settee, and Asher sat down beside me, so close our legs touched when he leaned forward, resting his elbows on his legs. Sitting across from Cecily like this, with Asher at my side, I felt a bit like an uneasy teenager being introduced to her new boyfriend's disapproving parents.

"Aren't you going to introduce me to your guests?" Cecily purred as she lounged back on the sofa, and her gaze lingered on Asher.

"This is my daughter Malin and her friend Asher." Marlow gestured to us.

"And I am Cecily Stavros, one of your mother's oldest and dearest friends," she said, laughing lightly. She rested her head on her arm, and a snake coiled around her wrist. "I understand you've come here asking for a favor."

"It's not a favor, exactly—" Marlow started to explain, but Cecily cut straight through the bullshit.

A snake in her hair began to hiss, and Cecily held up her hand to silence it. She asked, "Do you want something from me, or did you just come for a friendly chat?"

Marlow sat up straighter. "We only wanted information."

Cecily clicked her tongue, then narrowed her eyes. "And what shall I get in return?"

"What do you want?" Marlow asked.

"I want you to tell me when I'll die."

TWENTY-THREE

───◆───

M arlow took a deep breath, looking the gorgon directly in the face, and unemotionally answered, "I don't know. I don't know until the name shows up on my orders."

Cecily got up, walking across the room to a gold and glass serving cart. "But certainly my time must be up soon." She looked back over her shoulder at Marlow. "I can't be the only one that they allow to live forever."

She began pouring herself a drink, a dusty pink liquid from a lavish decanter, into a highball glass. From a small bowl she plucked two small globes that looked like ice cubes, but when she dropped them in her glass, they fizzed and bubbled.

"The math of the gods is a mystery to all of us," Marlow said simply.

"So what do you have to offer me?" Cecily asked. She walked past me and Asher on her way back to the sofa, and she paused in front of Asher to run her hand underneath her chin. "Did you bring me this delicious young man?"

All the snakes in her hair leered toward him, and he continued to stare at her impassively. But a small tick in his jaw made me suspect that it was taking a great deal of fortitude to keep from pulling back from her.

"I'm here because the information is of great benefit to me," Asher said.

Cecily threw back her head and laughed—a cheerful cackling sound—and then she strode back to return to her spot lounging on the sofa. "Don't be so serious, my dear boy. I'm only teasing."

"He's actually the reason I'm here," Marlow interjected, her voice sounding light, probably because Cecily seemed to have taken a liking to Asher.

His gaze turned stormy as he rested his blue eyes on my mother. "Not to argue semantics, but the reason we're here is actually because of *you*."

"Oh, there seems to be contention in the group." Cecily's eyes bounced excitedly between Marlow and Asher, and one of her snakes dipped its head into her glass, drinking. "Do tell all the juicy details."

"There isn't much to tell," Marlow replied, casting an irritated glare toward Asher.

"We're looking for the man that killed Asher's mother," I interjected, because I feared they would go around and around like this all afternoon. "Tamerlane Fayette."

Cecily tilted her head and sipped from her drink. "Name doesn't ring a bell. I've always been better with faces, anyway."

I pulled my phone from my messenger bag and quickly scrolled through until I found the picture of Tamerlane I'd saved to it. Then I walked over to her. Cecily touched the phone, moving it so she could get a better look, but she just shook her head.

"This isn't enough. I'll need more. Is there anything else you can tell me about him?"

Asher looked over at Marlow, and when she didn't say anything, he cleared his throat and said, "He's supposed to be dead."

Cecily's eyes widened with glee and her smile grew so wide, it looked painful. I don't know if I'd ever seen anyone quite as happy as she looked just then.

"Asher," Marlow hissed, with fury in her eyes. If she were any closer to him, she would've smacked him across the head, something I'd experienced firsthand plenty of times.

Asher shrugged. "It's the only other thing we really know about him."

"Did you let someone slip away, Marlow?" Cecily wagged her finger. "You dirty bird."

"It's a complicated issue, and I would like it if you could keep it between us," Marlow said.

"What's a little secret between old friends?" Cecily intimated as she took another drink.

Marlow smiled thinly. "Thank you."

"But now that you mention it, I have heard rumors about draugrs," Cecily said, and when Asher looked quizzical, she followed up with, "The undead."

Asher's brow furrowed. "You mean like a zombie or a vampire?"

"No. Not just immortals like vampires, or myths like zombies. Draugrs are undead in that they are immortals who managed to escape their fate and skipped their date with a Valkyrie," Cecily elaborated.

"So it has happened before?" I asked.

"There's talk of it from time to time, but most of the time it's only gossip and urban legends." Cecily waved her hand and tossed her head. "I've been alive for over half a millennium, and I've only met one draugr. He was a miserable old fool. Their time is up for a reason, and he eventually came to see me and asked me to turn him to stone. So I did."

She nodded toward a statue at the other end of the living room. He was marble perfection, with the chiseled physique of the gods, wearing only a loincloth, and with two large wings coming out of his back.

"Do you know anything about draugrs nowadays?" I asked, and Asher continued staring back over his shoulder at the statue.

"I had assumed it was nothing more than rumors or wishful thinking," Cecily admitted. "We immortals are always looking for stories about cheating death and ways to extend our existence here on earth."

The thing about immortals was that they never really died. There were ways to destroy their earthly bodies—either with the blade of a Valkyrie, or in various difficult tasks, like a vampire with a stake to its chest or a silver bullet for a lobishman. But once their bodies were dead, they merely moved on to the next plane of their existence—down to Kurnugia.

But Kurnugia was alleged to be dark and unpleasant, with several millennia's worth of angry demons and devils jostling for control and tormenting everyone around them. Without the Vanir gods and the Valkyries to intervene, it was chaos, and death wasn't an option anymore, so it was an endless nightmare.

There was a bastion of peace—a solitary fortress known as Zianna that was ruled by angels and other divine immortals. But with the population of immortals growing for all eternity, it was legendary for being nearly impossible to gain entrance. There were far too many immortals, and even discounting the huge swath that were too cruel and malicious to ever be invited in, it would be impossible to house all the saintly beings.

With the prospect of spending the rest of eternity in the cramped hell of Kurnugia, and with the doors of Zianna locked to them, most immortals preferred to live out their days on earth, where the sun was bright and pleasures were easy.

"What rumors have you been hearing?" Marlow asked.

"That there's a whole trio of draugrs stalking about the city," Cecily said.

"At least you're not the only Valkyrie shirking your duties," Asher muttered, causing Marlow to give him another dirty look.

"What is it they say?" Cecily asked. "Trouble always comes in threes?" Then she tilted her head. "Or is that death?"

"What are they doing in the city?" Marlow asked, returning the conversation to the topic at hand.

Cecily answered, "The same thing everyone else does here—get into as much trouble as you can without getting caught."

"Do you know anything about them?" Marlow asked.

"Not much." Cecily let out a dramatic sigh. "Only one of them I've heard of by name—Bram Madichonnen."

"Have you heard if he associates with Tamerlane Fayette?" Asher asked hopefully.

"Honestly, I haven't heard of this Tamerlane fellow at all, and the only thing I know about Bram Madichonnen is that he's allegedly a draugr and likes to hang out at the Red Raven."

"The Red Raven? Of course he does," Marlow groused.

I'd never been to the Red Raven, but the debauchery and sinister clientele there made it infamous around the country. It was a bar and dance club located in the Aizsaule District of the city, which had unofficially become an "impious-only" neighborhood. To top it off, the Red Raven was owned by Velnias—a demon who thought of himself as some kind of mobster.

Cecily leaned forward and set her drink on the coffee table. "Since we're old friends, I would *hate* to see you hurt. So it's as your friend I'm advising you to tread very carefully." The elation in her expression had fallen away, and she spoke gravely to my mother. "Draugrs are dangerous."

Marlow smirked. "I think I can handle an immortal."

"An immortal, sure," Cecily relented, but her gaze only grew more somber. "But draugrs are something different. They can't be killed."

"Of course they can," Marlow said with more conviction than I thought she should have. "Everything dies. One way or another, we all end up in the dirt or down in Kurnugia."

"Why do you think I turned him into a statue?" Cecily pointed sadly to the statue. "Poor dear Armaros had grown weary of this life, but nothing else worked. The Valkyrie blade couldn't cut him."

Asher leaned forward, resting his arms on his knees. "So you're saying that Tamerlane Fayette is immortal *and* unkillable?"

"If death marks you, and it misses you, who knows how long it will be before death comes around to mark you again?" the gorgon asked.

TWENTY-FOUR

---◆---

Once we'd all piled back into Marlow's car and she finally got it started—it was an old Jeep, with actual tires instead of hoverpads, and it always took a few tries before it finally started up—Marlow immediately lit up a cigarillo and let out a frustrated breath.

"So." Asher leaned forward from the backseat. "When are we going to the Red Raven?"

Marlow eyed him in the rearview mirror, looking at him like he was an idiot. "Not tonight. It's going to be a madhouse."

"Doesn't that make it the best time to go?" Asher asked. "It's almost guaranteed that this Bram guy will be there."

"A night like tonight, it's going to be rowdy as all hell," Marlow explained. "It's not worth the risk. If he hangs out there a lot, he'll be there another night when it's quieter."

Asher pressed on, "What if—"

"I said not tonight," Marlow snapped and put the Jeep in gear. "And that's final."

The rest of the car ride across town, none of us said anything, aside from Marlow cursing at other vehicles and pedestrians that she felt were slowing her down. When she parked in her spot by her house, she grunted a quick goodbye, and then headed toward her apartment without another word.

That left Asher and me standing awkwardly on the sidewalk.

"Thanks for coming today." He scratched behind his ear and glanced around. "You were helpful, I think."

"Yeah, no problem," I said, even though I wasn't sure I'd done anything at all. Then I turned to walk away.

"Are you going to the Red Raven tonight?" he called after me, and I turned back to face him.

Under the bright autumn sun, the blue in the darkness of his eyes glimmered. A smile played subtly on his full lips, and he moved closer to me. I couldn't help but notice that when he looked hopeful like this—his eyes both eager and nervous, his smile unsure but bold—he appeared strikingly handsome.

"Are you going?" I asked.

"I was thinking about it." He paused, chewing the inside of his cheek, before asking, "Would you care to join me?"

"Yeah."

"Now?"

I shook my head. "No, it's too early, and we can't go dressed like this anyway."

He glanced down at his jeans and distressed jacket. "Why not?"

"It's the Feast of the Dead. It's like demon New Year for them," I elaborated. "You gotta dress up for it, or you won't even get in the door."

"I guess I'll have to dig out my Sunday best, then," he said.

"Do you wanna meet me at my place at nine, then we can head out?" I suggested.

"That sounds like a plan."

I started to walk away, then stopped and called back to him, "Oh, and this should go without saying, but don't tell Marlow."

He waved in confirmation, and then he disappeared into a crowd of costumed characters. Presumably they were performers from the parade, based on their bright makeup and ornate regalia.

Back at the apartment, Oona interrogated me about visiting Marlow, and I filled her in as best I could, including all the details about meeting Cecily. After that, I enlisted her to help me get ready for the Red Raven. It wasn't the kind of event that I could skimp on.

Oona shaved the left side of my head, because Marlow had been right—it was getting long. Then she pulled out a dress that her mom had designed specifically for me.

This dress was a little black number with cutouts on the side and opaque black fabric laid at angles all over sheer black mesh, so it hinted at more skin than it actually showed. The sleeves were long mesh, hiding the bruises and injuries I'd suffered in the Amaryllis Mori encounter, but the hem was short and only hit my mid-thigh.

As I stood in front of the mirror, fixing my eyeliner and reapplying my Velvet Vampire lipstick, Oona stood behind me with her arms folded over her chest and a self-satisfied grin on her face.

"You're lucky you have me," she said.

I looked at her in the reflection of the mirror and said, "I know."

"You'd be totally lost without me," she reiterated.

"I really would," I agreed with a laugh.

"You could show your appreciation a little more."

I turned back to her. "Hey, I made you breakfast this morning, and I helped you work on your term paper for your Miracles and Visions course."

"That is true." Oona considered this for a second. "But I did stitch you up last night and shave your hair today, and I helped my mom make you that dress that looks amazing on you."

"Fair enough. I'll take you out for drinks this week?" I offered.

"Deal." She held out her hand to me and I shook it. "You really do look great."

"Thank you. You look . . ." I glanced down at her old leggings and oversized Ravenswood Academy T-shirt before deciding on the word, ". . . comfy."

Oona laughed. "Thanks. That's the look I was going for. Bowie's often impressed by this."

"I would invite you to join us, but . . ."

"No. I get it." She sat back on the couch. "I don't wanna get killed or punched in the face. Are you sure it's safe for you to go out tonight? I mean, if Marlow says it's too dangerous . . ."

I pulled my knee-high boots out of the pile of shoes by the door and sat on the couch beside Oona.

"It's not that she thinks it's too dangerous," I explained as I pulled on a boot. "She just doesn't want to deal with all the crowds and traffic. Plus, she really hates the Feast of the Dead."

"How come?" Oona asked.

"Because of everything I just said. Actually, now that I think about it, she hates most holidays."

"She sounds like a real hoot to have grown up with," Oona said dryly.

"You know it."

My right boot had gone on easy, but the left boot was a fight because my calf was still swollen and tender. I had to be careful, but I couldn't go out with a bloody bandage exposed, so I had to hide it under my boots.

"Marlow's anti-holiday rhetoric aside, it is going to be dangerous out there," Oona said. "The Red Raven isn't exactly known for being civilized."

"I know, but I can handle myself, and I'll have Asher with me."

"Yeah, but you don't really know Asher that well," she pointed out. "Can he even fight?"

"He seemed to handle himself when we scuffled." I'd finally gotten both boots on, so I turned to look over at her. "Plus, he was a Vörðr."

Her eyes widened. "Really?"

"I mean, I think so. He has a paracord bracelet with the Vörðr insignia on it, and I just get this vibe from him. It would also explain how he was able to get some of the classified information he showed me."

Oona thought about it and nodded. "Well, you did describe him as battle-weary before. You'll probably be safe, then."

"I think we can manage it," I said, hoping that I sounded more convincing than I felt.

If Oona noticed my ambivalence, she didn't say anything, and thanks to the knock at the door, she didn't have time to.

I answered the door to discover Asher standing there, clean-shaven and more handsome than ever. He wore a perfectly tailored suit that hugged his broad shoulders and tapered to his narrow waist. It was black on black, and he'd left the top buttons of his shirt undone, revealing just a hint of his chest.

I hurried to pick my jaw up off the floor and managed a smile before teasing, "So you can knock after all?"

"Yeah." He smiled crookedly, and I felt his eyes going up and down over me, causing a warm flush to spread through my body. "You look . . . you look great."

"Thanks. You clean up nice, too."

"I'm Oona Warren, by the way," she interjected, pushing herself between me and the doorframe to extend her hand toward Asher. "Marlow's best friend and roommate."

"Asher Värja." He smiled as he shook her hand.

"Take care of Malin, will you?" Oona asked, and I rolled my eyes.

"Of course." He stepped back and motioned to the hall. "Shall we?"

"Be safe, you two," Oona commanded as I grabbed my bag. "And don't stay out too late. The real trouble always starts after midnight."

TWENTY-FIVE

———— ◆ ————

Somehow, the Aizsaule District always seemed darker than the rest of the city. Maybe there was a hex over it, one that sucked up all the light. Even the sky above looked darker, without a single star showing.

The Red Raven was built out of some kind of shiny black stone, with an animated neon red bird above the door, moving up and down as if picking at the patrons. Two red searchlights roamed on either side of the door, but it wasn't as if the place needed help attracting more customers. There was already a line down the block, with all sorts of humans and supernatural beings dressed in their most gothic haute attire.

Fortunately, Asher and I looked good enough that we didn't have to wait very long. We'd been queued up for a little over a half hour, which wouldn't have been so bad if it weren't for the two Aswangs standing right behind us.

The Aswangs were particularly horrifying-looking humanoid creatures. The bottom half of their head was all mouth, filled with many jagged teeth and a long, serpent-like tongue. They also smelled like sulfur and rotten meat, and the two behind us had a particular lack of understanding of personal space.

They kept creeping up toward us, almost pushing Asher and me forward. He put his arm around my waist and moved back a bit, putting himself between me and the Aswang duo. It wasn't necessary, since I didn't need him to protect me, but I still thought it was a nice gesture.

And I especially enjoyed the way his hand felt on the bare flesh of my skin, exposed by the cutaway in the dress.

Periodically, a doorman walked down the line, plucking out those he deemed worthy enough for the Red Raven. He came over and motioned for Asher and me to go on in, and the Aswangs behind us let out an annoyed shriek, so I smiled and flipped them off.

Inside, everything was dim and glowing red, reminding me of an old darkroom for developing camera film. The Red Raven had several rooms—some private and off-limits, others looking far too S&M for my tastes—so we decided to bypass them and head for the largest main room.

It was about half the size of a football stadium, with a large dance floor in the center. A long backlit bar took up one whole wall, while booths and tables were lined up against the far wall and in the balconies that wrapped around the length of the room.

A stage at the end of the room had a band playing. The lead singer was a beautiful siren, accompanied by thrashing guitar players, a drummer, a keyboardist, and a DJ. The music was pulsing techno, with her melodic voice carrying through it.

"So how do we want to do this?" Asher asked, his voice in my ear and his hand around my waist, pulling me close to avoid us getting trampled at the edge of the dance floor.

"Let's go to the bar and start asking around," I suggested.

The bartender immediately came over—a chubby woman with

blue streaks in her jet-black hair. She leaned over on the counter, letting her large chest spill onto the bar from her skintight top. Something in the way she moved, the sultry turn of her lips, and the lure of her pheromones let me know instantly that she was a succubus.

"What can I get you?" she asked through her byzantine lipstick.

"What do you recommend?" I asked, trying not to be enchanted by the look in her eyes. As with the venom of the Jorogumo, I wasn't entirely immune to the charms of the succubus, but I did have a stronger resistance than the average human.

She pointed to a smoky red drink that another patron was drinking. "The Diablo's Dream is the special tonight."

"Two of those," I said.

She smiled wider, and I wanted to melt into a puddle of goo. "You got it."

"We shouldn't get drunk," Asher murmured, and the sound of his voice pulled me from the minor spell that the bartender had put me under.

"Drink slowly, then," I replied.

When the bartender returned, she set the drinks on the bar, and before she could even tell us how much it was, he set a fifty-dollar bill in front of her.

"Thank you." She smiled as she put the money in her bra.

"We were supposed to be meeting someone here." Asher leaned over the bar so she could hear him better. "He's supposed to be a regular. Maybe you know him?"

She shrugged. "I know some people. What's his name?"

"Bram Madichonnen," Asher said, while I tried my drink. It was all cherries and spice, but there was something else in it. Something thicker, warming my skin.

Her smile instantly fell, and the enchantment disappeared from her eyes. "Never heard of him," she replied blankly. She tapped the bar once, then started walking away. "You two have a good night, now."

"That was weird," Asher commented after she'd gone.

He left his drink at the bar, while I continued slowly sipping mine as we wandered around the room. We tried to seem casual, like we were just two people here celebrating the holiday, and we got a few demons and cravens to talk to us.

But as soon as we dropped Bram's name, the conversation would grind to a halt. No matter how much either Asher or I tried to flirt and play it off, it always ended the same.

"This isn't working," Asher commented.

"Maybe we should try loosening up more," I suggested.

I'd just finished my drink and left the empty glass discarded on a nearby table. Between the alcohol and the music thumping through the room, I felt fiery and free. A carnal heat rushed through me, setting my skin ablaze, and desire swelled in the pit of my stomach.

Asher leaned against the bar beside me, and even in the darkly lit room I couldn't help but notice how sexy and strong he looked. His suit fit him to perfection, hugging his muscular frame.

I'd been standing beside him at the bar, but leaned into him now, letting my lips brush against his earlobe as I whispered, "We could dance."

"We could," he murmured, and that was all the encouragement I needed.

I swayed my hips as I danced closer to him, subtly rubbing against him, and I put my hands on the lapels of his jacket. His hand was on my hip again, cool against my warm flesh, and I pressed against him as I danced. He pulled me closer, so close my lips were almost touching his, and I wondered what his full lips would feel like against mine.

Before I could find out, I stepped back from him. The air felt thick and electric, and I needed to put distance between us so I could think clearly again, because thoughts of Asher and what I wanted to do to him were clouding my mind.

Still dancing suggestively, I backed away from him, and he leaned against the bar, watching me with a mixture of bemused desire darkening his eyes.

He mouthed the words *Watch out*, but it was too late. I bumped into someone, their body firm and unyielding behind me, and I turned around to see Arawn—a demon powerful and famous enough that I recognized him immediately.

TWENTY-SIX

———————◆———————

Under the red light of the club, his long white-blond hair glowed a dull crimson. He wore a suit made of pure white, clashing with the color scheme of nearly everyone else here. He was handsome, the way many demons were, but his smile managed to freeze the heat inside of me.

"Are you having a good time?" Arawn asked in a voice like satin.

"I am," I said, pushing down the chill inside me and managing a flirtatious laugh. "How about you?"

"Always." His smiled widened, looking hungry, and he looped an arm around me, pulling me out to the dance floor with him.

He moved gracefully across the floor, somehow making me a more elegant dancer along with him. I wasn't exactly clumsy, but my movements had never felt so fluid as with his arm around me, guiding me through the steps.

With a hand on my back, he pressed my pelvis against his, then dipped me low. I relaxed against his arm, allowing my hair to drag on the floor, as he supported me and pulled me against him.

"You're a good dancer," Arawn mused, his lips mere inches from mine.

"Thank you," I breathed.

"What's a nice girl like you doing in a place like this?" he asked.

"I'm not so nice," I replied with a coy laugh. "But I was hoping to meet someone here tonight."

He gave me a predatory smile. "Well, you found me."

"Maybe if you play your cards right," I teased, keeping my voice as sultry as possible. "I was actually looking for Bram Madichonnen."

Arawn waited a beat before replying, "Haven't heard of him." His arm was still around me, but his eyes darted behind me. "Your boyfriend is getting jealous. You should probably head back to him."

I glanced back over my shoulder to see Asher standing at the bar watching us. His eyes were dark, and his lips were pressed into a grim line, but I read the expression for what it actually was—not jealous, but cautious and diligent.

"He's not my boyfriend," I said, and when I turned back to Arawn his smile had vanished.

He let go of me and stepped back before commanding, "You should head back to him anyway."

The crowd had parted a bit to make room for us to dance. Arawn was the kind of guy who demanded space. But when he walked away, he left me standing alone in a small circle on the dance floor, with leering eyes surrounding me.

I tried to play it off and walk as calmly as I could to join Asher at the bar.

"Who was that? He looked important," Asher asked when I reached him.

"He is." I ran my hand through my hair and exhaled. "He's a bigwig at the Kurnugia Society."

It had been named for the ancient word for the underworld Kurnugia, and it existed as a counterbalance to the Evig Riksdag. The impious believed that the Riks tended to land on the side of "good" more often than not, and they didn't want the divine inheriting the world.

The Kurnugia Society was basically a demonic version of the FBI, with a strong emphasis on making sure the impious and craven were treated "fairly."

"Did he know anything?" Asher asked.

"Oh, yeah, he definitely knows something," I said. "But he's not talking. As soon as I mentioned Bram, he shut it down."

Across the dance floor, Arawn had settled into a private booth, and he waved over a scruffy bouncer-looking guy. He leaned over as Arawn whispered into his ear, and then he turned toward us—his red eyes scanning the crowd before landing on me.

"They're on to us," Asher said.

"Maybe." I grabbed Asher's hand. "Let's dance and act normal, and then get out of here the second they stop looking."

We tried to get lost in the crowd, moving closer to the stage where the music was louder and the bodies were crammed closer together. There wasn't much room to move, so I pressed my body against Asher's and wrapped my arms around his neck.

His arm was around my waist, but this wasn't like before when we'd been dancing—this was protective and fierce. I'd never been around anyone who tried to protect me, other than Oona's motherly suggestions, but that didn't feel like this. My whole life, I'd always counted on my own strength to get me through anything, and so far, it had.

But for the moment, with Asher's strength enveloping me, it felt . . . nice. A new warmth grew inside me, softer and deeper, making me feel dreamy and romantic. I didn't need Asher's protection, but that's what made it all the more gallant. He knew how strong and capable I was, and he still cared enough to shield me.

He kept looking around, his eyes conspicuously darting, so I put my hand on his face, forcing him to look at me.

"Keep your eyes on me," I told him. "We're trying to look natural."

"Right." He nodded, and his eyes met mine.

I let my hand linger, caressing the scruff of his face, and his expression softened from fear to something else, something like when he'd been watching me while I danced. We swayed together, an island in a sea of people. Alcohol and adrenaline buzzed inside me, but that wasn't why I felt so wonderfully light-headed in his arms.

I imagined him kissing me then. The scruff of his chin scraping against my face and neck as his arms tightened around me. I wanted nothing more than to take him to a dark booth and give in to every urge that had taken hold inside me.

But I couldn't. Not then. Not with demons and monsters lurking around, waiting to pounce.

"Is he still watching?" I asked Asher, trying to break through the fog of my own lust.

"What?" He blinked at me, then looked around. "Oh. No. I don't know where he went."

Then I felt a hand on my shoulder, burning hot through the thin fabric of my dress, and I looked back to see the bouncer Arawn had been talking to. He looked even bigger up close and personal, with veins bulging through his dark skin, and his eyes were blood-red.

He was a Pishacha—a flesh-eating demon—and right now his carnivorous gaze was fixed on me and Asher.

"Mind if I cut in?" he asked.

"Yes, actually. I do," I said firmly.

"Maybe you haven't heard of me. I'm Cormac Kaur," he informed us, grinning like a wolf. "I'm the head of security around here. So why don't we go have a little chat?"

"What's this about?" Asher asked, trying to remain calm.

"It's easier if you just come with me," Cormac commanded, and, based on the look in his eyes, I knew there was no arguing with him.

TWENTY-SEVEN

———————◆———————

The back room was lit by a solitary bulb dangling from the ceiling, and the concrete floors were covered in rust-colored stains that looked suspiciously of blood. It even smelled of it in here—metallic and earthy.

The room was the size of an average walk-in freezer, and the steel door looked like it had once belonged to one. The walls were exposed brick, and there was nothing in it except for a single chair.

Cormac had led us off the dance floor, gripping me by the wrist so tightly it would've snapped if my bones hadn't been supernaturally strong from my Valkyrie blood. Asher followed at his heels, demanding to know what this was all about, but Cormac said nothing as he led us through the dark winding halls until finally shoving us into this back room.

"What do you want?" Asher demanded again, his fists balled up at his sides.

Based on everything I knew of Asher—his Valkyrie mother, his muscular physique, his possible experience as a Vörðr, his profes-

sion tracking down his mother's killer—he was a formidable oppo-
nent in his own right. But Cormac was a huge dude, with demonic
strength flowing through him, and he was used to dealing with the
unruliest patrons at the Red Raven.

There would be no way that Asher could win a fight against him.

"You've been annoying our clientele," Cormac informed us, and
he began circling us the way sharks circle their prey.

"How so?" Asher asked, feigning naïveté.

"You've been interrogating them about one of our patrons,"
Cormac said.

"So Bram Madichonnen is a patron?" I asked.

Cormac's self-assured smile faltered. "We don't discuss private
business here. We like to keep to ourselves. And you'd know that if
you were from around here."

"We're just looking for an old family friend," Asher said, trying
futilely to maintain our innocence.

Cormac ignored Asher and closed in on me. His red eyes bulged
out from his skull, and his lips were pulled back into a snarl, revealing multitudes of pointed teeth. The scent of raw meat radiated
from his breath, and I had to swallow back my urge to vomit.

"At first I thought you two were just curious humans, but you're
not. You're something else." Cormac tilted his head. "What are
you?"

"Look, we don't want trouble. We only want to find a friend."
Asher was at my side, but he moved, trying to wedge himself between
me and Cormac.

Annoyed, Cormac glared at Asher, and without warning, he
struck. He punched Asher, knocking him to the floor, and then I
lunged at the Pishacha. I hit him in the face, and a stunned Cormac
stumbled back, his fingers at the blood forming on his lip.

He growled, then charged at me. I dodged his punch, and kicked
him in the stomach. This time he fell back, and I kicked him in the

side again, just to make sure he was really down. Then I walked over and stomped my boot on his neck, pinning him there. My stiletto heel dug into the tender flesh of his throat, and he gulped as he looked up at me.

"Shit. You're a damn Valkyrie," he realized.

"I am," I admitted. "And now you know that I can kill you if you piss me off. Why don't you tell me where Bram Madichonnen is?"

Cormac laughed. "You're not allowed to kill me."

"Try me," I said, pressing my boot harder against his throat.

"Okay, okay," he croaked, and I let up a bit so he could talk more easily. "It's not like I have his home address."

"Tell me what you know!" I commanded.

"He hangs out with this Fallen girl," Cormac said finally, referring to the vernacular for fallen angels. "Eisheth Levanon."

"What do you know about her?" I asked.

"She's an ex-prostitute, but she used to work for some kind of archangel before she fell in with us," Cormac elaborated. "I don't know where she's staying, but if you find her, you'll find him."

"Thank you," I said, and since I knew he wouldn't let us just walk out of here, I pulled back and punched him as hard as I could. It didn't knock him out, not completely, but it would leave him dazed enough that we could get out.

"Come on!" I yelled and grabbed Asher's hand.

I didn't know where we were going, but I had to get out before Cormac alerted all the demons that there was a Valkyrie in their midst stirring up trouble. I darted down the narrow hallways until I finally spotted a door with a bright red EXIT sign above it.

I pushed through, still holding Asher's hand, and we ran out into the cold night to a deserted back alley. Despite the chill of the air, my skin was flushed with heat, and my body felt like a live wire, electricity surging through me.

Once we'd gotten outside, I let go of Asher's hand, and we stood under the dark sky, which was glowing red from the lights of the club. We stood together, both of us breathing deeply to catch our breath, and in that moment, the two of us alone in the alley, I couldn't recall a time that I'd ever felt more alive.

When I looked over at Asher, a sly smile played on his lips, and something in his eyes made me think he felt the same way.

"That was badass," he said, his voice a husky rumble, and he stepped closer to me, causing my heart to skip a beat.

I meant to thank him, but the words died on my lips. My pulse raced, and my breath came out shallow and shaky in anticipation—anticipation of what, I didn't know, but I felt it coming, or at least I hoped for it. *Ached* for it, really.

My legs felt weak, like jelly, but I also felt stronger than ever, like I had taken on an army of ogres and still came out on top. Everything was now in hyperfocus, as if time were slowing down. The world felt like it all might pitch to the side, but I wasn't scared at all, because I knew that Asher would catch me if I fell.

I was acutely aware of how close to me Asher was. So close I could reach out and pull him into my arms, if I wanted to. My thoughts raced back to the dance floor, when my body had been pressed against his, and I could still feel his hands, cold and rough on my hips, and I'd only wanted him—

Then he was there, right there against me, with his hand on my face. I sucked in a breath, breathing him, and the scent of his cologne suddenly transported me to a memory of my childhood, when I'd been lost in a dark forest outside of the city during a rainstorm.

It was the most frightening and exhilarating and enchanting memory of my life, and that's exactly what Asher smelled like now—woodsy and dark and crisp and alive. Like terror and happiness.

His eyes searched mine, and his thumb tentatively traced the outline of my lips. When his mouth finally found mine, it was like getting struck by lightning—I could actually feel the electric heat pulsing through me.

He pushed me backward, but I didn't stumble. I just clung to him, letting him lead me until my back pressed against the cold stone of a wall. As he crushed me against it, kissing me ravenously, I realized I'd underestimated his strength.

Asher was raw power and lust, and the intensity of his kisses and the insistence of his hands roaming my body sent shivers all through me. It all terrified me, but I couldn't get enough of it, enough of him, and I held him to me, lifting a leg to wrap around him and pull him closer to me.

He let out a low moan, a soft rumble in my ear, that made my stomach swirl with delicious excitement, and his lips brushed against my neck. His moved down, gripping the bare skin of the thigh that I'd wrapped around him, and his fingers dug into my flesh as he kissed me.

As abruptly as he'd started, he stopped, stepping back and leaving me gasping against the wall. My skin was trembling, and the mixture of pleasure and relief that washed over me reminded me of how I felt after I'd finished a job and had killed an immortal.

Except, of course, that Asher left me unsatisfied and desperate for more.

"Sorry. That probably wasn't appropriate," he breathed.

I shook my head. "No. That was . . . that was good." It was the most perfect, intense kiss of my life, but I didn't want to explain that to him. Not then.

Squawking—a robust cackle, really—from behind Asher finally made me pull my gaze away from him and his stormy blue eyes. A few meters behind him, in the otherwise deserted alley, a massive raven was perched on a dumpster.

The bird's dark, beady eyes were locked on me, and I realized it was the same raven I'd seen before. The one that had watched me kill Amaryllis Mori, the Jorogumo. I wondered dimly how long it had been here, how long it had watched me with Asher.

"We should get out of here," I told Asher, just as the raven cawed and flew off.

TWENTY-EIGHT

———◆———

I stumbled out of my bedroom, limping because my left leg was killing me, just as Oona was coming in the front door. Despite the overcast skies and rain hammering against the window making it look like night, the alarm clock on my bed assured me it was well after noon.

"Are you just waking up?" she asked, taking off her jacket and kicking off her shoes.

"I had a long night," I reminded her as I hobbled into the kitchen to make myself a cup of coffee. Bowie was hopping around my feet, begging to be fed, and I nearly tripped over him as I dumped a cup of Lagomorph Chow into his bowl.

"I was sleeping when you came in. Did everything go okay?"

"Yeah. As good as it could, I guess," I answered. "Where were you?"

"Brunch with my mom and my cousin Minerva."

"How'd that go?" I asked, pouring myself a huge mug of coffee.

"Fine, except my mom kept getting annoyed that me and Minerva were talking about thaumaturgy and all that." Oona stopped talking to eye me as I hobbled to the couch to sit down. "How is your leg?"

"Awful," I admitted, but I tried to gloss over it by immediately asking her, "Is Minerva the sorceress?"

"She is, and she gave me these cool protection crystals to try out," Oona said, but she was already turning and walking into her room.

A second later, she came out with the ocher-colored solamentum in the palm of her hands. She held them out to me, but when I reached for them, she closed her fist and pulled them back. "I'll give you two more of these, but you have to promise me that you'll go to the doctor tomorrow and get your leg checked out for real. Promise me."

"I promise," I said, but honestly, I would've agreed to most things if it meant I could take something to ease the throbbing of my leg. I downed them quickly before she had a chance to change her mind, and she sat down on the couch beside me.

"So, what all happened? Did you find out anything?" she asked.

I explained to Oona what had happened and what we had found out, deliberately leaving out the part where Asher had kissed me, but just thinking about it made my skin flush. It wasn't that I was ashamed or wanted to keep it a secret—there were just more important things at hand and I didn't want to waste time dissecting what was happening between me and Asher.

Especially since I didn't know what was happening with us. The kiss had been exhilarating and brilliant, albeit very brief, but after that there had been nothing. We left the club and drove around for a bit, partially to cool off and partially because the streets were so crowded it was hard to get anywhere quickly.

But then we'd just parted ways and agreed to meet up later.

"I could probably track her down," Oona commented, once I'd finished explaining that Cormac Kaur had said Bram Madichonnen was staying with Eisheth Levanon. "You could, too."

I shook my head. "I tried searching the Internet. But you know how the impious can be. They're either posting everywhere all over social media, or they're completely silent and working in the background."

"No, I mean, you could use alchemy," she corrected me.

"No, I can't." I groaned and leaned my head back against the couch. "Alchemy is so hard."

"You need to practice it more, Mal. You wanna be a Valkyrie? You wanna track down this guy that's turning the world upside down? Then you gotta get a handle on your alchemy."

"Can you just help me today, and tutor me on alchemy another day?" I asked hopefully.

Oona sighed. "Fine. First, what do you know about Eisheth Levanon?"

"She's a Fallen and Cormac says she's an ex-prostitute."

That made sense, because a lot of Fallen ended up that way. Some angels were allowed to live and love freely, but certain sects were required to be completely "pure" and abstain from all sorts of physical pleasure. If they gave in to their urges, they were booted out of their group and usually lost their jobs. And without any real skills, other than their former purity and goodness, many of them fell onto prostitution.

"She lives in the city?" Oona asked.

"Supposedly. A lot of Fallen live in the Wolf River District, so if she's here, she's probably staying somewhere in that area."

"Great. That narrows it down. I'll get my kit," she said, and she was already up and hurrying to her room.

Oona gathered up her alchemy toolbox and lugged it to the living room. She pulled out a mirrored tray and set it on the coffee table, then began rummaging through her toolkit until she pulled out several different-colored vials.

One of the largest bottles, curved and filled with a glowing lime-green liquid, sat near the top, and she picked it up and pulled out the glass stopper. Slowly, she poured it into the tray, filling it up to the edge of the lip. With deft movements I didn't understand, Oona waved her hand over the liquid, causing a glowing mist to rise above it and dissipate throughout the room.

"This isn't going to hurt Bowie, is it?" I asked.

My wolpertinger was sitting by the window, dutifully cleaning his long ears with his front paws. But at the sound of his name, he perked up and looked over at me.

"I would never do anything to hurt Bowie. He'll be fine just as long as he doesn't drink this."

She added a few more vials, saying a Latin phrase each time she poured one in. Taking a long stick from her box, she stirred the mixture before adding a vial of black crystals. The pool of liquid turned black and became smooth and reflective, appearing more like a television screen than a tray of potions and liquid.

Oona rubbed her hands together and cleared her throat. "*Ostende mihi Wolf River District.*"

"What'd you just say?" I asked, and she held up a finger to silence me.

The liquid began to swirl, changing from black to gray, and slowly an image began to take form. At first I didn't recognize it, but as the streets and old warehouses took shape, I realized it was an aerial view of the Wolf River area.

"*Lumino angelorum lapsus,*" Oona said, and buildings started lighting up, glowing bright green.

"What's happening?" I asked.

She motioned to the tray. "It's showing places where fallen angels live."

"That's like a hundred places or more," I pointed out. "Is there a way to narrow it down?"

"Well, I was hoping there would be fewer spots on here." Oona chewed the inside of her cheek. "What else can you tell me about Eisheth?"

"Um, she's supposedly been hanging around with this Bram guy a lot lately," I said.

"Would you say she was his consort?" Oona asked helpfully.

I shrugged. "Maybe?"

"And what do you know about Bram?"

"Just that he's a draugr. Allegedly."

"Oh, right." Oona thought for a minute, then leaned over the tray and cleared her throat. "*Lumino consorcio immortui.*"

Many of the lights blinked out, but about two dozen still glowed.

"I think that vampires and a few other types of the impious are being lumped in because I had to use the word for 'undead,' since I didn't know the one for draugr," Oona explained. "So I need something else."

"Can you just say Eisheth?" I asked.

Oona shook her head. "It doesn't work like that. Beings go by many different names. You have to describe *who* they are, not *what* they're called."

"Cormac thought she used to work for an archangel, if that's helpful."

"I'll try it." She rubbed her hands together again and incanted, "*Lumino servi archangeli.*"

With that, all the lights went out, except for one.

"*Adducet eam ad me,*" Oona said authoritatively, and the image in the pool zoomed in, bringing us just above the glowing building. "That's where she is."

"So where is that?" I asked, tilting my head.

"What does that look like?" Oona leaned over the pool, squinting at a street sign. "I think that says . . . Lake Street and . . . Canal Avenue." She sat back on her knees, looking proud of herself. "Eisheth lives in a building at the corner of Lake Street and Canal Ave."

I was about to thank her, when something occurred to me. "Why can't we do this with Bram or even Tamerlane Fayette?"

Oona shook her head. "They're way too powerful. This kind of thing only works on low-level supernatural beings, like Manananggals or the Fallen. I doubt it would've even worked on Tamerlane Fayette *before* he became a draugr."

Angels were divine and immortal, but once they became Fallen, they gave up their immortality and all their authority. That would make Eisheth Levanon easier to deal with once we found her, because she wouldn't need a Valkyrie sword or a kill order for me to be able to end her life, if that became necessary.

I leaned back in the couch, exhaling deeply. Bowie came over and hopped onto my lap. He ruffled his feathered wings, and I absently petted him, smoothing them out.

Oona propped her elbows on the table and looked up at me. "What's your next move?"

"Wait for the pain meds to kick in, and then go tell Marlow that we found a link to Bram Madichonnen," I decided.

"Are you gonna contact Asher?" she asked.

I shook my head. "Not today."

Things were already strained enough between Marlow and me right now. I didn't need to add the tension surrounding Asher and all the mixed feelings about his quest. Besides, I was only going to relay some info to my mother. It'd be simple and quick, and nothing exciting should happen. He didn't need to be there for that.

TWENTY-NINE

———◆———

"Y ou didn't have to come with me," I told Oona as she
huffed up the flight of stairs behind me.

She'd wanted to drive me here because she didn't think
I'd properly be able to drive the luft with my injured leg since I'd
overdone it last night, even though I'd been coping pretty well the
last couple days. But if it made her feel better to tag along, I was
happy to let her.

"No, no, I got this," she insisted, jogging up the last few steps to
catch up with me. "I do really need to start working out more. It's
ridiculous that it's harder for me to go up those sixty steps than it
was for you with your injured leg."

"I do train for this kind of thing," I reminded her, pausing at the
landing outside Marlow's apartment to give Oona time to catch her
breath.

"Maybe I should start training with you." She reached out to
touch my bicep, firm and brawny underneath my light jacket. "Wow.
Maybe I could start out slower, like with a spin class."

I knocked at the door, and Marlow answered relatively quickly, at least for her. Her hair was still wet from a shower, and she was makeup-less, other than her usual dark red lipstick. She leaned on the doorframe, sighing at me.

"Don't you ever call anymore?" she asked.

"You never answer when I call," I countered, which was true. I'd tried calling her three times before I came over, but she literally never answered her phone.

Marlow raised an eyebrow. "Doesn't that tell you something?"

"That's a real nice way to talk to your daughter," I muttered before plunging into my spiel. "I just came to tell you that we found out something about one of those draugrs, but if you don't wanna talk—"

She instantly straightened up and her eyes narrowed. "What do you mean, you found something out?" Then she glanced over at Oona. "Oh, fine, come in. The both of you."

Marlow walked into her dim apartment, which was still fairly clean from Asher's visit, though there were several empty alcohol bottles piled up around the sink. So either she had cleaned out a closet, or she had gone on a minor drinking binge after parting ways with Asher and me yesterday.

Some exercise equipment—free weights and a stair-stepper— was strewn about the living room, and she had on her stretch pants and a loose muscle shirt. The armholes hung low, exposing the black of her sports bra and a nasty scar that ran along her ribs below it.

Oona and I sat down on the couch, but Marlow remained standing, lighting one of her cigarillos.

"How are you doing, Oona?" Marlow asked. "Is your mom still running that dress shop?"

"I'm good," she said, sounding exaggeratedly chipper. Like most people who had met Marlow, Oona was intimidated by her. "Yes, she is still sewing and tailoring."

Marlow nodded, taking a long drag of her tobacco. "That's good. Tell her hi when you see her."

"Will do," Oona replied.

"So." Marlow cast her gaze on me. "What is this exciting new piece of information you discovered?"

"Last night, Asher and I went to the Red Raven—"

"You did what?" Marlow growled, instantly tensing, and Oona shrank back on the couch beside me.

"It wasn't a big deal," I said, trying to play it off. "We were both fine."

"I specifically told you not to! It's too dangerous!" Marlow shouted at me.

"Well, we were fine, so it wasn't that dangerous," I argued. "And you didn't seem to care that much about my well-being when you sent me out to face Amaryllis Mori on my own."

She shook her head and began pacing slowly across the living room. "That was different."

"How is that different?" I asked.

"You're supposed to handle Amaryllis on your own," Marlow contended. "You trained for it, have a sword for it. Hell, you were born for it! You can't just go taking on the demon underbelly by yourself."

I let out an exasperated groan. "We were fine! I don't even know what you're so mad about."

"Because you didn't wait for me when I asked you to," Marlow said, speaking to me like I was either stupid or a small child, or maybe a particularly stupid small child.

"We're not just going to wait around forever for you," I told her. "Tamerlane Fayette has already killed at least one Valkyrie. We need to stop him before anybody else gets hurt."

Marlow finally stopped pacing. She flicked her cigarillo in a nearby ashtray, and her entire body slackened. Staring down at the floor, she rubbed her temples and exhaled heavily.

"You need to be more careful," she said.

"I am," I insisted.

She looked at me like she wanted to argue, but she took a resigned breath instead. Her normally hard steel eyes were misty when she said, "I know I'm not much of a mother, Malin. But I just want you to be safe."

I opened my mouth, wanting to say some sort of word of comfort, but I couldn't think of anything. I wasn't used to any tenderness from her and didn't know how to react.

But she was still my mother, and I did still love her.

"So what did you find out?" Marlow asked finally.

I explained everything Asher and I had found out at the Red Raven, which caused her to respond with several eye rolls and tongue clicks. Then Oona chimed in to explain the incantations she'd done to track down where Eisheth Levanon lived.

"Well, I suppose we ought to get going, then," Marlow said abruptly when we'd finished.

I glanced over at Oona in surprise before asking, "Right now?"

Marlow put out her cigarillo, then went over to her pantry. That's where most people stored their food, but hers was filled to the brim with weapons. She grabbed several knives, including her sword Mördare.

"You were asking around the Red Raven last night and caught the attention of Arawn," Marlow explained as she laid out her weapons on the kitchen table. "It won't be long before Bram Madichonnen and any other draugrs know that you're looking for them. And then they'll either skip town or go on the offense and come after us."

"So you're saying that we need to get to them first?" I asked.

"Exactly," she replied. "Oona, are you coming with us?"

"I can, in case I might be able to help if you guys get lost," she offered.

Marlow held a jagged knife toward her. "Then you better take this, just to be safe."

Oona did as she was told, while Marlow headed back to her bedroom to finish getting ready. I went over to the weapons cabinet to start picking out a few knives for myself. Oona stared down at the knife with nervous eyes and chewed her lip.

"Stay close to me, and you'll be fine," I promised her.

THIRTY

———◆———

The large square brick building before us had once been a warehouse—an old luftfahrrad factory, Marlow thought—but it now housed over a hundred small loft apartments. Or at least that's what the property manager had claimed.

Oona's magic had gotten us to the building, but it was Marlow's old-fashioned detective work that got us to Eisheth's door. She'd gone in to the property manager's office and, using a combination of flirtation and threats, was able to ascertain that Eisheth Levanon lived in apartment 21B, and even got the manager to buzz us into the building.

The lights in the hallway hung below the exposed pipes and kept flickering on and off. In the last few seconds before Eisheth finally opened the door, we were submerged in total darkness.

For a moment the only light came from her loft, and she stood backlit in the open door—a dark shadow with wings towering over her. The silhouette of a demon.

Then the hall lights flicked on and revealed a beautiful young woman standing in the door. Her long dark hair cascaded past her shoulders, and two black leathery wings extended from her back. She wore a white sarong, loosely tied up around her neck, so her ample breasts were all but falling out the sides, and the sarong was sheer enough that her nipples were entirely visible.

She parted her lips slightly and tilted her head. "I didn't buzz you in, did I?"

"No, the manager let us in," Marlow explained. "We just wanted to chat with you."

She laughed hollowly. "I've already met my lord and savior, and I don't have any money to buy anything else you might be selling. Sorry."

Marlow put her hand on the door, stopping Eisheth from closing it. "No, we're not here to convert you or sell anything."

Eisheth narrowed her eyes, but didn't try closing the door farther, so I took that as a good sign and plunged ahead by saying, "We only wanted to know if Bram Madichonnen is around."

Instantly her expression hardened. "I don't know anyone named Bram." She tried to slam the door, but Marlow held strong, and the door wouldn't budge.

"We know you're lying," Marlow warned her.

"How could you possibly know that?" Eisheth demanded.

"I'm a sorceress," Oona piped up confidently. "I know all kinds of things."

Eisheth gave up and sighed. "Fine." She turned and walked back into the loft, her hips swaying subtly under her dress. "You can come in if you want, but Bram's not here. And when he gets here, if he doesn't like you, he'll kill you."

The loft was sparsely furnished, with thick black drapes covering the large windows and blocking out any light—and keeping out any prying eyes. The décor felt very bohemian, with lots of draping, beads, and mandalas. There were no traditional tables or chairs—only cushions and pillows on the floor.

Candles had been set out all over the space. Kitchen counters, the mantel, the floor, nearly ever surface had a candle on it, burning dimly. Melted wax was dripped onto everything.

"I'd offer you something to drink, but I don't want you here, so . . ." Eisheth laughed lightly at her own joke, then fell back onto the "bed," a collection of overstuffed pillows and blankets.

I walked to the center of the room, close to where Eisheth lounged. Oona followed me more slowly, careful not to step on any open flames or freshly melted wax. Marlow began circling the edge of the room, taking slow, deliberate steps.

"We don't mean to intrude, and we don't plan to be here long," I said.

"Mmm-hmm," Eisheth murmured, lounging back on her pillows.

"When do you expect Bram back?" Marlow asked, stopping to admire a large art piece made out of macramé.

"Soon," Eisheth replied indifferently.

"How long have you known Bram?" Marlow tried again.

"I'm not telling you anything about him," she said. "If he wants you to know, he'll tell you himself."

"That sounds fair," Oona said.

Eisheth turned her narrowed eyes on Oona. "Are you really a sorceress?"

Oona nodded. "Yeah."

"Show me something," Eisheth commanded.

Oona smiled nervously. "I'm not a magician. I don't just perform feats for simple entertainment."

Eisheth leaned forward, resting on her arms, and looked up at Oona. "If you show one of your tricks, I'll tell you something about

Bram." Oona glanced back at me, so Eisheth added, "If it's something really good, I'll tell you *three* things."

Oona chewed her lip, thinking. "Okay. I got it." She dug into the pockets of her jacket and pulled out a small satin bag. "My cousin Minerva just gave this to me today, so I'm not entirely sure it will work."

"Show me what you got, Magic Man," Eisheth teased.

Oona dumped the bag into her hand, filling her palm with tiny amethyst crystals, looking like purple grains of salt. She closed her eyes and began slowly rubbing her hands together. Her lips were moving, but I couldn't hear any words.

Finally she opened her eyes and held her hands far apart, up in the air, and all the purple crystals were gone.

"*As ypárchei skotádi,*" Oona whispered, and the candles went out—every single one, plunging the loft into near-total darkness.

"*Kai egéneto fos,*" she breathed, and all the candles lit up again. Only this time, for a few seconds, they burned bright purple before changing back to their normal amber flame.

Eisheth threw her head back, cackling with glee. "That was great!"

"I held up my end of the deal," Oona said proudly. "Now tell us three things about Bram."

"Okay." Eisheth sat up a bit. "I've known Bram for two years. He hates surprises, and . . ." Her smile widened, growing more seductive. "He's going to kill you when he gets home."

That caused her to burst out laughing again, and Oona looked nervously at me. I was about to tell her that everything would be okay when the door to the apartment opened. Eisheth barely managed to stifle her giggles as a man strode into the room.

His eyes were hard, but his smile was bemused. His dark hair had begun graying at the temples, and though he looked much like a mortal man, he was much taller and more broad-shouldered.

When he caught sight of Marlow standing in front of his fireplace, he let out a warm chuckle.

"You're not Bram Madichonnen," Marlow said, and I could hear the struggle in her voice to keep its tenor even. "You're Tamerlane Fayette."

He grinned more broadly. "You're in luck. I'm both."

THIRTY-ONE

—◆—

Marlow took slow, deliberate steps away from the fireplace, putting herself between where Oona and I stood and where Tamerlane had entered the room. I did the same, moving so I partially shielded Oona.

As soon as Marlow said his name, I recognized him from the pictures I'd seen, but he did look different. In photos, his skin was tawny and warm, but now it had a dull blue tone to it, making it appear ashy and gray.

And somehow, he seemed bigger. Larger and more imposing.

"You don't look happy to see me," Tamerlane commented. "Or are you just unhappy that I'm still alive?"

"Why would I be unhappy?" Marlow smiled, and very slowly the two of them began circling each other. He would step closer, and she'd step away—keeping the distance between them the same. "I'm the one that let you live."

"Oh, I haven't forgotten." He scratched his head, seeming very nonchalant, and I noticed the ends of his fingertips were scarred—

he'd burned his fingerprints off to help mask his identity. "I've been meaning to thank you for that. But I hadn't been able to find your address. You Valkyries are always so secretive about where you live."

I tensed, even more so than I already was, and Oona gasped softly behind me. While we'd been hunting down the draugrs, it hadn't occurred to me that they'd be hunting *us*.

"You've been looking for me?" Marlow asked calmly.

"How else could I send you a gift of gratitude? Maybe a bouquet of flowers?" Tamerlane mused. "You seem like the kind of woman that would appreciate a few dozen red roses."

"That's very kind but unnecessary," she demurred, opting for flirtatious, even though I knew that she was furious.

"I only recently came back to the city." Tamerlane paused to give her a puzzled look. "How did you know I was here?"

"I didn't," she replied. "It was just serendipity. Why did you come back?"

He smiled slyly. "I thought you might have some regrets about me."

"Now, why would I?" Marlow asked.

"Someone's been looking for me," Tamerlane told her. "I've heard rumors of my name, of people searching for me, and you're about the only ones left alive that knew I hadn't died."

My breath caught in my throat. Asher—in his search to avenge his mother—had brought attention back to us. If he hadn't found me when he did, there was a very good chance Tamerlane would've gotten to us first.

"What about your family?" Marlow asked. "I let you live so you could care for them."

Tamerlane's expression fell, but only for a moment, and he was quick to erase it. "Those are things of the past. I no longer have ties to anything on this earth. My work has become much greater than that."

"And what is your work?" she asked.

"I don't think you'd approve." He grinned. "Or even understand."

Eisheth laughed at that, a hysterical cackle rising deep from within her, as she lay on the bed watching this all unfold with rapt attention.

"Try me," Marlow replied.

"I would really love to catch up with you. Honestly, I would love to hear how you've spent the last four years of your life, while I've been toiling away as a draugr." Tamerlane held his hands up, shrugging helplessly. "But I haven't got the time."

Marlow had moved so she was standing between Tamerlane and the door, blocking his escape, and she was facing me.

"You know I can't let you leave alive," she warned him. "Not again."

"If you really wanted me dead, you had to kill me back then," Tamerlane contradicted her. "Now it's too late."

"We'll see about that."

Sheathed on her hip, my mother's sword began to glow red. It was much duller and muddier than normal, but Marlow reached for it. She pulled it out just as he moved toward her, but it was already too late.

It only took a matter of seconds—Mördare was pointed at Tamerlane, and then he was on Marlow, grabbing her wrist and breaking it with an audible snap. He turned my mother's own sword on her and drove it through her stomach. From where I was standing, I saw her eyes widen with pain and shock, and her mouth hung open.

"No!" I cried out.

Oona wrapped her arms tightly around my waist, trying to hold me back. I began dragging her across the floor as I ran toward Marlow. I screamed as her body started to slip backward, going limp, and I reached for my own sword.

"*Tin prostasía mas me to fos sas!*" Oona shouted as she held on to me with all her might.

Suddenly the candle flames turned dark purple and exploded around us, throwing me and Oona back against the wall. Eisheth screamed as hot purple smoke filled the room, burning my eyes and lungs. The windows exploded outward, and Oona bent over me, trying to shield me from the flames and glass.

"Eisheth, we leave now!" Tamerlane shouted.

I lifted my head just as the fires went out, and tiny bits of glass were still falling to the floor, like the room was raining glitter. Eisheth grabbed on to Tamerlane, and she ran toward the window, her large wings already flapping, and leapt out into the night.

I scrambled away from Oona, crawling through the smoke and melted wax to where Marlow lay on the floor. Her blood had already begun pooling around her, and Mördare left her stomach glowing red.

"Marlow," I said, brushing back the hair from her face.

A line of blood trailed down from her lips as she stared up at me. Her mouth was moving, but no words came. Her body twitched slightly, like she was having subtle convulsions.

"Marlow, it'll be okay. Just hang on," I told her.

Her back arched, and she stopped trembling. Her eyes changed from dark gray to pure white—no pupil, no color. An inhuman voice came from her mouth, sounding twisted and angry, saying, "Remember that we all must die."

Then she gasped once, and her body collapsed back on the floor. She went limp, and her head lolled to the side.

"Marlow!" I wailed, shaking her as if that would help somehow. Oona had crawled over to my side, and she put her hand on my arm.

So I turned to her, screaming, "Help her! Oona, you have to help her!"

"I can't!" Oona said with tears in her eyes. "I'm sorry, Mal. But I can't. I can't bring her back from the dead."

"Why didn't you use that spell sooner?" I demanded. "Why didn't you save her?"

"I couldn't." She shook her head, tears streaming down her cheeks. "It all happened too fast, and I didn't realize until it was too late. I'm sorry."

Then a strange weakness came over me, and I collapsed into her arms, sobbing. Oona stroked my hair, repeating, "I'm so sorry," over and over.

THIRTY-TWO

———◆———

"Who do we call?" Oona asked, her voice soft and comforting as she gently rubbed my back. My mother's body lay a few feet away from us, and her blood was staining the knees of my jeans. "Mal? Who do we call?"

"What are you talking about?" I asked.

"I don't know what to do," Oona said simply. "Do I call the police? Or . . . we can't just stay here with Marlow like this. Tamerlane might come back."

I sat up slowly, and I felt like I was waking from a horrible dream. I hadn't been sleeping, but it still felt like none of this could be real. My eyes were raw from crying, and I rubbed at them as I looked around at the disaster that had become of Eisheth's loft.

"Who do we call?" I repeated.

"Do you have a number? I can call, if you need me to," Oona offered.

I stood up, thinking that somehow that would make me feel better, and I stumbled over toward the windows. The wind was blowing in, making the curtains billow into the room and letting the amber glow of the city stream in, along with the icy night air.

"Mal?" Oona called after me, sounding worried.

"Samael," I said thickly.

I dug my cell phone out of my pocket and pulled up his number. Then I stood waiting, rubbing my temple and hoping he answered, because I didn't know what to do if he didn't. This was too much of a mess, and I didn't trust anybody else.

"This is Samael," he answered.

"Samael, it's Malin." I sniffled and closed my eyes. "I need you to come down here, and I think we need . . . we need a cleanup crew."

"What are you talking about?" Samael asked. "What's going on?"

"Everything went to shit," I said. "And Marlow—" My voice cracked on her name.

"What about Marlow?" Samael asked, and I could already hear the panic edging into his voice.

I let out a shaky breath and finally forced myself to say, "She's dead."

There was a long silence on the line, so long I was afraid the call had been disconnected, but I didn't have the strength to say anything. So I just waited, and finally Samael asked, "Where are you?"

I gave him the address, and he promised to be here as soon as he could. I don't know how long it took him to get here. Maybe five minutes. Maybe an hour. All I knew was that by the time he arrived, the loft had gotten very cold, and Oona was worried that I might get sick. She wanted me to step back from the window, but I wouldn't. I couldn't, and I didn't know how to explain it to her.

And then Samael came, and I don't think I'll ever forget his expression when he saw Marlow. His face went white, his eyes widened, and I don't think he breathed or moved for a long time. The cleanup crew—a group of lower-level angels who took care of this kind of thing—stayed outside the door, and when they asked to come in, Samael barked at them to stay put until he called for them.

As he stared down at my mother, fighting back tears, I think that was the first time I really knew that he was in love with her. I'd known for a while that they had some kind of flirtation, but I could see now, as he realized she was gone . . . he was devastated.

When he asked me what had happened, I thought about lying to him. For a moment I really considered hiding the truth to protect my mother. Nobody else needed to know what she'd done, that she'd failed at her job and it had gotten her killed.

But Tamerlane Fayette was still out there, and he wanted to kill everyone who knew he was alive, which now included me, Oona, Asher, and Asher's grandmother. Not to mention any other innocent people who got in his way.

So I told Samael the truth. I told him, and I watched his expression change from shock to horror to disappointment to horror again. I didn't leave out anything, even the parts I wanted to, and he listened patiently.

"We need to keep this quiet," he said once I'd finished, and the air had gotten so cold, I could see his breath when he spoke. "I can do that, and I will. No one outside of this room can know the truth. Not yet. Do you understand?"

I nodded. "Yeah, I do."

"Do you have someone you can go home with?" he asked. "I don't think you should be alone."

I motioned to Oona, who'd been standing beside me the whole time, but Samael looked at her like he'd forgotten she was there. This was all a lot to take in for him, I supposed.

He nodded, then, brusquely, he reached out and hugged me, pulling me close to him. I closed my eyes for a moment. He smelled

of autumn leaves and campfires, and his arms were so warm and
`strong. I realized that I couldn't remember the last time my mother
had hugged me, or what she smelled like, other than cigarillos.

"I'll take care of her," he promised me, then he let me go. "You
go home and take care of yourself. We'll talk soon, okay?"

I nodded because I didn't think I could talk without crying, not
anymore, and I let Oona take me out of the apartment. I don't remember leaving or walking or any of the way home, but I know that
eventually we made it home. The first thing I said was that I didn't
know if I was an orphan or not, because my mother had never both-
ered to tell me much about my father. That never seemed like a
big deal before, and I was always fine that it was just the two of us,
except now it wasn't just the two of us.

It was just me, and it would only be me from here on out.

"That's not true," Oona insisted as I stared out the window at
the vast city below us. "You have me. You'll always have me."

"Nobody really has anybody," I told her. "We all must die, and
we all die alone."

THIRTY-THREE

———◆———

I lay on the sofa in my living room, staring blankly ahead. Bowie kept nuzzling my hand, trying to get me to pet him, but I couldn't muster the energy.

"You need to eat something," Oona told me, standing before me with a bowl of harira soup. The scent of savory tomatoes, ginger, and lentils was usually enough to whet my appetite, but right now it only made me more nauseated.

"No, I don't," I said.

"Mal." She sighed and set the soup on the kitchen counter. "You've been lying on that couch since we got home yesterday. You can't just stay there forever."

I rolled over, burying my face in a throw pillow, and muttered, "Watch me."

After a long silence, Oona gently said, "I can't even begin to pretend to understand how you feel."

"Then don't try," I snapped.

"Fine. I'll leave you be. But when you want to talk, I'm here."

I heard her footsteps retreating to the other side of the apartment, toward her bedroom, but a knock at the front door halted her progress. I didn't bother to roll over and instead just lay buried in the couch, listening as she answered it.

"Asher," Oona said in surprise.

"I heard about Marlow, and I wanted to see how Malin was doing," he said.

"That's how she's doing. You can try talking to her, but I don't know if she'll talk back," Oona offered bleakly.

I rolled over to see Asher standing in the doorway. His normally handsome face had aged under the burden of remorse. Dark circles under his grave eyes, deep creases of worry on his forehead, and lips pressed into a grim frown.

"How'd you hear about Marlow?" I asked.

He took that as an invitation and stepped into the apartment. Oona closed the door behind him before quietly retreating to her room, giving Asher and me some space to talk alone. There was an awkwardness about him, a tension that hadn't been there before, and it wasn't from Marlow's death.

I could almost feel him wanting to reach out and comfort me, but he managed to suppress the urge, instead restlessly rubbing at his thumb as he stood in front of me.

"I have some friends who are on the Vörðr force," Asher explained. "They said they're keeping it under wraps how she died, but it's still big news on the inside that a Valkyrie was killed."

I sat up on the couch and, without the potency it deserved, I mumbled, "Tamerlane killed her."

For a moment Asher said nothing. Slowly, almost weakly, he sat down on the couch beside me and gaped at the floor. "You found him?"

"Yeah, but only long enough for him to kill Marlow and then escape again."

He grimaced. "I'm sorry I dragged you into this."

"You didn't drag me into anything. This was all Marlow's fault, remember?" I said. "And besides that, Tamerlane admitted he was in search of Marlow, so it was only a matter of time until he found her. Her death was inevitable."

My mind went back to the conversation I'd had with Sloane Kothari, where she admitted that she didn't believe in free will, and that meant the whole world moved in predestination, with someone—or something—controlling everything.

I wondered again if that was true, and if there was anything I could've done to prevent Marlow's death, or if this was the way it was always supposed to be.

Maybe she'd broken free from her track, and her punishment had been death. Because if the whole world exists rotating in a perfect order, there is no room for someone going rogue. Eventually she was bound to be ground up and destroyed inside the machine.

"I'm still sorry it happened," Asher said, pulling me from my thoughts.

I shrugged emptily. "Yeah, well, you know how it goes."

"When my mom died, it was the worst day of my life. I didn't know how I would ever get through it," he said.

I rubbed my eyes and snapped, "But you did, and I know that I will, too." I was in no mood for a pep talk or an inspirational speech about the strength within or how I'd always carry memories of Marlow with me.

"I never doubted that you would," he responded. "You're strong and resourceful."

"Thanks."

"But it does make it easier if you let people help. My grandma—"

"You had a family to help you," I cut him off. "I don't."

"Family doesn't have to just be blood," Asher contended. "You have your friend Oona. You have me. I'm sure you have others you can count on."

"Marlow told me that Valkyries didn't do well with long-lasting relationships," I replied, and even as I was arguing against him, I knew there was truth in Asher's words. Oona had been my best friend for years, and I'd always be able to count on her.

But at the moment I didn't feel like agreeing with him. I wanted to be isolated in my pain. That's what Marlow would do.

"I don't know about all Valkyries, but that is true for some," he admitted.

I laughed hollowly. "Good to know Marlow wasn't wrong about that."

"But you can make your life what you wish. My mom did."

Asher looked at me—really looked at me, for the first time since he'd come over today. Before, his eyes had been focusing just off to the side, as if looking at me directly would spur an awkward conversation about our kiss the other night and how that played into our relationship, which was now further complicated by my mother's murder.

He was now stuck in the terrible position of comforting me over the death of someone who had caused the death of his own mother. But when he looked at me, there was no anger, no sense of justice or retribution. Only compassion and hurt and warmth.

His normally stormy eyes were like a calm sea, inviting me to join him in peace, where the two of us could cling to each other for comfort. So, when he reached over, taking my hand in his, I let him. It made me feel . . . safer and less alone.

"Well, your mom sounds more progressive than mine," I said.

"Marlow seemed like a very complicated, strong-willed, independent woman." He spoke slowly, as if choosing his words carefully.

"She was. She was all those things and so much more," I agreed.

Then, rather abruptly, I said something that had been digging at me since she died, since before then, really, but since her death it had been a sharp dagger twisting inside my chest: "I don't think she loved me."

The realization of that coupled with Asher here, attempting to comfort me and care for me, only compounded the brutal truth that I didn't think anyone had ever really loved me. Maybe Oona had. Probably, actually. But sometimes I needed more than one solitary friend in the whole entire world who really and truly loved me.

"I . . ." Asher took a deep breath. "I honestly didn't know her. I want to tell you that she did love you, in her own way, and I think that's probably true, but I don't know."

"It's okay," I lied as tears welled in my eyes. "I think I always knew that she didn't love me. And I was okay with it, because I thought, *That's normal. Valkyries can't love. This is just what we are.* But deep down, I always knew that was a lie. Because I loved her."

Asher put his arm around me, pulling me close to him and letting me cry into his shoulder. He held me fiercely in a way that I couldn't remember anybody else ever holding me, and he kissed my hair.

"I know nothing I can say will take your pain away," he whispered. "But I promise you that I will do everything in my power to avenge Marlow and my mother. Tamerlane Fayette won't escape death again."

THIRTY-FOUR

———◆———

In the Rosehill Cemetery, bodies were piled on top of each other. The population explosion of the last few centuries had created the need for alternative burials, with cremation and shared graves becoming the top affordable options.

Fortunately for me, that was one thing I didn't have to worry about, thanks to my mother's status as a Valkyrie. All Valkyries—whether they died in the line of duty, by accident, or simply from old age—were buried in the Mausoleum av Veteraner Från Kriget Mot Odödlighet.

The crypt sat on a large hill in the center of the cemetery, surrounded by rosebushes, which had already begun to wither and die with winter around the corner. It was a large square building made of white marble, with the only decoration being the coat of arms above the door—a shield emblazoned with the three horns of Odin and nine swords fanned out behind it.

Inside the mausoleum were hundreds of white marble drawers, all labeled with simple gold letters stating each name, year of birth, and year of death. Nothing more, nothing less. Near the end of the hall, in a spot four rows from the bottom, was my mother.

MARLOW GRACE KRIGARE

Her letters were brighter and shinier than the others', since they were newer. Fresh flowers stood on a pedestal near her tomb, and an Eralim in a black uniform stood to the side, presiding over the funeral.

It was a sparely attended funeral, the way many Valkryies' funerals were, but Marlow had even fewer connections in life than most, I suspected. There might have been more mourners, but Samael was doing everything in his power to keep the news of her death from spreading.

Valkyrie deaths could be rather public spectacles if allowed to be, but in Marlow's case that would only lead to questions and suspicions and unwanted attention for myself and Asher. So Samael kept it quiet, and only eight people had shown up, including Samael and his two guards, Atlas and Godfrey.

Oona had come with her mother, Rhona, and they stood on one side of me, while Asher and his grandmother Teodora stood on the other. Both Oona and Asher seemed ready to reach out and steady me, should I need it, but I held strong throughout the service, and never shed a tear.

The Eralim presiding spoke of living a life of honor and virtue and dedication, and I wondered if any of those words even applied to Marlow. He finished up by talking about how Marlow was at peace now, and I hoped at least that part was true.

"I'm so sorry about your mother," Rhona said after the service had ended, and she squeezed my hand tightly. "I can't imagine how difficult this must be for you."

Atlas and Godfrey offered similar sentiments, giving me their sympathies for my loss, and I realized that nobody really had said anything about Marlow. I appreciated that. I didn't need them lying to me about how kind or generous she was. She didn't need her memory to be exalted higher than how she lived her life.

Teodora smiled thinly at me, pulling her black cloak around her. "I know your mother and I had our differences, to put it lightly, but I would never wish this upon you. Losing a loved one is never easy."

"Thank you for coming," I mumbled, because I didn't know what else to say.

Asher looked like he wanted to say something, but Samael stepped up, edging his way in.

"Mind if I speak to Malin alone for a moment?" he asked.

Asher looked to me, his gaze protective and warm, and I nodded to let him know it was okay to leave my side. "Sure, of course," he said, squeezing my hand gently before turning to take a few steps away. The other guests had gone outside, leaving the three of us alone in the mausoleum, and Asher lingered nearby with just enough distance between us that he wouldn't be eavesdropping.

Samael's eyes were red-rimmed and his umber skin was unusually pale, and though I don't think he could ever really look bad per se, this was the worst I'd ever seen him. Even his lush curls seemed lifeless today. He fidgeted with his handkerchief and stared down at the floor, which was covered in petals from the dying flowers left on the doors of other tombs.

"What do you want to do?" Samael asked finally.

"What do you mean?" I asked.

He lifted his aquamarine eyes to meet mine. "About Tamerlane."

"I plan to kill him," I replied honestly.

"You don't have to," Samael said, then he hurried to correct himself. "I mean, I can take care of him. I *will*, if that's what you want."

"I appreciate that, but I think I would rather handle it myself," I said.

Samael nodded. "I thought that's how you would feel. But I wanted to let you know that I'm here to help you as much or as little as you need. I want to end this bastard just as much as you do."

"I do need help finding him," I admitted.

I'd spent the twenty-four hours after Marlow died numb and unable to think of anything, really, and then Asher came over and woke up the pain inside me, and it all came tumbling out. Since then, I'd only really been thinking of one thing—how to find Tamerlane and kill him.

The only speed bump in that plan was that I had no idea where to look. Marlow was the one who had connections—she'd introduced us to Cecily Stavros, who was able to point us in the direction of Tamerlane.

But without Marlow, I didn't know where to start.

"I'm already on it," Samael assured me. "I have feelers going out as far and wide as I can, and as inconspicuously as possible, of course. And just so you know, I'm also having a few off-duty Vörðr keep an eye on you and Oona, in case Tamerlane comes looking for you."

"I don't really think that's necessary," I objected.

"I'm not doing it for you," Samael said with a pained smile. "It's what Marlow would've asked me to do. She wanted you safe."

I lowered my eyes, since I couldn't argue with the wishes of a dead woman. "I'll just keep a lookout for them, then."

The clacking of heels echoing through the mausoleum caused me to look up, and I saw Quinn Devane walking slowly toward us. She wore all black, and managed to somehow look beautiful, even on a day when I didn't think I'd be capable of finding beauty in anything.

"I'm not interrupting, am I?" Quinn asked, chewing her lip.

"No." Samael shook his head, then touched my arm gently. "I'll let you know when I found out anything, Malin. Take care."

"Thank you," I said, and I watched him walk away, disappearing outside into the overcast afternoon. Only then did I finally force myself to look back at Quinn.

· With her silver hair cascading around her shoulders, she had an extra ethereal quality to her to beauty, and I realized that I couldn't remember the last time I'd seen her in the daylight. So much of our relationship had been done clandestine, with stolen kisses in dark bedrooms, both of us with busy schedules and me afraid of what the higher-ups at Ravenswood would think.

Seeing her here like this reminded me of seeing a teacher outside of class or an actor out of costume. It was disarming, and suddenly I felt uneasy. I looked over at Asher, who still lingered down the hall, reading the plaques on the wall, and just knowing he was nearby gave me the strength to face Quinn.

"What are you doing here?" I asked finally.

Her eyes were filled with sympathy as she softly said, "I heard about Marlow, and I wanted to make sure that you're okay."

"I'm fine."

Her shoulders sagged, and her lips twitched slightly. "Malin, I know you're hurting. Why do you have to shut me out like this?"

I ran my fingers through my hair and tried to think of all the things I wanted to say to her, all the emotions I couldn't form the words for. The contradictions of missing her and being afraid of her. Wishing she hadn't come here and also grateful that she still cared.

Feeling edgy, I glanced from Quinn to Asher, and I realized the key difference between the two of them—Quinn left me breathless and invigorated and pushed me too far so that I never felt safe, and Asher left me breathless and exhilarated and made me feel . . . certain in a way that she never had.

Quinn was always a question, and Asher was the answer.

But right now I couldn't deal with it, so I just looked up at her and asked, "Do you really think now is the best time to do this, Quinn?"

"No, of course not. I'm sorry." She lowered her eyes and shook her head, her fair cheeks reddening subtly with shame. "I only wanted to . . . I wanted to let you know that I'm here for you, if you need me. For anything at all."

"Thank you, but . . ." I began, but then I realized we weren't alone. A man was wandering through the vast halls of the mausoleum, carrying a large bouquet of flowers. It was so big, it looked like he might nearly topple over.

"Sorry," he said as he approached us. "I have a delivery for the Krigare funeral?"

"It's over now," I told him. "But I'll take them."

He apologized profusely as he handed them to me. "Sorry about that. The order just came in, and we rushed as quickly as we could."

He left me, struggling with a heavy vase full of two dozen red roses, the exact same shade as the lipstick Marlow always wore. Hardly anyone had come to Marlow's funeral, and as far as I knew, she didn't have that many friends in the world, so I couldn't imagine who would send them.

"Who are they from?" I asked Quinn, since I was too busy trying to hold them to look at the card.

Quinn moved around the roses and found a small card, matte-black with a message inscribed in gold ink. "It only says, *With all my love, Tamerlane.*"

THIRTY-FIVE

———— ◆ ————

Dead mother or no, Oona had decided that I'd put off going to the doctor long enough, and I was inclined to agree with her. I'd woken up the day after Marlow's funeral with a nasty infection brewing in my leg and all sorts of unpleasant sights and smells going on underneath my bandage.

But after the taunting bouquet of flowers Tamerlane Fayette had sent to the funeral, I didn't feel I could put off plotting to find him, either. Oona and I came to the agreement that while I was at the doctor's, she would gather information and call people, so that when I was done we could have a discussion and figure out what to do about Tamerlane.

A few hours later, I came back from the hospital with a freshly irrigated wound and a bottle of very strong antibiotics to find Asher and Quinn sitting on my couch. That was exactly what I wanted to deal with today. My ex-lover and my maybe-sorta-current-lover together. Discussing things about me. Without me.

Oona had set out a vegetable tray on the coffee table, which

Bowie was sneaking a carrot from. I must've looked as shocked as I felt, because Oona offered me a sheepish smile.

"How'd it go?" Oona asked.

"Great," I said, feigning a smile.

"Why don't you have a seat?" Quinn suggested, patting the spot between her and Asher. He actually scooted to the side a bit, to make room between the two of them, and the thought of that made me feel more claustrophobic than I ever had before.

"Nah, I think I'll be good over here." I went into the kitchenette area of our apartment and dragged an old kitchen chair into the living room, so I could sit across from Quinn and Asher.

"So, I was doing research about Tamerlane and how to handle draugrs, like we talked about," Oona explained as she sat cross-legged on the floor beside me. "And I realized that this is such a vast undertaking, it might be helpful to have more people, so I called over Asher and Quinn."

I scratched the back of my head, doing my best not to look as annoyed as I felt. "Uh-huh. That makes sense."

"And Oona filled me in about everything that's been going on," Quinn said, but she didn't need to. I could already tell by the worry in her eyes and the grim downturn of her mouth. "I really wish you would've come to me sooner. I could've helped."

"I didn't want it getting out," I said. "I was afraid about what would happen to Marlow, but . . . now that doesn't really matter."

"Tamerlane is the one who sent the flowers yesterday?" Quinn asked.

After I'd gotten the roses, I'd thrown them on the floor of the mausoleum. The vase shattered, and I stomped all over the flowers while Quinn kept asking me what was wrong. I was too irate to see straight, so I'd stormed off without explaining anything to her.

Oona groaned in disgust. "I can't believe he did that. That's so messed up."

Angry bile rose in my throat, and I was barely able to swallow it down before muttering, "He did say he ought to thank her by sending her flowers."

"So does anybody know how to kill Tamerlane?" Asher asked, smartly changing the subject before I lost my shit again.

"Back when I was going to Ravenswood, I took an elective on Mythology and Urban Legends," Quinn said. "We briefly discussed zombies and the undead then, but it wasn't anything too in-depth. The only thing I really remember is them saying that the Valkyrie sword would no longer work on them."

"That seems to be as much as I've been able to find, as well," Oona agreed. "Only information on what does *not* kill them, which isn't helpful at all."

Asher leaned forward, resting his arms on his knees. "When we were talking with the gorgon the other day, it got me thinking about things in a way I hadn't before, so I started going through my grandmother's books. She has hundreds of these really old books from our homeland, and in a book filled with fables and stories I found a chapter on draugrs—"

Quinn interjected, "You guys keep mentioning draugrs, but I haven't heard anyone use that word before today. What does it mean, exactly?"

"I just looked it up, actually, and learned it's an old Norse word meaning 'again-walker,'" Asher explained. "They were thought to be like zombies."

"But zombies don't exist," Quinn argued. "'That which is dead cannot rise.' That's Supernatural 101."

She was right. That was one of the first things we were taught about the world we lived in. To maintain order in a world where immortals lived alongside humans, we were all only given one life—with humans lying in their tombs, while the immortals were shuttled down to the underworld.

But both were given the same commandment: The dead must stay dead. That which is dead cannot rise.

"They're not exactly zombies," Asher continued. "Just immortals that found a way around the Valkyrie loophole."

"But those are just old Scandinavian stories," Quinn reminded us.

"Well, me and Oona saw Tamerlane," I pointed out. "He's alive, when he should be dead, and he killed *two* Valkyries, which shouldn't even be possible. We're now in an uncharted world where the impossible has become possible."

Oona frowned as she considered this. Bowie had given up on stealing carrots and hopped over to sit on her lap, where she absently began to stroke his feathered wings.

"Did the book say anything about how to stop them?" Quinn asked, resting her emerald gaze on Asher.

"Not really. But it did have this passage—I wrote it down so I would remember it exactly." He pulled out his phone and scrolled through it. "It says, *From whence the draugr rose, only that will make the draugr fall. If his master waits in Helheim, it is his sword that makes the call.*"

We all sat silently for a minute, thinking about what Asher had read and trying to decipher whatever coded message might be hidden in it. Quinn played with her long hair, something she did when she was agitated, and she grew rougher with it the more she thought.

Finally, she broke the silence and asked, "What does that mean?"

"Helheim was the Norse afterworld, which I get," Asher supplied. "But if we assume that Tamerlane Fayette is a draugr, who is his master?"

I shrugged. "Supposedly he's hanging out with two other draugrs, but I don't know if any one of them is really a 'master,' or who they would answer to."

"Who is the big head honcho around here?" Oona asked, her eyes darting between the three of us.

"Velnias has a lot of sway in the demonic community, and he's the head of the Kurnugia Society," I said. "But I doubt he'd talk to us, after the way everyone at the Red Raven shut us out when Asher and I went there."

"And if Velnias is Tamerlane's master, I seriously doubt he'd help us fell Tamerlane, anyway," Asher added.

I rubbed a hand over my face and slouched back in my chair. "Figuring out how to kill Tamerlane is almost a moot point, since I don't know if we'll ever find him again. I'm sure after all this he's going to burrow even deeper underground."

"Maybe not," Oona argued. "Sending flowers to Marlow's funeral was pretty bold. Not to mention the stuff that happened with Amaryllis Mori."

Asher turned to me, his gaze a mixture of curiosity and concern. "Who's that?"

"She was a Jorogumo that I killed for work, but she almost bested me, and her venom was more powerful than it should've been," I explained. "And she told me that the tables were turning, and the underworld was growing stronger."

"Tamerlane might not feel the need to hide," Quinn pointed out hopefully. That was just like her—trying to look for the bright side in a completely impossible situation.

"Well, he has been staying in the city using the alias of Bram Madichonnen," I countered.

Oona sat up straighter, gently knocking Bowie off her lap, so he hopped angrily to the other side of the room. "So, I've been thinking about that, and I looked into it more, because I was curious as to *why* he chose the name that he did."

I shrugged. "What does it matter?"

"Marlow spared him because she thought he was good and pure, and now he's a megalomaniac who killed the person that saved him," Oona said. "Something changed."

"Yeah, he became a draugr," Asher replied.

Oona shot him a look but continued. "Yes, but the name he chose loosely translates to 'cursed father.'"

"Why would he pick that?" Quinn asked.

"Before being a draugr, by all accounts, he was a happy father who helped run an orphanage," Oona said. "Now his family is dead, brutally murdered, and his orphanage is closed. Everything that mattered in his life is gone."

"When he became a draugr, he had to give that all up," I said. But that was something we already knew.

"And based on his name, I'm thinking that might not have been his choice," Oona reasoned.

I thought back to the confrontation I'd witnessed between Marlow and Tamerlane. He'd been cool and casual right up until the moment Marlow mentioned his family. That was the only time his mask of nonchalance slipped—only for a moment—and then right after that everything had fallen apart.

"He did seem really touchy when Marlow mentioned his family," I remembered.

"So, he begged Marlow to spare him so he could take care of his family and be with them because he loved them and all that," Oona went on, sounding more excited as her idea came together. "Then he became a draugr, and . . . then what? Did he kill his family? Did he have a change of heart? Or did someone else make him do it? Or did someone else do it to send him a message?"

"Maybe all of the above?" I said. "If what Amaryllis Mori was saying is true, there is something brewing in the underworld."

"But you can't return from Kurnugia," Quinn maintained. "That's one of the rules. When humans and mortals die, we're just dead. When immortals die, they get to go to Kurnugia, but they can't return."

"Well, we all know they've never been too thrilled about the Valkyrie and Kurnugia arrangement," Asher pointed out dismally.

"If they're working together to form some kind of underworld uprising—which is scary as hell—then they must have some kind of leader," I said. "And now all we have to do is figure out who that is to either kill them or get them to kill Tamerlane, and then we'll be all set."

"And we should probably also work on quelling that uprising in Kurnugia," Oona added.

Quinn smiled, trying to remain optimistic, but the twitch at the corner of her crooked lips gave away her unease. "Well, if anyone can handle all that, it ought to be the four of us, right?"

THIRTY-SIX

———◆———

After hours of going over who might be Tamerlane's master—throwing out names from Velnias to Odin, and even delving deeper into the underworld with figures like Ereshkigal, Hai-uri, and Erlik—we were no closer to figuring out who it might be, even assuming there was a master. There was even a chance that Tamerlane was his own master, but I wasn't exactly sure how that would work.

As the conversation went late into the night, Oona grew tired and eventually fell asleep. She lay on the floor with a throw pillow under her head and Bowie curled up beside her. When she started snoring softly, I woke her up and helped her get to bed.

After Oona mumbled a sleepy good night, Asher excused himself to use the restroom, and Quinn stood up and stretched. Her shirt rose up, revealing her taut stomach, and I noticed a collection of black stars tattooed just above her hip.

"New ink?" I asked, motioning to her hip. It had been only six months since we'd last been together, and I vividly remembered tracing my hands over every inch of her. I could still remember every freckle and scar that marked her skin, so I definitely would've recalled a tattoo.

"Yeah." She smiled demurely and ran her fingers seductively over her hip. "It's the constellation for Capricorn."

"Capricorn?" I asked in surprise. "But you were born in August. Aren't you a Virgo?"

Her smile deepened, looking pleased that I still remembered her birthday.

"I did, but I was officially sworn in as Valkyrie on a cold day in January two years ago," Quinn explained. "I just finally got around to getting a tattoo to commemorate that."

My mind flashed to a time when we'd been lying in my bed together, our arms intertwined, with the early morning light spilling in through my bedroom window. Her head had been resting on my chest, and I curled up close to her. Her hair had been dyed lavender then, and I remembered breathing her in and thinking it fitting that she smelled like lilacs and summer.

We'd been sharing war stories from our childhood. While I had plenty of anecdotes about Marlow, Quinn had very little to say about her own mother, and instead focused most of her stories on school bullies and ex-girlfriends. She had pulled herself closer to me, her arm wrapped around my waist and her cheek pressed against my bare skin.

"But that's all behind us now," she'd told me in her husky voice, as rich and sweet as honey. "We've come out of it and we're on the other side, stronger and braver for it."

"You really think that?" I had asked her, and she tilted her head to stare up at me with her wide green eyes.

"I do. Sometimes I think of my existence as two lives," she had explained. "There was the time before, when I had no control and I was dragged around the world, feeling unloved and un-wanted.

"And then there's the life when I became a Valkyrie," Quinn had gone on. "The day my life became my own. Sure, I have orders to obey and responsibilities, but my fate is in my own hands. Some-times I feel like my real life didn't begin until then."

"Well, I'm glad that I'm a part of your real life," I'd teased her.

"Of course you are." She moved, propping herself up so she hov-ered above me, smiling down at me. "You're the main reason that I know this is my real life, that everything before this was just prac-tice for what was to come. Because you're here, and the way I feel about you is the truest thing I've ever known."

She'd leaned down and kissed me then, and while her kisses felt wonderful and left me dizzy, this one had been different. This one had filled me with an urgent panic that I couldn't explain, and I couldn't breathe.

I was overwhelmed by her—she'd always overwhelmed me, but before, it had felt exciting. But in that moment, it just felt terrifying and heavy and too much.

Though Quinn had begged me to stay in bed with her, I had made some excuse about why I had to go. Two weeks later, I had broken up with her.

Now, standing in my living room, Quinn's smile faded, maybe because she was thinking of the same memory, or maybe she was just tired, as she suppressed a yawn.

"It is getting late," she said. "I should probably head home."

"Thank you for helping," I told her as I stood up and walked her out.

She lingered in the doorway, toying with her Vegvisir amulet hanging around her neck.

"You're a very good friend," I added, trying to reaffirm that distance I'd put between us.

"I know." She nodded once, smiling sadly at me, and then started backing away. "I'll see you around."

Once she had gone, I closed the door and leaned back against it, breathing in deeply. I closed my eyes, trying desperately to push down all the confusing feelings that whirled inside me.

THIRTY-SEVEN

⸻◆⸻

"Is everything okay?" Asher asked quietly, and I opened my eyes in surprise. For a moment I'd actually forgotten that he was still here, and I hadn't heard him come out of the bathroom.

"Yeah." I forced a smile. "Everything's fine."

"I should probably leave you be," he offered.

But even though I'd sent Quinn away out of fear of the complexities of our past, I didn't really feel like being alone. I knew sleep wouldn't come easy for me—it hadn't since Marlow died—and I didn't want to sit up alone all night, thinking my horrible thoughts and worrying my terrible worries about what may come of the world.

"No, you don't have to," I said, which was as close as I could get to asking him to stay, and walked toward the kitchen. "Do you want a drink?"

"Uh, sure. What are we drinking?" he asked.

"Oona's got an old bottle of wine in the fridge she said I could finish off." I pulled out a large black bottle, simply labeled with BOAL MADEIRA in big white letters.

"Sounds good."

Oona and I didn't have much in the way of dishes, since we ate a lot of takeout, and I grabbed a large beer mug and a glass decorated with the logo for the Ravenswood Academy soccer team, the Raging Raptors. Oona had gone on a mini-shopping spree after getting accepted into the academy, so we had all kinds of random stuff with school logos.

"So," I said, as I filled up both the glasses. "Tell me about yourself."

"There's not much to tell." He shrugged.

"Oh, I doubt that." I took a big gulp of my wine, then walked back to the living room to get more comfortable on the couch. "Especially since I know next to nothing about you."

"My childhood was mostly normal and uneventful," Asher elaborated disinterestedly. "I was born twenty-one and a half years ago to a Valkyrie who loved me very much, and a mercenary. My mom raised me on her own, because my father was off doing his own thing, and I grew up just south of the city. My first job was as a bike messenger, but that didn't last long."

"Why not?" I asked.

He took a long drink, then stared down at his cup. "Because my mom died."

I grimaced. "Sorry."

"After that, I basically threw myself into finding her killer, and now here I am with you." He smiled crookedly at that.

"You can't just brush over the last three years," I persisted. "I know you had adventures. You told me you searched all over the country."

"I did," he admitted, scratching his cheek. "I became a private investigator, to help fund my own investigations, but mostly I was hired to look for spurned lovers."

He turned to look at me. "The other night with you, at the Red Raven. Now, *that* was an adventure."

"That wasn't much of an adventure. It didn't last very long." I was leaning my head against the back of the couch. My knees were pulled up nearly to my chest, my glass of wine cradled between them, and my feet pointed toward him.

"Yeah, but you were badass," he said, sounding wistful.

His eyes were the darkest shade of blue I'd ever seen, like the sky just before it completely gave way to the black of night. Whenever he grinned, it drew attention to the scar on his lip, a tiny blemish on his otherwise flawless skin that somehow made him even sexier, and that felt like the perfect analogy for Asher himself.

Then, rather abruptly, he turned bashful—lowering his gaze and smoothing out nonexistent wrinkles in his pants. His cheeks flushed slightly, and his dark lashes landed on them heavily.

Asher cleared his throat. "I wanted to, um, apologize."

"For breaking in? I thought you already had," I said with a laugh.

"No." He licked his lips. "For kissing you the other night. I shouldn't have done that."

"Why not?" I asked, then added, "I wanted you to."

He lifted his head, his eyes filled with an unexpected eagerness and hope that made him appear more youthful. "You did?"

"Do you think I would've kissed you back if I didn't like it?"

"No, I don't suppose you would," he admitted with a small laugh. "But you just seemed too cool for it."

I raised an eyebrow. "Too cool for kissing?"

"Too cool for kissing *me*," he amended.

I laughed again. "I don't even know what that means."

"I don't know." He furrowed his brow, like he couldn't think of just the right words to say. "You seem above everything, sometimes."

I frowned. "I'm not." I took another drink. "But I think I know why I seem that way. Sometimes—well, most of the time, really—I'm afraid to feel things."

"What do you mean?" Asher asked.

My mind went back to a memory, a time when I couldn't have been more than five or six. I had a crush on this girl at school, and when I told her, she made fun of me in front of all her friends.

I came home bawling, and Marlow knelt down and looked me square in the eye, and told me, "Don't be a crybaby. You're a Valkyrie. Valkyries don't cry over petty shit like this, and they don't fall in love. You're stronger than this."

She meant it to be encouraging, but all I learned was that I should suck it up and shove down any feeling I had.

I took a deep breath and stared down at the wine in my cup. "I don't think I know how to have feelings, real ones like passion and anger and sadness and all that. Marlow always taught me that real Valkyries don't feel like that. That those emotions are just for humans. But I do feel them, and I always have, even when I tried not to."

Asher moved closer to me, putting his hand soothingly on my leg. "Real Valkyries do feel. My mother was emotional and passionate, and she was damn good at her job."

Suddenly tears were forming in my eyes. I didn't know why, and I hurried to wipe them away. "I know. I've only just begun to realize that this was another thing that Marlow was wrong about."

"I didn't mean to make you sad," he said, his voice low and soft.

"I'm not. It's okay," I insisted, sniffling a little. "These last couple weeks have just been so very long."

"I'm sorry. I shouldn't be here bothering you and taking up your time." He started to move away from me, but I reached out, putting my hand on his forearm to stop him.

"No, don't go," I said, and even I could hear the desperation in my own voice. It wasn't something I normally felt, but right now with Asher, that's exactly how I felt. Desperate to feel close to someone. For someone else to care about me and worry about me, so that, even just for a little bit, I didn't have to take care of myself.

He glanced at the doorway, as if having an internal debate, and he bit his lip before asking, "You sure?"

"Yeah. Right now, I really want you to stay."

"Okay," he said, and there was something about the way he said it—the weight of his words, the depth of his voice—that made me certain he knew exactly what I was asking.

He set his glass on the table and moved closer to me on the couch. I slid into him, so he wrapped his arm around me, pulling me to him. I curled up in his arms like that, relishing how strong and safe and warm I felt.

And he held me in a way that no one ever had before, not even Quinn. She would get feisty sitting still too long. But Asher seemed to have boundless patience inside him. He didn't try talking or kissing me or moving. He never asked a single thing from me—he just held me as long as I needed him to.

But eventually I realized I needed something more. I tilted my head up toward him, and his lips found mine, and all I wanted was to lose myself in him. I pressed my body against him, kissing him more deeply, and his hands were all over me, tracing the contours of my body.

It was less electric and insistent than our first kiss had been, but that didn't make it any less wonderful. It was gentler. Deeper. More intimate. This wasn't lust and adrenaline. It was something else.

His hand was on my cheek, and when we stopped kissing, he was looking me right in the eyes. He was right there with me, so close, and I felt a familiar panic inside my chest. I wondered painfully why it hurt so much to feel close to someone.

But at that moment, I thought it would've hurt more to be away from him. All I wanted to think and feel and be was with him, in the safety of his arms, until everything else just fell away and it was only me and only him and only us.

"Let's go back to my room," I told him breathlessly.

He lifted me up, and I wrapped my legs around him, allowing him to carry me to my bed before we both collapsed onto the mattress, ditching our clothes in a flurry.

THIRTY-EIGHT

The blinds in my room were open slightly, letting in the blue light from the billboard across the street, and I lay in Asher's arms in the sapphire afterglow. My head was on his chest, and his hand ran down my bare back.

In the dim light, I noticed a few jagged scars across his chest— all small and curved, dotting his smooth skin like angry bits of punctuation. I traced my fingers along the bumps, and Asher shivered involuntarily, but he didn't ask me to stop.

"What happened there?" I asked.

"It was from when I was a Vörðr," he said.

I tugged at the paracord bracelet he still had around his wrist, the one with the Vörðr emblem. "I was wondering when you were going to get around to telling me about that."

"Yeah, I was a Vörðr," he admitted with a sigh. "But it didn't last long."

"Why not?" I asked.

"It's hard to explain."

I tilted my head to get a better look at him. "Try me."

"I'd always wanted to be a Vörðr, ever since I was a little kid," he explained. "I couldn't be a Valkyrie, so I thought this was the next best thing. Proving my mettle, protecting and serving, saving the world. It all sounded so appealing."

"But it wasn't what you thought?" I asked.

"I don't even think it was that," he said. "After my mother died, everything changed. *I* changed." He paused. "I went after it anyway, because I didn't know what else to do, but my heart was never really in it. All that fighting and anger and death . . . it just didn't seem worth it anymore.

"No offense to you," he added in a hurry. "I know how important your job is, better than most people, actually. It just . . . it wasn't for me anymore."

"No, I understand," I assured him, pressing myself deeper into his arms, but something about his words hurt in a way I couldn't explain.

Maybe it was because he'd been able to get tired, to decide that violence wasn't for him, to leave it all behind, but for me it was in the very core of my being.

I had been born with an urge to kill, a calling inside me that intensified as I became a teenager. Getting rid of immortals brought me immense pleasure, and I couldn't imagine ever giving it up.

It was a strange, cold thing to realize I was born to be a murderer.

"Hey," Asher said softly, sensing the tension in my body. He reached down, putting his hand under my chin and gently forcing me to look up at him. "You are strong, and you are good. You are more than your job, and you're not your mother."

"You don't know that," I whispered around the lump in my throat, desperate for his words to be true even though some deep, dark part of my heart was certain that he was wrong.

"No, I do know that," he insisted with a gentle smile. He must've seen I was about to protest because he explained, "My grandmother said that sometimes our ancestors—those that died before us and love us—leave us truths when we most need them."

"How?" I asked, staring up at him skeptically.

"It's a thought that comes in, but it's truer and brighter, and it becomes branded across my heart." He brushed back the hair from my face as he looked down into my eyes. "And when I met you, I just knew," he said as his fingers trailed down my temple. "I *knew* you were good, and I knew you were who I was looking for."

Somehow, he'd known how to say exactly what I needed to hear at the moment, so I kissed him gratefully and wrapped my arms around him. I wanted to stay like that forever, with him.

When I was with Asher like this—in the quiet moments between plotting to fight a demonic draugr—he made me feel like a girl, in a strangely wonderful ordinary way. I wasn't some monster or machine or tool of the gods. I was just someone he cared about, and for a little while, that was all that mattered.

Eventually Asher drifted off to sleep beside me. I lay awake, thinking about everything and listening to him breathe. But the sound of flapping outside my bedroom window drew me from my thoughts.

It was actually more than flapping—something was pecking at the glass. I sat up and peered through the blinds to see the large black raven, stalking me. It stared right at me, unblinking, and I swear it could see straight into my soul.

"What do you want?" I whispered, but it only squawked in reply, then flew off into the night.

THIRTY-NINE

———————◆———————

Coming into class three minutes before it was set to start seemed like a good move on my part, but when I entered Professor Wu's class for the first time since my mother's death, I instantly regretted it.

Almost all the other students were already in class, and they had been talking among themselves. When they spotted me, there was hushed murmuring before the class fell silent, and I could practically feel their eyes burning into me.

Samael, I was certain, had done his best to keep the news of my mother's death and the circumstances surrounding it as secret as possible. But even within the Riks, hot gossip and rumors had a way of making its way through the city—and nothing was more scandalous than anything that happened with Marlow.

"Malin," Professor Wu said, and even his tone sounded off—more unsure and tight. He didn't seem to want to look directly at me, his eyes landing in the general area around me as I slowly took my seat. "We didn't expect you back so soon."

He had definitely heard something. How much he really knew—and how much of it was misinformed conjecture—I couldn't say, and I wasn't about to ask him. There was no point in explaining Marlow's actions, because the truth was damning enough, so I just had to keep my head down and barrel my way through the whispers and the stares.

"Getting behind in school wouldn't help anything," I said, dreadfully aware of all the ears hanging on my every word.

"If you need more time, you should take it," he persisted.

"I'll be fine," I maintained.

"Well, all right, then." He smiled cheerlessly, then turned to the whiteboard at the front of the class. "Since everyone seems to be here, we might as well get started. As we were talking about on Monday, there is one way for immortals to willingly return to Kurnugia, and that is through the Gates of Kurnugia—a city under impious control located just north of the equator, created by Ereshkigal a millennium ago."

As he began writing on the board, his demeanor returning to his usual dapper intellectual self, I heard two nearby students whispering. They meant to keep their voices down, but they were just loud enough that I could overhear them.

"I heard they killed her mother because she wouldn't do her job," one of them, a moody vampire, was whispering.

My heart pounded in my chest, causing my ears to flush with heat, and I bit my lip to keep from shouting out. The vampire wasn't wrong, not exactly, but I still didn't need to hear him gossiping about my mother so soon after her death.

"That's so weird, because she was just asking about what would happen if Valkyries didn't do their job last week," his friend agreed. "Do you think they were in on it together?"

"Hey," Sloane Kothari snapped at them. "Can you keep it down? Some of us are actually trying to learn here."

Professor Wu glanced back over his shoulder. "Thank you, Miss Kothari. If you don't want to be here, you don't have to be, but please don't distract the other students."

Sloane turned back to look at me, and instead of the usual disdain in her eyes there was sympathy, and something else. Worry, maybe? Her lips pressed into a thin smile, and I realized with some dismay that she might be the closest thing I had to a friend in this class. And as word got out about the suspicions regarding Marlow, I wondered how many friends I would have in the future.

For the rest of class, I kept my head down and dutifully copied the notes that Professor Wu told us to write and listed the chapters he told us to read. But otherwise I couldn't remember a single thing he said. My heart kept racing so loud I could hardly hear my own thoughts.

The second he told us we were excused, I bolted out the door, with no intention to try to stick it through any more of my classes. I hurried down the long halls, my footsteps echoing off the marble floors, when I spotted something that made me freeze in my tracks.

On one of the sterile white walls there was a large rectangle of white, even brighter and more stark than the surrounding area. Beneath it was a smaller rectangle where a plaque had been taken off, leaving an unpatched blemish in the plasterboard.

I looked around the hall, suddenly feeling disoriented and dizzy, and noted that all the other art pieces were still in place. All the paintings and sculptures created by former students remained exactly as they had been since I had started going to Ravenswood Academy.

All of them, except for one. The one titled *The Desire of the Valkyrie* had been removed, leaving only the white space behind it. Marlow's painting.

The school was already distancing itself from her. In life, she had been a hero, a mentor, someone to aspire to be, but now, in death, she would become a villain to be ostracized, to be hidden away.

"Malin," Sloane said, pulling me back to reality.

I turned to look at her, blinking a few times to assure me this was all real. Sloane stared at me, appearing as prim as she always did. Her black curls were pulled back in a tight ponytail, and her lips were pressed together in a thin line.

"I just wanted to say that I'm sorry about your mom," she said, and it sounded like she really meant it.

"Thanks . . . I think," I replied, narrowing my eyes. "Why are you being so nice to me?"

She glanced around, confirming that we were alone. This part of the hall was just far away enough from the classrooms that it was generally deserted, and today was no exception.

"Most people here know that my dad is a Deva," she said. "That's fairly common knowledge, because I've worked really hard to keep it hidden that my mom was an Apsara."

I hadn't known that, but I also didn't know why it mattered. Apsaras were immortals, known for their beauty, their love of nature, and their lack of inhibitions. They were sort of like muses, in that they often inspired people to do more and create more.

"There's no shame in being an Apsara," I told Sloane in confusion.

"Just as there is no shame in being a Valkyrie," she agreed. "But your mother wasn't just any Valkyrie, nor was my mother just any Apsara."

Glancing back at the blank space on the wall where Marlow's painting should be, I realized bleakly that I was going to have to get used to feeling shame when I thought of her. Before, it had only been pride and fear. But never shame.

"Because of the very nature of the Valkyries' existence, my

mother did not believe she had free will, much like me," Sloane explained. "The fact that a being exists that decides when she should die meant that her life had to be preordained, at least to some degree. But she got it in her head that if she overthrew the Evig Riksdag, we would all be free to live as we wanted. That without the Eralim giving orders and the Valkyries to carry them out, nothing could be preordained or controlled.

"Though she held no vendetta against the Valkyries personally, she couldn't see a way to coexist with them and truly be free," she went on. "So she mounted an attack against the Riksdag, and it failed miserably, so you've probably never heard of it. She was thwarted almost before she began, and she was killed instantly."

I gaped at Sloane for a moment before managing a meek, "I'm sorry. I had no idea."

"I'm not looking for your pity," she replied haughtily. "I am only telling you this because I know what it's like to love someone and also be mortified because of their actions."

I felt a lump growing in my throat. "That is hard to explain or know how to feel. I don't even fully understand it myself."

Sloane went on, "There is also the bitter irony that if my mother was right about free will, it is not her fault that she did the things she did. She did what she was always meant to."

"I know how you feel about predestination, but I just can't believe that this is what my mother was meant to do." I shook my head. "Marlow wasn't perfect by any means, but her greatest mistake was letting someone she believed to be good live.

"But he's not good, not even a little," I said. "He's in bed with something evil, and if left unchecked, he could destroy so much. How could that possibly be the plan?"

"It may have been your mother's destiny to set evil free," Sloane said. "But it may also be yours to stop it."

"How?" I scoffed. "I'm barely even a Valkyrie, and I have no idea how to find who I'm looking for. I don't even know for sure who I am looking for."

She chewed her lip. "If it is your destiny, you'll find a way."

I waited for a minute, expecting her to say something more. There was a look of perplexed uncertainty on her face, pinching her eyebrows together and creasing her forehead. But she didn't say anything else, and while I appreciated her kindness—especially on a day when no one else seemed to want to show me any— I didn't have much use for her platitudes and proverbs.

So I nodded once and said, "Thank you for your support. But I should get out of here, so I can start finding my destiny." I took a few steps backward from her. "I'll probably see you around."

She just stared at me, chewing her lip and looking indecisive. I offered her a small wave and turned around, walking away from her. I'd made it halfway down to the garage when I heard her calling after me.

"Malin! Wait!" Sloane jogged over to me, and when she reached me, she was out of breath, and her tawny skin had paled some. "I don't know if I'm doing the right thing, but my father says it's impossible for any mortal to know for sure what is right."

"And what exactly are you doing?" I asked.

She started digging through her bag as she spoke. "Since I heard about what happened to your mom, I got to thinking about all kinds of things, and I felt compelled to go through my mom's stuff, and when I found this—"

Sloane pulled out a rectangular stone. Twice the size of a matchbox, it looked like an ice cube with imperfections mottling its transparency. It sat flat on the palm of her hand as she held it out toward me.

"—I took it as a sign," she said. "And then you just happened to be in class today, the day after I found this, and you're saying you're looking, and . . . and I just feel like you should have it."

I stared down at the stone, trying to figure out what it was, since Sloane was treating it with such reverence, but I had no clue.

"What is it?" I asked finally.

"A sólarsteinn," Sloane said. "It's a sunstone."

But she hadn't needed to add the explanation. As soon as she said sólarsteinn, I realized exactly what it was. The sólarsteinn was a fabled stone that worked similarly to a magic compass, in that it could show you exactly where to find whatever it is you're looking for.

"I thought these were only in legends," I gasped.

"Well, they're real, apparently," Sloane said. "My mom planned to use it in her failed attack on the Riksdag, but she got caught before she even got in and got to use it."

"How does it work?" I asked.

"You have to be close to your target, and you have to *really* want to find it, like it has to be your heart's strongest desire," she elaborated. "Then you just hold the stone up to the light, and whatever you're really looking for will show."

"How close to my target do I have to be?" I asked.

Sloane shrugged. "I don't know for sure. I would guess at least within the same city."

Gingerly, I picked up the stone and held it so it would catch the light from the bright chandeliers in the halls. "So you think I can use this to complete my destiny?"

"I think it's the only chance you've got."

FORTY

———— ◆ ————

After Sloane gave me the sólarsteinn, I spent every moment finding out everything I could about it. As soon as Oona got done with class, I enlisted her help, since she knew more about talismans and enchanted objects than I did.

We tried all sorts of different things, but no matter what I felt or how I held it up, I never got the damned thing to glow, or whatever the heck it was supposed to do to show me where Tamerlane Fayette was hiding.

"Maybe he left town," Oona said, coming out of her bedroom wearing her green polo with the name DILLINGER'S CORNER MARKET & APOTHECARY embroidered on the chest.

I lay on the floor of the kitchen, holding the stone up toward the window where the setting sun streamed in. Bowie lay sprawled out beside me, sunbathing as much as he could with what little light filtered in through the smog.

"But he sent flowers to the funeral just the other day," I reminded her.

"He could've called from anywhere in the world," Oona pointed out. "Or he could've left right after the funeral. It doesn't make sense for him to stick around here, not when he knows that you and other Valkyries are probably coming after him."

"That assumes he considers us a threat," I muttered. "Or maybe this damned thing doesn't work. Do you think Sloane could be screwing with me?"

"Maybe, but I doubt it." Oona stood over me, with her hands on her hips. "Are you going to be okay while I'm at work?"

I set the stone down on my stomach so I could look up at her. "Yeah, why wouldn't I be?"

She shrugged. "This is the first time I'm leaving you alone since . . . you know."

"I'll be fine, Oona. I'm just in mourning—I'm not suddenly a toddler."

She rolled her eyes, and she started walking toward the door. "Just don't do anything stupid while I'm gone, okay? And I'll be home in five hours."

"I never do anything stupid," I insisted, but she just laughed as she left.

If Oona was right, and the reason the sólarsteinn wasn't working was because Tamerlane was out of range, then I didn't know if the stone would ever really be of help. How could I ever get close enough to Tamerlane to find him, if I didn't know where he was? I'd be stuck in cyclical reasoning forever.

But if I couldn't get to Tamerlane, maybe I could get to someone close to him. I closed my eyes and tried to redefine my greatest want. I'd been trying to focus directly on Tamerlane, but now I broadened it to include anyone I felt was responsible for my mother's death, which included Eisheth Levanon.

If Eisheth hadn't been abetting Tamerlane, he wouldn't have gotten away so quickly, and maybe Oona and I could've stopped him.

Or at the very least held him until Samael got there, and he could've done something.

I squeezed my eyes shut tighter, focusing on her face and her name, and since I wasn't entirely sure how the sólarsteinn worked, I started chanting inside my head, *Show me where the fallen angel Eisheth Levanon is. Bring me to her.*

Then I took a deep breath and opened my eyes. Bowie had sat up beside me and leaned forward, sniffing the stone with his big ears cocked at odd angles below his antlers.

"Here goes nothing, Bo," I said as I picked up the stone and held it toward the window. My wolpertinger sat up on his hind legs, sniffing the air, which I decided to take as a good sign that something magical would happen.

A sliver of sun broke through the clouds and passed through the skyscrapers that surrounded us, perfectly striking the sólarsteinn. For a moment nothing happened, but then slowly a prism of color began to grow inside it.

I closed one eye, so I could see it better, and very clearly a rainbow of light was cast out from it, pointing back toward the inner city. It was pointing me where to go.

I leapt to my feet, panicking that the stone might change its mind and stop working. I ran around the apartment in a flurry, scribbling a note for Oona so she wouldn't worry, dumping a cup of food in Bowie's bowl, and filling my messenger bag with knives and my baton.

"I'll be back as soon as I can," I told Bowie as I pulled on my boots. "Stay out of trouble, and if I don't come back, be good for Oona."

With the sólarsteinn in my pocket, I raced down to the street and hopped on my luft. Every few blocks, whenever I was stopped at a red light, I'd pull out my stone and check it. The prism of light remained pointed in the same direction.

It led me deep into the heart of the city, a few blocks away from the Evig Riksdag. The light began to glow brighter, and I decided to finish the journey on foot, so I could keep my eye on the stone. I parked my luft and hurried along the sidewalk.

Downtown was buried in darkness, since the sun had dipped low enough past the horizon that the buildings blocked out its last rays. But the city was never truly dark—buildings and streetlights and traffic kept it twinkling at all hours.

Then I spotted her. Her big leathery wings stood out on the crowded street. She was waiting at a crosswalk, and I pushed through the other pedestrians, running as fast as I could to reach her.

Eisheth's gaze was focused on light across the street, waiting for the walk signal to flash green, and she didn't even notice me at first.

"Can we talk?" I asked.

She looked over, and when she realized it was me, she sneered and shook her head. "We've got nothing to talk about."

"We've got lots to discuss."

"Well, I don't agree, so get lost," she replied dismissively, and started across the street, a split second before the light turned green.

I reached into my pocket, holding on to the dagger I had stashed there, and ran across the street after her. As soon as I caught up to her, I grabbed her by the arm and threw her against the plate glass of the storefront beside her.

Through the window I could see people getting their hair and nails done, and they all gasped when Eisheth's big wings were splayed out against the glass, but I didn't care.

"Ow!" Eisheth winced as I held her pressed against the salon window. "What the hell are you doing, you little freak?"

I don't know why she called me "little," since I was bigger and stronger than her, and I slammed her again to remind her of that.

Then I pressed the dagger against her ribs, which were exposed underneath her cropped shirt. Angels had hearts that were larger and lower in their chest cavity than humans, and it would be easy to drive the knife between her ribs, into her massive heart.

Before she had fallen, I would've needed my Valkyrie sword to slay her (along with specific orders from an Eralim to do so), but now all it took was a dagger made of forged iron, which I just happened to have in my hand. The blade was ancient and dull, but I would easily be able to slide it through her flesh and into her oversized black heart.

"You think I won't I kill you, right here and right now?" I asked. "But I don't care anymore. You can scream for help, but you'll be dead the second the words escape your lips."

Her eyes darted around at the people passing by. Some had slowed, but nobody stopped. That was the wonderful and terrible thing about living in a city as crowded as this—you were often alone and unnoticed on the busiest of streets.

Eisheth finally relented and glared at me. "What do you want?"

"Where is Tamerlane?" I demanded.

She scoffed. "How the hell should I know? After you showed up, he ditched me and skipped town. I haven't heard from him since."

I pressed the blade harder against her skin, enough to draw blood, and she cringed back against the glass. "I don't believe you."

"You think I like admitting to you that he used me and threw me away like some piece of trash?" Her lip curled in disgust, trembling slightly, and it looked like tears were forming in her brown eyes.

I might've felt bad for her, if she hadn't been laughing while she watched her boyfriend kill my mother.

"Did he have you convinced that you were some special snowflake?" I mocked her.

Eisheth blinked back tears as she confessed, "He told me he loved me. He promised me that when the new world was established, I would be by his side. He would make all the humans and useless immortals bow before the one true queen."

I smirked. "You thought he was going to make you queen?"

Now she laughed, that same unstable giggling she'd done in her loft. "No, not me. We would serve *her*."

Out of the corner of my eye I saw a woman come out of the salon. She leaned against the open door and held out her phone toward me, as if threatening me with it. "What's going on out there?" she asked in an authoritative voice.

"Mind your own business!" I barked at her.

"I'm calling the cops!" she announced.

"Stop talking about it and call them, then!" I yelled. The woman huffed at me, then went back into the salon, presumably calling the police as she did, and I turned my attention back to Eisheth, whose full lips had twisted into a bitter smile.

The buzzing had started growing around my heart, and electricity raged through my veins as my pulse quickened. The urge to kill her was growing inside me by the second.

"Her who? Who are you going to serve?" I asked, barely able to restrain myself.

"You don't know anything, do you?" Eisheth asked.

"I know that I'll kill you if you keep playing these games with me," I warned her, digging my knife deeper into her skin, and I could feel her blood warm on my fingers.

Eisheth pulled her shoulders back and stared at me defiantly. "Go ahead and kill me. You think I even care if I live or die? This life means nothing to me anymore."

"If that's as you wish," I said, twisting the knife, and Eisheth grimaced in pain.

"Don't," a woman commanded beside me.

"I already told you to mind—" I began, but it wasn't the woman from the salon.

Quinn had somehow snuck up, and she was standing right beside me. Her eyes were grave, and she put her hand on my arm, strong and unyielding.

"Don't," Quinn repeated. "This isn't your job. This is murder. And there's a ton of witnesses."

I stared at Eisheth, into her dark eyes, knowing that I could take the light from them with the simple push of my wrist. But, using all my willpower, I lowered the knife and stepped back from her. "Go on. Get lost."

Eisheth put one hand over her wound and used the other to flick me off before disappearing into the crowded street. I wiped the blood off on my black shirt, and then put the knife back into my messenger bag.

It would only be a matter of time before the cops arrived, so I started walking quickly in the opposite direction that Eisheth had gone. Besides that, walking fast helped lessen the buzzing around my heart, so I didn't feel quite as much like I would explode if I didn't kill Eisheth.

"What are you doing here? How did you find me?" I asked as Quinn easily kept pace beside me.

"I've been trying to keep tabs on you," Quinn said. "I wanted to make sure you were safe."

I raised an eyebrow at her. "You mean you've been following me?"

She raised a shoulder, shrugging it coolly. "On and off. I lost you a few blocks back, but I'm glad I found you when I did."

"I guess it was probably for the best," I reluctantly agreed.

The world would most likely be a better place without Eisheth

Levanon in it, but one of the main tenets of being a Valkyrie was that that kind of thing wasn't my call to make. I didn't get to decide who lived or died.

"Actually, I was going to come get you around now anyway," Quinn said. "I just needed to wait for the sun to go down."

I stopped walking so I could look at her directly. "What for?"

"Come on." She smiled and took my hand. "I'll show you."

FORTY-ONE

---◆---

The alley led to a dilapidated stairway leading underground, then to an old subway system that had long since been shut down. The awning above was rusted, and most of the glass had been broken out.

Quinn let go of my hand to hang on to the rail as she led the way down the steps, explaining as she went, "I couldn't stop thinking about that thing that Asher read yesterday: *From whence the draugr rose, only that will make the draugr fall. If his master waits in Helheim, it is his sword that makes the call.*"

"Right, but we have no idea who his master is," I said. "Eisheth did just say something about a queen."

We'd reached the platform underground, which was filthy and full of leaves, trash, and presumably any number of vermin. Even though the subway had been closed for decades, it was brightly lit by kerosene torches hung up on the wall.

"A queen?" Quinn asked, stopping just before the turnstiles to look back at me.

"Yeah. She said she and Tamerlane serve one true queen, who-ever that is."

She scowled. "Oh."

"What? Why do you seem so disappointed?" I asked.

I mean, I wasn't exactly thrilled about the idea of tracking down this one true queen who had some sort of plan for world domination, but I didn't know how that specific piece of information could put a wrench in any of Quinn's plans.

She shook her head and jumped over the turnstile, apparently deciding that her disappointment wasn't enough to halt our travels.

"Because I was looking into things, and I discovered who I thought was Tamerlane's master," she explained as I jumped over the turnstiles behind her. "But he's male."

"Who's his master?" I asked.

Quinn reached the edge of the platform and jumped down onto the tracks. When I got to the edge, I hesitated, so she held her hand out to me.

"You'll be okay," she promised me. "I'm here."

I took her hand, then leapt down. I stumbled in my landing, but Quinn was there to catch me, pulling me into her arms. For a moment I was pressed against her, with her arms wrapped around me, and heat flushed over me before I managed to untangle myself from her. I cleared my throat and started walking slowly down the tracks.

"As for Tamerlane's master," Quinn said, "I was thinking more of who created him in the first place, and less of who he works for since he's become a draugr. *From whence he rose* to me implied at first that it was your mother—who didn't kill him, thus making him a draugr—but since she wasn't able to kill him when she tried, I was thinking that line was referencing something further back."

"You mean like going back into the Petro Loa lineage?" I asked.

She nodded, and the flames from the kerosene lamps made her silver hair glow like a halo. "Exactly. And I discovered this guy Kalfu was the first true Petro Loa, and he spawned all the other Petro Loas that exist today."

"Great. So where is this Kalfu?" I asked.

"Well, he died," she replied matter-of-factly. "A Valkyrie returned him around seven hundred years ago."

"So you're saying that there's no one alive that can kill Tamerlane? This all seems like terrible news." I glanced over at Quinn, who was stepping carefully along the tracks while smiling her lopsided grin. "I don't understand why you look so happy."

She waved me off. "No, I'm not saying that. I started putting out feelers, and I contacted this old friend of mine, Gable Tawfik."

Ahead of us, the subway tunnel descended into total darkness, but there was a well-lit hole in the side of the tunnel, with another set of cement stairs leading even farther down. Quinn started going down them, but I stopped short.

"Where are we going, by the way?" I asked, for the third time since I'd started following her away from my confrontation with Eisheth Levanon. So far, Quinn had avoided answering me, but it was getting to the point where I wouldn't keep following her without an answer.

She must've realized that, because she stopped and told me, "To the Avondmarkt."

"You mean the black market?" I asked.

"It's not the *black* market. It's a night market," Quinn corrected me. "Where they just happen to sell illicit and difficult-to-find antiquities, potions, and other various properties."

"Uh-huh. And why exactly are you dragging me there?" I asked.

"To meet Gable. He found something."

With that, she turned and jogged down the stairs, and I hurried to keep up with her. As I reached the bottom, I could already hear the noise—talking, laughing, movement, the sounds of a marketplace.

At the bottom of the stairs, a narrow hallway opened into a spacious underground bazaar. The high ceilings were two stories above us, and they were covered in backlit glass that gave the airy impression of having a skylight for a roof.

It was as busy as any marketplace I'd ever seen, with people crowding the walkways and vendors with stands taking up every available inch. As Quinn descended into the crowd, I reached out and grabbed her hand so I wouldn't lose her.

Every booth was overflowing with exotic and strange wares, like dragon's breath in a bottle, bones that allegedly belonged to Hercules, and the quills of a thunderbird. Someone was selling a smelly paste that they claimed was made from the liver of the Batutut, a Bigfoot-like creature that was protected under the Endangered Cryptids Act by the Evig Riksdag.

There was even a living Kting Voar calf for sale. It was a small, fluffy baby cow with a mouthful of angry-looking fangs. The man selling the calf had it on a leash as he proclaimed, "Get your Kting Voar, and all your snake and vermin problems will be gone forever! This Kting Voar will eat anything pestering your household!"

Quinn took us to a table covered in antiquities, with weapons and jewelry that appeared to be hundreds of years old. The jinn standing behind the table had his back to us when we approached, but when he saw us, he broke out in a wide smile.

He was very striking, with thick lashes and deep olive skin. In another realm, he probably would've been a model, if it wasn't for his height. He couldn't have been more than five feet tall, if that.

"Hello, Quinn Devane!" He grinned broadly at her, his dark eyes sparkling. "You are looking especially lovely today."

"Thank you, Gable. You're as handsome as ever," she said with her smile that could charm anyone, and his cheeks reddened a bit as she motioned to me. "This is my friend Malin."

"Any friend of Quinn's is a friend of mine," Gable assured me.

"It's nice to meet you," I said.

"I think I have found what you are looking for." He bent down and pulled a small trunk out from underneath the table. He set the box on the table, then opened it, revealing an oblong object wrapped in a burgundy satin cloth.

"Can we see it?" Quinn asked.

He gestured toward it. "But of course."

She carefully pulled back the cloth, and there sat a dagger with a jagged blade of black tourmaline. It looked like it had been broken from a chunk of stone, with sharp angular edges. The hilt was a deep red, with a symbol carved into it, right in the center of the quillons.

I wasn't sure if I had seen this exact symbol before, but in researching Tamerlane and Petro Loas, I'd learned enough to know that this appeared to be a Vévé symbol. This sword had definitely belonged to a Loa of some kind.

"You're certain this was Kalfu's dagger?" Quinn asked.

"I am as certain as you are beautiful," Gable told her, making Quinn smile.

"This does look real," I agreed.

"You will be taking it, then?" Gable asked hopefully.

"How much is it?" I asked.

"We already discussed the price," Quinn told me as she dug through her bag and pulled out a fat stack of cash wrapped in rubber bands that she handed to Gable. "Here you go. It's all there."

"Thank you." Gable bowed slightly to her, then wrapped the dagger back up in the satin cloth before handing it to her. "It is always a pleasure to do business with you, Quinn, as I do love making your every wish come to fruition. Please do not hesitate to contact me if you are in search of something in the future."

She handed me the dagger, which I placed deep in the bottom of my messenger bag, hiding it as best I could. Quinn said her goodbyes to Gable, then took my hand to lead me through the crowded marketplace.

"How much did you pay for that?" I asked as we climbed the stairs up away from the Avondmarkt toward the subway tunnel.

"It doesn't matter."

"It seemed like a whole lot of cash," I pressed, following her. "How could you afford it?"

"You remember my Vegvisir amulet?" she asked, and I realized with dismay that for the first time since I'd known Quinn, she wasn't wearing it around her neck.

"The one that had been in your family for generations?" I asked.

"I sold it."

"You sold it?" I stopped so I could yell at her incredulously. "Quinn! Why would you do that?"

She stopped and took a step back down, so we'd be at eye level. "Look, Malin, Tamerlane Fayette is bad. He's a draugr who might be able to bring about the end of the world. And this weapon might be the only thing that can kill him. An old amulet seems like an easy price to pay."

I shook my head. "Quinn. I have to pay you back. That's too much."

"No, you don't. I wanted to do this. I want to protect you. Why can't you just let me?" She moved closer to me, so her breasts were nearly touching mine, and the light from the lamps danced in her emerald eyes.

"I don't need—"

"Don't tell me you don't need it," she cut me off. Her voice was low and husky as she brushed back my hair from my forehead. "I don't know why you have to be so stubborn all the damned time."

"If I were perfect, it would be too much," I replied, trying to make a joke, but the air suddenly felt thick and I couldn't even muster a smile.

With her eyes still on mine, she leaned down and kissed me. Her mouth felt soft and eager against mine, and her tongue parted my lips, hesitant, tentative at first. But then I was kissing her back, and her hand moved, her fingers knotting in my hair as she pulled me to her.

It was strange, because I expected her to taste different, but she didn't—her lips were cool and sweet, and she smelled of fresh lilacs, the way she always had. Everything felt the way it was before.

My heart pounded erratically in my chest. There was an ache inside me, a familiar mixture of pain and longing, because I had missed her desperately. Since we'd been apart, hardly a day had gone by that I didn't think about her.

But being with her still petrified me, and my stomach didn't know whether to twist into horrified knots or leap in elation, so it did both, until I couldn't take it anymore. As amazing as it felt kissing Quinn, I was terrified that I might throw up, so I used what was left of my willpower to pull away from her.

As I stepped back, both of us gasping for breath, we stood staring at each other in the poorly lit stairwell for a few seconds. I could see the conflict in her eyes—she wasn't sure whether to kiss me again or not, and if she did kiss me, I wasn't sure that I'd have the strength to say no again.

Finally, she said, "We should go. This isn't a safe place to loiter."

She turned her back and started running up the stairs without waiting for me as I struggled to catch my breath and slow the racing of my heart.

FORTY-TWO

———◆———

So this is what we've got," I told Oona, setting the sólarsteinn and Kalfu's dagger down on the table in front her.

She sat at the kitchen table, with one knee pulled up to her chest and a bowl of cereal in front of her. She'd been awake for all of twenty minutes this morning, and I was already pestering her.

After the Avondmarkt last night, Quinn and I had parted ways. She had been distant since the kiss, probably because she didn't know how I'd react, which was just as well, because I didn't know how I'd react, either.

Then I had come home with the full intention of looking up everything I could on Kalfu and his dagger and how to stop draugrs like Tamerlane, and I did manage to, for a little bit. But then the exhaustion of the past week came crashing down on me, and I passed out before Oona had gotten home from work.

Now Oona sat half awake at the kitchen table as I laid out my plan.

"Where'd you get that knife?" she asked, eyeing it suspiciously.

"Quinn gave it to me," I said, deciding to abbreviate what had happened to avoid a lecture. I summarized everything I knew about the dagger and Kalfu, and assured her that Quinn had gotten it from a reliable source.

"So this"—she tapped the stone—"will show you where Tamerlane is, assuming you know the general area he's in and get close enough to him, and this"—she touched the dagger—"should kill him, assuming that you can find him and that he doesn't overpower you the way he did Marlow."

Oona said that last part gently, since she wasn't trying to be cruel about Marlow's death. She was merely pointing out that a Valkyrie with much more experience than me hadn't been able to stop Tamerlane.

"You sound skeptical," I said flatly.

"No, that's not it." She set her spoon in the bowl and pushed it away from her. She pursed her lips as she thought, making the studs above her lips twist and sparkle. "I'm just worried we're getting in over our heads."

I took a step back and folded my arms over my chest. "Quinn and I are both Valkyries, and Asher's had tons of training as a Vörðr, not to mention he has Valkyrie blood from his mom. And you know all kinds of potions and tricks because of your familiarity with alchemy and thaumaturgy."

"All that may be true, but Tamerlane is a draugr. Don't you think that's beyond our skill set?" Oona stared up at me helplessly.

"No one has experience with draugrs," I reminded her. "And individually we wouldn't be able to handle him, but together I think we can."

She sighed and ran her hand through her short black hair. "It's just early in the morning, and I'm worried. We don't even know where Tamerlane is. How are we going to find him?"

"Well, we—"

The ringing of my phone interrupted me. I was planning to let it go to voice mail, but the screen was face-up on the counter, with the name SAMAEL on it in big bold letters, so I rushed to answer it.

"Malin, it's Samael," he said when I answered. "How have you been holding up?"

"Okay, I guess." I had my back to Oona, but I could feel her eyes watching me expectantly. "How are you?"

There was a long pause before he finally said, "I've been better. But I was wondering if you could come in and talk?"

I shifted my weight from one foot to the other, balancing on my noninjured leg. "Do you have another assignment?" I asked, hoping that he didn't, because I had no idea how I would fit one in with everything else that was going on.

"No, you won't be getting any more assignments. Not until we find you someone new to apprentice under," Samael told me, and my heart plummeted.

I hadn't wanted to deal with a new assignment right now, but I had been so busy mourning Marlow's death and attempting to avenge her that I hadn't really considered what her death meant for my career. She was my mentor, my teacher, and without her—and with her name now tarnished—I didn't know if I'd ever be able to find someone else willing to apprentice me.

So, on top of everything else, I was just coming to the bitter conclusion that my career as a Valkyrie might be over before it even started.

"Okay," I said once I managed to find my voice again. "What's this about, then?"

"It's about Marlow," he said. "When can you come in?"

"I can be there in a half hour."

"Good. I'll see you then," he said, and hung up the phone.

"Was that Samael?" Oona asked, right behind me. "What'd he want?"

"I don't know. He said it's about Marlow." I turned back to face her.

She was standing with her hands on her hips, nodding as her eyes darted around. Whenever she was working something out, she'd play with her piercings, pushing the studs with her tongue so they bobbed as she thought. I could almost see the wheels turning inside her head.

"Okay, so you wanna do this? You wanna track down Tamerlane?" she asked.

"Of course."

"Samael will help, right?" Oona asked, looking at me hopefully.

I nodded. "He told me he wanted to catch Tamerlane as badly as I did."

"Great." She exhaled, looking relieved. "He works for the Riks, so he has all kinds of access to information and weaponry. You need to get everything you can from him."

"I can do that," I said.

Oona started walking, pacing the kitchen as she spoke. "While you're gone, I'll do my best to gather what I need for protection spells, and I'll see if I can do anything for tracking. But you have to get Samael to give you as much as possible."

"I will," I assured her.

I hurried to get dressed, and Oona was already flying around the apartment, digging through her thaumaturgy kit, and pulling out old grimoires that had belonged to her ancestors. I promised her I'd be back as soon as I could, but she barely mumbled a goodbye and kept her head buried in a book.

FORTY-THREE

───────◆───────

Godfrey and Atlas were posted on either side of Samael's door, as usual, but they'd added black armbands wrapped around their massive biceps. The same way they did whenever a comrade had fallen.

It was a simple gesture, a common one, but it wasn't something I expected to see done for Marlow, and I felt a pain in my chest as I tried to swallow back unwelcome tears.

"He's waiting for you," Atlas told me, forgoing his usual small talk to offer me a sympathetic smile.

"Thank you," I said.

Godfrey reached for the bronze door to open it for me, but he paused, his solitary eye resting solemnly on me. "Your mother was a very intimidating woman," Godfrey said, his voice a low rumbling bass. "I liked her."

I smiled gratefully up at him. "I think that's the truest thing anyone's ever said about her."

Inside Samael's office, he was sitting behind his long black desk, but he stood when he saw me. "Malin. It's good to see you."

Samael strode across his office with quick strides, and before I could say anything, he pulled me into a hug. Then he released me, looking directly into my eyes in a way that made me nervous that he could read my mind. "Are you sure you're holding up all right?"

"I'm all right." I rubbed the back of my neck and avoided his gaze. "What did you want to see me about? Did you find out anything?"

"I did, actually. But let's start at the beginning." He gestured toward his sofa. "Shall we sit and talk?"

I sat down on the couch, and he sat beside me. His usual boyish face seemed to have aged even more since I last saw him, and I wondered if sadness affected him more greatly than time.

"Did you know that Tamerlane Fayette is a draugr?" he asked me directly.

I wavered a second before nodding. "I suspected as much, yes."

He leaned back on the couch, his aqua eyes appraising me. "How long have you known?"

"Not long," I admitted. "Marlow had told me a few days before she died that she hadn't killed Tamerlane as she was instructed to, and it was only after that I really even learned what a draugr was."

"I've had feelers going out about any news on draugrs, and I've been getting word back that they're heading to the Gates," Samael said.

"You mean the Gates of Kurnugia? The city in Central America?" I asked, and the knot in stomach only twisted harder.

"Yes, and as you may know, it's under impious control."

I rubbed my forehead. "Are they trying to enter Kurnugia?"

"Possibly, but it's not something they can just go in and out of. The doors exist the same way a door exists on a safe or even to this building." He motioned vaguely toward his office doors. "But not just anyone can walk in. And in the case of the Kurnugia, the doors to it are very rarely allowed to open, and no one is ever allowed back out."

"Do you know why they're all heading down there?" I asked. "They must be planning something."

"I agree, but I'm not sure what." He shook his head sadly. "I talked to the higher-ups about sending help down to investigate, but they said this was not a matter for us to interfere. They believe that we need to let the mortals and immortals handle whatever conflict may be brewing themselves."

"But draugrs aren't even supposed to exist," I argued. "And by the Rikdag's own decree, Tamerlane Fayette is supposed to be dead. Don't they just want to take care of him themselves?"

Samael frowned. "I tried to reason with them, but they are unfortunately rather orthodox, and they like to live to the very letter of the law, which means being as hands-off as possible in this case, even if it's to the whole world's detriment."

"So Tamerlane Fayette is headed down to the Gates?" I asked.

"Yes, assuming he isn't already there."

I chewed the inside of my cheek, mulling over everything I knew about Tamerlane that might give me some hint as to what he was up to. The only things I really had were Amaryllis Mori's claims that the underworld was planning an uprising, and Eisheth Levanon's certainty that they were following a queen.

"Do you know of anyone that the draugrs might be serving?" I asked Samael. "I heard that Tamerlane says he's working for the one true queen."

He raised his eyebrows. "A queen?"

"Yeah. If they're planning to get through the city and into Kurnugia, I'm guessing she's connected to the underworld. Maybe a spurned goddess?" I suggested.

"An underworld goddess?" He exhaled deeply before he began

listing them off. "Mictecacihuatl, Laverna, Ereshkigal, Sedna, Nyx, Hine-nui-te-pō, Dewi Sri, Nephthys, Hel, Maman Brigitte, Marzanna . . . And those are just the ones I can think of off the top of my head."

I groaned. "So that doesn't exactly narrow it down."

"Unfortunately, no," he agreed pessimistically. "Not unless you have more information."

"None yet," I said, slouching back on the couch.

"Do you want me to go with you to the Gates?" Samael offered.

I considered this a moment before asking, "Can you do it without attracting attention?"

"No," he admitted. "Eralim are very rarely granted any kind of leave of absence."

"Then it'll probably be best if I go without you. I don't want anyone stopping us from going after Tamerlane simply because you're with us and they don't want you interfering."

Samael leaned forward, resting his arms on his knees, his forehead pinched with worry. "You're not going alone, are you?"

"No, I have friends that are fighting with me." I looked at him hopefully, remembering Oona's request for more weapons. "Do you have any weapons that might be good for fighting a goddess or draugrs or whatever other demonic jerks we might go up against?"

He smiled at that and stood up. "I do, actually, have just the thing."

Samael went over to the wall that was lined with shelves. On a lower shelf that came to his waist, he moved an antique totem to the side, revealing a small touch screen. He tapped in a few numbers, then put his hand down to scan his print.

The screen let out a happy bing of recognition, and a second later a thin concealed drawer slid open, revealing a hidden cache of ancient weapons, carefully cushioned on black velvet.

"This is Tyrfing." Samael pointed to the first sword, one with a long blade with a golden hilt. In the center of the pommel, a triquetra symbol had been engraved. "This sword has been endowed with a power so that it never misses a target, no matter who swings it."

He moved down the line, pointing to the next sword. It was shorter than the first, with a beveled blade, and both the blade and the hilt appeared to be made out of a singular piece of a black obsidian-like material.

"This is Kusanagi," he went on. "This is a very powerful sword, forged inside a dragon, and it's believed to control the wind."

The next sword also had a black blade, but the hilt was a deep red, and the cross guards were shaped to look like flames coming out of the grip.

"This is Dyrnwyn, and legend has it that if whoever wields this sword has a quest that is pure, the blade will burn," Samael said. "The user will remain unburned, but the flames will destroy the enemy."

"But what if their quest isn't pure?" I asked, since I really had no idea how this particular sword might feel about what I was planning to do to Tamerlane.

"Then it's just a regular sword, albeit with a very powerful blade," Samael said, then moved on to the next weapon.

Unlike the first three, this was not a sword. It was a mace with a long bronze staff with a rather gruesome-looking spiked head made of iron attached by a chain.

"And this is Sharur," he said. "It's enchanted so that it will fly great distances to its owner, should its owner need it to, and it has a very precise aim."

"You think these will be able to kill whatever the hell is brewing down in Kurnugia?" I asked.

"If any weapons on earth can help, these will be the ones to do it," Samael said. "They're all enchanted, and most were gifts from the Vanir gods, back in times when they still deigned to interfere with mortal matters."

"So it's all right if take them?" I asked, glancing down at the cache of invaluable weaponry before looking back at Samael. "I can't guarantee that I'll be able to return them, though I'll try as hard as I can."

His eyes were grave. "I told you that I'd do whatever it took to bring that bastard down. If that means losing a few ancient trinkets in the process, that is a price I am more than happy to pay."

"Thank you."

Samael went to retrieve something to carry the weapons in, so I wouldn't be walking down the street with an armload of swords like some kind of maniac. He came back a few moments later with a long black case with padded cloth sides, so it appeared similar to a duffel bag, only longer and more rectangular. Then he helped me carefully load up the weapons.

"Is there anything more I can do for you?" he asked.

I shook my head. "You've given me weapons and a direction to head in. That's more than enough."

"Let me know if there's anything more I can do, anything at all."

He walked me to the door, but when I was about to leave, I hesitated. The bag of weapons weighed heavy on my shoulder, but there was something nagging at me that I couldn't let go of, no matter how hard I tried.

"Can I ask you something?" I asked. "It's not about the weapons or Tamerlane."

He spread his arms wide. "You can ask me anything."

"Was Marlow kind to you?" I asked him awkwardly.

He thought for a second before answering. "I believe that she was, but I suppose it depends on your definition of *kind*. Are you asking was she soft and affectionate with me? As much as she could be, but honestly, that wasn't nearly enough."

"But you still cared about her."

"That's the funny thing about love," he said. "It doesn't wait for perfection—the heart loves who it loves, exactly as they are, faults and all."

"Do you . . ." I hesitated, since it felt uncomfortable to ask, but I had to know, so I pressed on. "Do you think she loved you?"

He smiled then, but there was a pained edge to it, so it didn't quite reach his eyes. "I don't think any of us could ever truly know what was in Marlow's heart, not even her."

FORTY-FOUR

———◆———

W hat on the good green earth is that?" Quinn asked, wrinkling her nose at me. Her long silver hair was pulled back into a ponytail as she stood outside the Tannhauser Towers, leaning against her black hovercraft. It was rebuilt from a vintage sedan, replete with suicide doors, rounded fins, and a heart-shaped grille.

Oona had come out ahead of me, and she was already loading up Quinn's trunk with all her thaumaturgy gear, along with an over-night bag crammed with as much clothes and necessities as she could fit into it.

I hobbled out of the apartment complex with a backpack filled with my personal stuff, the padded case of weapons, and a pet carrier containing my twenty-plus-pound wolpertinger, along with a bag of his food.

"This is Bowie," I said, setting a few things down on the curb before I accidentally dropped everything into the canal.

"I know who Bowie is, but you can't possibly think it's a good idea to bring a rabbit along," Quinn said, picking up my bags so she could put them in the trunk.

"First off, he's not a rabbit," I corrected her. "He's a wolpertinger. Second, we're not bringing him with, but I can't exactly leave him at home by himself when we don't know if or when I'll ever be back."

"So where is he going?" she asked.

"We have to make a pit stop."

Once we had the car loaded up, I hopped into the backseat so I could sit with Bowie, while Oona took shotgun. Bowie had never been fond of traveling, and I calmed him down by sticking my fingers through his cage and stroking his nose as I directed Quinn on how to get to Galel's Garage.

She parked in the tiny parking lot beside the auto body shop and offered to help me carry everything, but I didn't want to deal with the awkward interactions between Quinn and Jude, so I told her that I could handle it myself as I hurried to gather Bowie and his things together.

When I got out of the car, Jude Locklear was just coming out of the garage. His coveralls were unbuttoned at the top, revealing a thick black tattoo across his chest. His dark hair hung down in waves behind his ram's horns.

"Malin." He smiled at me as I approached. "I haven't seen you in a while. How have you been?"

"I've been better, honestly," I said as I set Bowie's carrier down near his feet. "My mom's dead, and I have to leave town to take care of some business."

His face fell. "Oh, no. I'm sorry to hear that. Is there anything I can do for you?"

"Well, believe it or not, you're one of the few people in the world that I actually feel like I can trust, so I'm going to ask you a really huge favor," I said.

Jude eyed me warily as he asked, "What is that?"

"Can you take care of my wolpertinger, Bowie?"

He puffed out his cheeks before exhaling and put a hand on his chin. "I've never taken care of a wolpertinger. I don't really know anything about them."

"It's a lot like taking care of a cat," I assured him. "Bowie's nice, and he's litter-box-trained. I brought a bag of his food, but he also enjoys carrots and cucumbers. I have the emergency number for his vet on his carrier, so you can call them if you have any problems. And you can look up anything else you might need to know about wolpertingers online."

Jude crouched down so he could get a better look, and Bowie sniffed the door. "He is mighty cute."

"He is," I agreed as Jude scratched his nose.

"All right," he relented and straightened back up. "If it will help you and make you feel better, I'll take care of him."

"Thank you. It really will." I was so grateful I almost hugged him, but I was all too aware of Quinn's prying eyes behind me in the car.

"How long are you going to be gone for?" Jude asked.

"It should only be a few days. But if I don't come back . . ." I stared down at Bowie's cage and cleared my throat. "Maybe try to find him a good home, if you can't care for him."

"If you don't come back?" Jude's voice was tight with worry, and he stepped closer to me. "What's going on? Do you need me to come with you?"

"No, I think I've got this covered." I flashed him my most reassuring smile. "Just take care of Bowie."

"Okay," he said reluctantly, and I turned to walk away. "Hey, Malin, you always were my favorite customer."

"I know." I smiled back at him. "Goodbye, Jude."

With that, I jogged back to the hovercar and jumped into the backseat. Quinn drove off, while I sat staring out the window, wondering if I'd ever see Jude or Bowie again.

"So that guy's not your boyfriend?" Quinn asked, and I looked up to see her watching me in the rearview mirror.

Her eyebrows were slightly pinched, and her slender lips were pursed together. No doubt her mind was on the kiss she and I had shared last night, the one that conspicuously neither of us had addressed.

"Nope. He's just a friend," I said as I settled back into my seat.

"Now where to?" Quinn asked.

"Down to Hegewisch to pick up Asher," I informed her.

Before I had left the Evig Riksdag, I had texted both Quinn and Asher to see if they were up for a revenge trip down to the Gates of Kurnugia, and when they'd both given me their enthusiastic yeses, I told them to be ready ASAP. Quinn agreed to pick us all up, since she had a car while I just had a luft, and Asher texted me his address.

"Oh, so Ash is coming with?" Quinn asked, and the tension lines deepened across her forehead.

"Yeah, why wouldn't he? Tamerlane killed his mother, too," I reminded her.

"I just thought . . . I don't know." She sighed, and there was an unmistakable sadness in her voice. "No, it makes sense. We need all the help we can get."

My heart skipped a beat. I didn't know what Quinn had figured out, but she definitely knew there was something between Asher and me. Which was just great. I didn't even know exactly how I felt about my ex-girlfriend or my current sorta-beau, and now we were all going on a road trip together to avenge our mothers and save the world.

FORTY-FIVE

———— ◆ ————

When Quinn pulled up in front of the tiny, cozy little house that Asher shared with his grandmother, Asher was already sitting on the front steps, waiting with a duffel bag beside him. It was warm, almost exceptionally so for October, and he wore a pair of jeans with an old T-shirt that pulled taut over his arms and chest.

"Hey," he said as I walked over to greet him.

Behind me, Quinn and Oona were waiting in the car, arguing about what music we were going to listen to, and it suddenly hit me as Asher stood up, smiling sheepishly at me, that this was my first time I'd seen him since we'd slept together.

His hands were shoved in his pockets, and he stared down at me with a look in his eyes, one filled with such warmth and affection, it actually made me feel strangely gooey inside, and I wondered if anyone had ever looked at me like that before.

Quinn's amorous gazes tended to be hungry and demanding, but Asher's were soft and gentle. Quinn wanted to throw me up against a wall, and Asher wanted to pull me into his arms. The problem was that I wanted both at different times.

"How are you doing?" Asher asked.

"Excited. Terrified. Nauseous."

He laughed softly. "Yeah, me, too."

I was about to ask him if he was ready to go when the front door to his house opened behind him. His grandmother, Teodora, strode out with her arms folded over her chest and a rather severe expression on her face.

"Is that it?" she asked as she slowly descended the steps toward us, her white hair ruffling in the wind.

"Is what it?" Asher asked, glancing around.

"That's your whole team?" Teodora motioned vaguely toward the car, where Quinn and Oona were bickering loudly about what constituted rock music. "Your whole plan to defeat this draugr?"

"*Amma*, we already talked about this," he said.

She shook her head adamantly. "No, I talked about how I didn't want you to die at the hands of the same madman that killed your mother, and you didn't listen to me!"

"This isn't just about Mom, not anymore," Asher said, trying to keep his cool in the face of her distress. "If an immortal is allowed to escape and live on, everything could fall apart. The whole world could be undone."

Teodora gestured wildly. "So let it be undone, then."

"That doesn't even make sense," he said. "If the world ends, that includes me and you, *Amma*. I'm going to die either way."

"Maybe, but maybe not. And if you do die, you'll be here with me." She reached up, touching her grandson's face with tears in her eyes. "We'll be together."

"I have to do this," Asher insisted. "But I'll come back. I promise you."

She exhaled a shaky breath, then turned her attention toward me. "I don't hold your mother's actions against you. Asher has told me that you're kind and you share his strong sense of justice. I hope that he is right, and I am asking you to succeed in protecting him, where your mother failed with my daughter."

I swallowed hard and somehow managed to speak around the growing lump in my throat. "I will do my best."

"Wait here one moment." She held up a finger toward Asher and me, then started back toward the house. "I'm going to get something."

"What's the holdup here?" Quinn asked, leaning over Oona to yell out the car window.

"Seriously?" Oona asked. "He's saying goodbye to his grandma. Give him a second."

Quinn sat back down in the driver's seat, but I could still hear her arguing with Oona. "We've only got thirty minutes to make it to the Overland station, so if we're gonna catch it, we gotta go."

"I've always liked you, Quinn, but you can be very pushy," Oona commented.

A moment later, Teodora came rushing out of her house carrying a large shield. It appeared to be made of a heavy dark iron with a Norse symbol of protection engraved in the center.

"Here," she said, handing it to Asher. "This was my grandmother's shield, and her grandmother's before her, and so on. We call it Rök, and it can withstand most any supernatural attack. Since I'm too old to be going with you, this is the only way I can still protect you."

"Thanks, *Amma*," he said, and she kissed his cheek before he grabbed his bag and dropped it in the trunk.

Asher got in the backseat beside me and looked out the window at the receding figure of his grandmother, all of us knowing that this might very well be the last time he ever saw her. I reached over and took his hand, and when he looked back at me, he seemed a bit relieved.

"Let's do this, then," he said.

We arrived at the station for the NorAm Overland Express with only seven minutes to spare, which led to a frantic run through the depot and up to the raised platform. The Overland was neither a train nor a bus, but rather an odd hybrid that made travel much faster and easier.

The double-decker carriage straddled several lanes of the highway, with a three-meter gap underneath large enough to accommodate the average hovercraft. It ran on rails located on either side of the highway, with a fixed route similar to that of a train, and it could reach speeds as high as 125 miles per hour.

Quinn led the way, up to the second story of the double-decker carriage, which was slightly less crowded than the main-level cabin had been. Fortunately, there were several rows of seats still open, so we would all be able to sit together.

Quinn put her bags up in the overhead bins that ran between large skylights in the roof. I took a seat by the window, and Oona, in her infinite wisdom, took the seat next to me, thus sparing me from the awkward situation of being stuck directly between Quinn and Asher.

Asher finished loading up the bags, while Quinn excused herself to use the restroom located at the back of the carriage.

"You know, there's a saying," Oona said, giving me a knowing look. "You don't shit where you eat."

I gaped at her for a moment, since I hadn't told her anything about my recent romantic entanglements with either Asher or Quinn. She'd known about my previous relationship with Quinn, obviously, but when she asked anything about my feelings toward her now, I always denied them.

But Oona knew, and really, it had only been a matter of time. Somehow, Oona always managed to figure things out. Maybe that was one of the consequences of being best friends with someone for over a decade. She knew me better than I knew myself, and I couldn't hide anything from her.

"I don't know what you mean by that." I feigned ignorance, since now didn't seem like the best time to be having this conversation.

"It means," she said, lowering her voice, "don't go hooking up with *both* of the people you need to help you complete your mission."

"I didn't," I insisted, which wasn't exactly a lie, but it wasn't entirely the truth, either. "It's over with one, basically, kind of, and . . . okay, so I accidentally maybe started something with the other. But this is important. We're all focused on what we need to do, so nothing else matters. Not even who is sleeping with who."

"What are you talking about?" Asher asked, taking the seat on the other side of Oona.

"Nothing," Oona and I replied in unison.

FORTY-SIX

———◆———

The Overland horn let out two long bleats as a final warning that we were about to take off, and I settled into my seat for the long ride south. Just as the express lurched away from the station, a hulking figure with a familiar face lumbered up the stairs—Atlas Malosi, one of Samael's personal guards.

As soon as he saw me, a relieved grin spread out on his face, and he walked down the aisle toward us. He hurriedly shoved his suitcase in the overhead bin, then rather clumsily slid past the other passengers in the row so he could take the seat directly in front of mine, right by the window.

"What are you doing here?" I asked him.

"You know this guy?" Oona tilted her head as she looked up at him, kneeling awkwardly on the seat in front of me so he could look at me, but his large frame hardly fit in the seats to begin with. "I thought I knew everyone you knew."

"This is Atlas, he works for Samael." I gestured vaguely toward him.

"I'm Oona." She leaned forward so she could shake his hand, and his hand was like a massive bear paw enveloping hers.

I returned to the question at hand that he still hadn't answered: "What are you doing here?"

"Since Samael would draw too much attention if he attended to this personally, he sent me along in his stead," Atlas explained, smiling sheepishly at me. "He thought you needed as much help as you could get, and he told me that I was the best he could send."

"That's very generous of him, and you." I smiled as gratefully as I could, since it was a nice gesture—and probably a necessary one, given what we were up against.

It still felt vaguely awkward having Atlas tagging along, knowing that he'd most likely be reporting everything that happened back to Samael, and it was also kind of embarrassing having my boss/my mom's-sorta-boyfriend checking up on me.

"Welcome aboard the Revenge Express to Hell," Quinn replied cheerily and leaned over Asher to shake Atlas's hand. "I'm Quinn, and we're happy to have another body with us."

Asher squished back in his seat to avoid getting Quinn's breasts shoved directly in his face, and he was still leaning back a bit even after she sat back down.

"That's all well and good, and we really do appreciate your help," Asher said carefully. "But how did you know where we were? On this exact Overland at this exact time?"

"Samael told me where you'd be, but that I'd have to hurry if I was going to catch you," Atlas said with a shrug. "I don't know how he got the information, but he has his ways of finding out most anything he wants to."

"Good to know," I said under my breath.

"Do you guys wanna go over a plan or anything?" Atlas asked.

Quinn motioned to the people sitting around us. "I think it's best if we wait until we get where we're going."

"Right. Of course." Atlas turned back and sat down in his seat, but a few moments later, he craned his head back around to look at us. "I have snacks up here, if any of you guys want any."

"We're good for now, but thanks," Oona told him with a smile.

Atlas finally settled into his seat, and Oona pulled out a thick, heavy book that smelled of dust and burnt sage, with the title *Sorcellerie Grimoire* embossed on the front. It had been a gift from her cousin Minerva, and she was studying up on it to prepare for what lay ahead for us.

Meanwhile, Asher was on his tablet and looking up maps of the labyrinthine city of the Gates of Kurnugia. It had been deliberately designed to be confusing and maddening, to keep immortals from escaping and to keep mortals from invading their space.

And at the far end of the row, Quinn had put her earbuds in and stared down at her phone, presumably watching a movie.

With everyone otherwise occupied, I was finally able to relax for a bit in my seat, knowing these might be some of the last truly peaceful moments of my life. I looked out the window at the decrepit, overcrowded landscape of the city as the Overland whizzed through the south-end slums.

Eventually we escaped the shadows of the skyscrapers, and as the buildings started thinning out, so did the smog that shrouded the city. The darkness of the metropolis gave way to deserted plains, cracked dry earth that had been overfarmed and underwatered.

The vast wastelands that stretched between the various megacities were virtually uninhabitable, leaving the several billion mortals, immortals, and various creatures that lived in the United States to overcrowd the cities.

Through the skylights above, I watched as the dark clouds moved in, blotting out the orange sun, and they rumbled loudly with the threat of an oncoming storm. I closed my eyes against the world and tried to get some sleep while I still could.

I awoke sometime later with stars twinkling above. I yawned and lifted my head, blinking to focus, and I was startled to find that I had been sleeping with my head resting on Asher's shoulder.

"What's going on?" I asked, glancing around the dim carriage of the Overland Express. "Where are we?"

"You were out for a while," Asher explained in a hushed voice. "We all kind of moved around so we could get more comfortable."

He motioned to a row over, which had been filled with passengers when I passed out, but now only had Quinn. She had lifted up the armrests and spread out, napping with her coat bunched under her head as a pillow.

In the seats right in front of me, I could hear Oona—her voice soft and excited as she argued with Atlas about the proper ways to fight a demon.

"Where are we?" I asked, since it was dark and the carriage had obviously emptied out quite a bit.

"We're almost to our stop."

I sat up sharply and looked out my window, at the night landscape and the dark desert outside that had subtly begun to shift to waving fields of grass under a full moon. "This is Mexico? How long was I asleep?"

"No, our express stops just short of the border, so we're spending the night in Sugarland, and we'll catch the next express down to the Gates first thing in the morning," he told me.

"So tomorrow." I took a deep breath and settled back in my seat. "Tomorrow we'll get there, and hopefully, soon, this will all be over."

Asher took my hand in his, sharing his quiet comfort with me. I cuddled up next to him, resting my head against his shoulder, and he kissed my temple.

I relished the brief moment of affection before turning my attention back to avenging our mothers. "What were you working on?" I asked, gesturing to the tablet resting on his lap.

The screen had gone black, but he tapped it to reveal detailed floor plans of a building that reminded me of a cathedral, almost, except the entire structure appeared to be made out of bones, if the designs were to be believed.

"This is the Bararu Mutanu Ossuary," Asher explained, and he swiped away from the blueprints to show me a full-color picture of the exterior.

"It blocks the entrance of Kurnugia," I said. I'd learned about it in school, but I didn't think I'd ever really seen pictures of it, not like the ones that Asher was looking at.

"Right." He started scrolling through the pictures, flipping past one skeletal room after another. "It's rumored to be impossible to get through, but if Tamerlane is trying to get into Kurnugia, he'll have to go through here."

"But I thought he was just hiding out nearby. Why would he want to get in?" I asked. "I mean, he could've just let my mother kill him, then."

"Maybe he didn't think she could kill him and he just wants to find a way in on his own," Asher offered, then paused. "Or maybe he's not trying to get *in*—maybe he's trying to let someone *out*."

FORTY-SEVEN

———◆———

The view from the motel window was of a crowded parking lot. We were on the fourth floor, and it felt too close to the ground, the skyline too short without towering skyscrapers surrounding us. Sugarland looked as if the mega-cities I was used to had been squished down and compacted, with a thinner layer of smog allowing the stars to shine through.

We were in an older motel, with paint chipping off the stucco sides and an outdoor walkway to the rooms. Our room was on the highest floor. The walkway outside was lined with a rust-covered railing. The doors, at least, had microchipped keys, so it would be harder for anyone to break in. Hopefully.

"That sure is a weird-ass painting for such a small-ass room," Atlas commented behind me, and I turned back to survey the room.

The hotel room was two narrow queen-sized beds jammed against the wall with a door in the corner leading to an economy-sized toilet/shower combo. Above the beds was a massive drawing of a woman, framed with ornate obsidian.

We'd gotten another room as well, one door over, but we were all packed in this one like sardines now. I'd wanted to pace—my legs were restless from the long ride and anxiety was kicking in, electrifying my skin. But there wasn't enough room.

Atlas's hulking frame blocked the door, while Oona sat cross-legged on one bed with Quinn sprawled out beside her, letting her shirt ride up and her jeans hung low on her hips.

"So what now?" Oona asked.

"We could sleep," Asher suggested, barely suppressing a yawn, from where he leaned against the slim dresser beside me.

Quinn took her hair down, slowly shaking her head to set her long silver locks free. "We shouldn't have slept so much on the train."

The large framed drawing above the beds was photorealistic and managed to be both completely captivating and totally unnerving. It showed a gorgeous woman with dark brown skin lying back, with her hair shaved on either side of her head, leaving her with a short curly Mohawk. She was naked except for the fur blanket that swathed her.

At the bottom, larger and more centered than the artist's signature scribbled in the corner, was the title:

Ereshkigal in Repose

The air in the room began to feel thinner, and my breath came out shallow. I had the strangest sense of vertigo, like the entire room had pitched to the side, only my gaze fixed on the painting keeping me upright.

Suddenly I felt hot—not just flushed with warmth, but *burnt*. The heat rose from the soles of my feet, scorching my skin as it traveled painfully up my thighs, and the scent of fire and smoke filled my nostrils. My mouth tasted of fresh blood—metallic and warm— as panic surged through me.

I was terrified and in pain, but I couldn't move or scream or do anything. I stayed totally frozen, my eyes locked on the woman in the painting.

Then I heard a voice like satin in my ear: "Remember that we all must die."

"Mal?" Oona was saying—almost yelling, sounding afraid—and rather abruptly everything stopped.

The heat. The fear. The taste of blood. It all fell away. I was just standing in the hotel room with four concerned faces staring at me. Asher touched my arm, meaning to comfort me, I was sure, but I nearly jumped out of my skin.

"Malin?" he asked. "Are you okay?"

I shook my head, trying to clear it. "Yeah, I'm fine. I just . . . I think I need to get some fresh air."

"We could grab something to eat, maybe?" Atlas suggested, and his voice was cheery, but his dark eyes were anxious. "It might be good to get out and move around for a while."

I motioned to all our bags and gear piled up on one bed, including the one from Samael filled with irreplaceable weaponry. "But we can't just go out and leave all the stuff here."

"I'll stay and watch the stuff, if you're worried," Asher offered; he was still close to my side, in case I might need him to steady me or pull me from another trance.

"You sure?" I asked, but really I didn't want to wait to hear his answer. I didn't want to stay inside a second longer. I needed to get out, to move, to breathe.

"Yeah," he assured me with a smile. "I'll be fine."

I wanted to look at him directly, to see if there was any hesitation in his eyes, but I didn't trust myself to look at anybody. Everything still felt strangely off-kilter, and so I just nodded, taking his word for it, and stepped out to the hallway balcony.

A few moments later, Quinn, Oona, and Atlas followed suit.

Quinn said she considered staying behind to help Asher, but she felt as pent-up as I did. Oona didn't want to leave me on my own, and it sounded as if Atlas was essentially my bodyguard at this point, even though I did not need a bodyguard.

"What happened in there?" Oona asked me, her voice low as we descended the stairs toward the street below, with Atlas and Quinn a few steps ahead.

"Just exhaustion and stress, I think," I replied vaguely.

I shook my head, and I wasn't trying to brush her off, but the truth was that I didn't really remember, not exactly. It was like, waking from a vivid dream, when you tried to tell someone about it, you only had a few fragmented images to hang on to.

So I had to chalk it up to my own mind playing stress-induced tricks on me, because what else could it be?

The weather in Sugarland was cool, but it lacked the crispness of back home that I so wanted right now. At least the streets were less crowded here—you could take three or four steps before bumping into another person. But it was still busier than I expected for an outskirt town like this.

We'd only walked a couple blocks when Quinn stopped short. She'd been leading our small group, since the rest of us didn't feel like taking charge. After she stopped, I could see why.

Across the street from us was a large adobe building, where a small crowd had amassed trying to get in. They looked much like the clientele I would see at the Carpe Noctem bar back home, but with more cowboy boots and hats.

The bright pink and green neon sign in the front read DEL SUDOR Y PECADO, and it featured an animated demon with horns and a forked tail taking off his hat and saluting the patrons as they entered the bar below him.

"How about this place?" Quinn suggested, hooking her thumb at it.

"This doesn't exactly look like a restaurant," Atlas said.

"Yeah, well, I don't need food to help me sleep," Quinn muttered, and without waiting for the rest of us to respond, she walked ahead into the bar.

FORTY-EIGHT

———— ◆ ————

Shots?" Quinn suggested with a raised eyebrow, her eyes darting between the three of us.

We stood at a high-top table next to a table full of squealing Nephilim celebrating a bachelorette party, and discarded peanut shells and sawdust crunched underneath our feet. A strange fusion of country and death metal blasted out from a high-tech jukebox that glowed red in the corner, and everything smelled vaguely of sweat and wood chips.

"Hunting a demon with a hangover doesn't sound ideal," I said, nearly shouting to be heard over the music.

"He's not a demon—he's a draugr," Oona corrected me as her gaze followed a waitress walking by with a tray of brightly colored drinks, and I could almost see her salivating.

"That changes everything, then," I said with a sigh.

"Nobody's getting drunk. Just one shot," Quinn promised, holding up her index finger. "Just to take the edge off."

Oona was staring at me hopefully, and I knew her belief that alcohol made everything better was very skewed, to say the least, but something to calm my nerves did sound necessary at this point. Especially after my weird freak-out at the hotel.

"Fine," I said, and the words had barely escaped my lips before Quinn was off, flagging down a waitress to procure the shots.

A few minutes later she returned, carefully carrying our tiny cups of red liquid with bright orange flames dancing out of the tops.

Atlas took a shot from her and wrinkled his nose. "What is this?"

"Who knows? The waitress says it's the best, so blow out your drink and swallow it down." Quinn raised her glass and waited for the rest of us to do the same. "To saving the world!"

We clinked our glasses, blew out the flames, and I tossed my head back, gulping down the sour liquid as fast as I could.

"There," Quinn said, smiling at me as I grimaced. "Isn't that better?"

"Maybe. Give it a second to kick in."

While I waited for the liquid to do its job and soothe my frayed nerves, I noticed Oona eying a guy at the bar. He was shirtless, which actually didn't appear to be out of the ordinary for this bar, and he looked like he'd been chiseled out of marble. He leaned against the bar, casually sipping a beer with his cowboy hat cock-eyed on his head.

"Wow." Oona leaned forward, resting her arms on the high tabletop as she ogled him.

"He's an immortal. Maybe a demigod?" Quinn guessed.

I shook my head. "No. I don't recognize his lineage, so he's something lower-level. Maybe a warlock?"

"I didn't realize you guys read people that easy," Atlas said, looking at us both with bemused amazement. "I usually don't get to hang out with Valkyries outside of work."

"It's something we just . . . know." Quinn shrugged, because there really wasn't a better way to explain it.

"Can you tell if he's gay?" Atlas asked with a raised eyebrow.

"Or straight?" Oona chimed in hopefully.

"Nope," Quinn said. "You'll have to figure that one out on your own."

Oona and Atlas exchanged a look, and apparently decided to give it a go. Oona grabbed one of the brightly colored drinks from a waitress as she and Atlas made their way over to the ripped immortal, presumably hoping to come back with a better understanding of which one of them had the best chance with him.

"You wanna dance?" Quinn asked, looking at me with that crooked smile of hers.

"I don't know if I should." I tried to decline, but the drink was finally starting to kick in, making my muscles feel loose and easy.

A warm relaxation had settled in over me. My smile came easier, and saying the word *no* suddenly felt so much more arduous than it had a few moments ago. Even the music that had seemed so grating when we first came in actually made sense, and I found myself swaying with it involuntarily.

"Will another shot get you to dance?" Quinn arched her dark eyebrow.

"Maybe, but I definitely won't be doing that," I said, using all my willpower to refuse. "I need to be clearheaded for tomorrow."

"A dance it is, then."

She took my hand, leading me through the bar to a clearing in the center. I wasn't sure if it was really a dance floor, exactly, but several folks were dancing there—a few drunk young ladies on their own, and a few couples grinding against each other.

At first Quinn and I danced much like the drunk girls—our only connection being where our fingers were linked loosely together as we moved and swayed. But when the song switched to something melodic, less angry and more electronic, Quinn pulled me to her.

She looped one arm around my waist, pulling us together, and

I wrapped my arm around her neck. And I didn't know if it was her or the shot, but it all hit me at once. Her skin was so soft against mine—how was her skin so soft, how was it even possible?—and she smelled of lilacs and alcohol in a way that seemed to be so perfectly Quinn.

Then her fingers were on my face, gently caressing my cheek and jawline, and I looked at her. I wanted her to kiss me, and she *knew* it, so she didn't. Not right away. She just held me to her, letting her hand trail over my skin underneath my shirt.

I couldn't take it anymore, and I pulled away a bit. "I'm not drunk enough for this."

Hurt flashed through her eyes like lightning, darkening her face, and she stepped back from me. "What is that supposed to mean?"

"I just meant dancing," I said lamely, and the fog of the drink and her touch was making it hard for me to argue.

"Did you? Or did you mean you're not drunk enough for me?"

"Come on, Quinn." I ran my hand through my hair. "When we were together, you were the only thing that I was ever really drunk on."

"Is that why you ended things with me? You didn't like the hangover the next day?" Her husky voice was quiet, barely loud enough to be heard over the music, and pain made it tremble slightly.

"It's not like that," I said, because I didn't know what else to say, but the truth was that she wasn't far off the mark.

Being with her was wonderful and exciting, but she never gave me space to breathe, and after we'd spend a weekend together I'd end up feeling exhausted and drained. She cared too deeply, too fiercely, and I could never keep up. I could never be who she needed me to be.

"Why did you end things? You never explained it. Everything was so good. *We* were so good."

"Were we?" I asked, almost plaintively. "It wasn't all roses."

"Even roses have thorns, Malin. We were *good*." She reached out, brushing back my hair from my face.

Then she was pressed up to me again, her mouth on mine, kissing me fiercely the way she always did, and as much as I wanted to give in and kiss her back, I just couldn't. I pulled away and put my hand on her shoulder, pushing her from me.

"This just isn't the right time," I insisted.

"I know the timing is terrible, but this might be it, Malin. You do realize that, right? What we're going up against, there's no way we can all make it out alive. So the time is now or never." She stared at me. "Do you want me or not?"

"That's not fair."

"I'll take that as a no, then." She started walking away, so I grabbed her hand, stopping her.

"Quinn, it's not that simple."

She whirled on me. "No, for me it is that simple! I've wanted to be with you since the day we met, and I knew it. You've never been able to figure out what you really want. I kept waiting for you to know and I was certain that one day you'd come to your senses, but . . ."

"I never asked you to wait!" I shot back, and her face fell, like I had punched her in the stomach.

"You're right. You're absolutely right," she replied thickly. "I will always care about you, and I will gladly follow you into whatever battle may come tomorrow. I won't let you die and I won't let the whole world come crashing down because of what's happening between us. But I can't keep doing this dance with you. I know it's my fault. I know I kept hanging on long after I should, but . . . I'm done now."

"Quinn . . ." I tried to argue, but there was nothing I could say. Especially since she was just saying what I'd been trying to say for the past six months, but somehow hearing it aloud, and seeing the look on her face . . . it hurt so much more than I expected.

Without saying anything more, she turned and walked away, disappearing into the crowd, and suddenly I didn't feel like being there anymore. I pushed my way out into the night air, which was much cooler and cleaner than inside the bar.

I'd only taken a few steps when I heard Oona calling my name.

"Mal, wait!" she shouted, so I turned to look at her. "What's wrong?"

I shook my head. "Nothing. I'm going back to the hotel to get some sleep. Stay. Have fun. Don't get too drunk, and I'll see you in the morning."

Her eyes were narrowed in concern, but I didn't wait for her to say more. I just turned and practically ran back to the hotel. I wasn't in a hurry, really, it just felt better to run. When I made it back, my legs felt like jelly and my skin was flushed, both from the booze and the jog.

We'd quickly discussed sleeping arrangements when we got here, so I went to the room that I would share with Oona and Asher, while Atlas and Quinn would take the other one farther down the hall.

Asher lay on the bed farthest from the door, shirtless, with his back to me. In the moonlight streaming through a gap in the curtains, he looked so serene and peaceful.

Wordlessly, I took off my shoes and pants before sliding under the covers beside him. We hadn't talked about whether I would be sleeping in his bed or bunking with Oona in hers, and I hoped he didn't mind. I wrapped my arm around him and pressed my head against his back.

For a few moments we lay that way, with me trying to quiet the anxiety raging in my head, until finally he said, "Are you okay?"

"I just don't want to be alone tonight," I admitted.

He took a deep breath, then put his arm over mine. "Okay."

FORTY-NINE

———◆———

The next day the NorAm Overland Express took us as far as Belmopan in Belize, and from there we had to take a cab. We all piled into an old van. I sat in the seat farthest back, squished between our luggage with Oona, while the others made do with the seats in front.

Everyone else had slept on the express down from Sugarland, except for me. But I was glad I was awake. Halfway through the long ride, the desert scenery had given way to the most beautiful, lush landscape I'd ever seen. Tall vibrant trees lined our path, and I'd even spotted a few howler monkeys hiding in the branches as we zoomed past.

When we had finally gotten off, everyone had commented on how strangely gorgeous it was here. It was like being transported into another realm, a fairy-tale land. The air was thick and humid, and it smelled sweetly of flowers. Even the sun seemed to shine brighter here, so Oona had bought a pair of oversized sunglasses at the station. It was so unlike the city back home.

During the cab ride, I leaned out the window, staring in awe at all the green that surrounded us, and at a flock of bright red birds taking flight.

Among the greenery were stunning homes and buildings made of limestone with ornate architecture, and massive stone temples looming in the distance. Eventually the trees thinned out and high-rises replaced the rain forest.

Farther on, the buildings began to look rougher and older and became smaller and were crammed closer together. The air became drier and hotter, like sitting too close to a fire, as the paved roads gave way to bumpy dirt. The area lost all pretense of being stable and devolved fully into a shantytown.

"El Noveno Anillo," the cabdriver explained to us, motioning to the homes made of mismatched plywood and sheets of corrugated metal. "This is, uh, how you say—*afueras*?"

"The suburbs," Oona translated for him, and he snapped his fingers in excitement.

"*Si, si.*" He nodded, and with a push of a button, he rolled up all the windows of the van, sealing out the growing stench of sewage and decay. Then he blasted the AC to keep the heat at bay. "This is the suburbs of the Gates."

"Why is it called El Noveno Anillo?" I asked, but he couldn't hear me over the racket the air-conditioning was making.

"It means 'the Ninth Ring,'" Oona answered. "I imagine it's a reference to Dante's *Inferno*, with the ninth circle of hell being the final one before the devil."

The cab moved slowly through the town, since the narrow winding roadway was filled with potholes and pedestrians who paid no mind to any kind of traffic laws. The inhabitants appeared to be an even mixture of humans and immortals, but they were all ragged and dirty, and they stared at me through the window with angry glares.

Not that I blamed them. Living in a place like this had to be awful.

Finally the van rolled to a stop just where the dilapidated homes were buttressed against a tall adobe wall. Directly before us was a large archway, with the view inside only revealing more rust-colored walls.

The driver hit the meter and turned back to us. "This is as far as I go."

Oona stepped out, taking off her sunglasses, while I paid the driver and the others started unloading our gear.

"So this is it?" She looked back over her shoulder at me. "I just expected there to be actual gates, or something. But this is just a big open entryway."

"It's actually a poor translation," Quinn explained, referencing something we'd both been taught at the academy. "Originally, when it was first settled thousands of years ago, it was called *In Sabatu Kurnugia*, but someone mislabeled it on a map as *Baba Kurnugia*, and Baba meant Gates. Eventually that took hold, and whenever English became the standard language around here instead of Sumerian, it officially became the Gates of Kurnugia."

"Well what does *In Sabatu* mean?" Atlas asked.

"Rings," I said and pointed to the walls. "They didn't have a word for 'labyrinth' back then, so it was referring to the maze of walls that encircle it, making it difficult for anyone to find their way through."

Oona considered this for a moment as she looked ahead. "So it's really the Rings Around Kurnugia."

Just as she said that, a creature walked by the entrance, on the inside of the Gates. It was a massive reptile, with dark emerald scales and four long legs. With a long snout filled with jagged teeth, it looked like a cross between a crocodile and a velociraptor.

I'd never seen one in real life before, but based on the pictures I'd seen in textbooks, I guessed it was a mahamba.

"What is inside there"—the cabdriver motioned toward the Gates—"the physical world cannot hold it. A gate would do nothing. It is the *brujería* that keeps them inside."

The mahamba stared at us a moment longer—its large green eyes with slit-black pupils locked on us. Then it blinked and turned to walk away, disappearing behind the adobe wall that separated us.

The very second the van was empty, the driver turned around and sped off down the road, going much faster on the way out than he had on the way here.

While most of El Noveno Anillo had seemed heavily populated, the area just around the wall seemed deserted, but that was just as well, because I preferred to get ready with some modicum of privacy.

Oona's large backpack of thaumaturgy gear was almost toppling her over, so Atlas traded his much smaller backpack for hers. She kept a few protection and healing potions in his bag, in case we needed them on short notice.

I crouched down over the bag I'd gotten from Samael, preparing to dole out weapons before we entered the Gates. We'd already discussed who would get what, trying our best to align the best weapon for each person's skill sets.

Tyrfing—the Norse sword that never missed its target—went to Oona; Kusanagi—the sword forged inside a dragon—went to Quinn; Dyrnwyn—the flaming sword—went to Asher; and Sharur—the enchanted mace—went to Atlas.

I kept Kalfu's dagger—the smallest weapon but the one that could hopefully kill Tamerlane Fayette—for myself, sheathing it on my right side, while my Valkyrie sword Sigrún was sheathed on my left, and the rest of my belongings were in my knapsack on my back, aside from the sólarsteinn, which I put in my pocket.

"You should have this." Asher held his grandmother's shield Rök out to me, but his eyes were downcast.

This morning, when I awoke, he'd already been out of bed, and he'd hardly spoken to me, other than a few monosyllabic replies to questions I asked. On the express and in the van, he seemed to avoid sitting by me.

Something was definitely up with him, but I didn't know what it was, and I didn't have time to deal with it. Not now.

"Thanks, but I don't—" I began, but he cut me off.

"You need this more than I do." He cast me a slanted look. "Just take it."

"Thank you," I said, because I didn't want to argue, and I hooked it onto the bag on my back.

"Should we do this, then?" Quinn asked, which was also about the first time she'd spoken to me today. But the encouraging look in her eyes let me know that she'd put our fight last night behind her.

I glanced over at my other friends and saw a similar look in their eyes, even Asher's. Supportive. Nervous. Brave. Whatever had happened between us before didn't matter now. We had a mission— arguably the most important mission any of us had ever been on—and we were going to complete it to the best of our abilities.

The heat was already getting to me, so I pulled my hair up in a ponytail, and then took the sólarsteinn out of my pocket. Holding it tightly between my hands, I closed my eyes and began chanting inside my head: *Show me where the draugr Tamerlane Fayette is. Show me how to find him.*

Then I took a deep breath and opened my eyes.

At first there was nothing, and my heart pounded in my chest.

But slowly I saw it grow—a prism of color and light shining through, pointing straight ahead, toward the very center of the demon-controlled city.

"He's in there," I said, feeling both relieved and completely terrified. "Let's go get him."

FIFTY

———◆———

As we passed under the archway, a strange tingling sensation ran through me. It wasn't exactly unpleasant—sort of like the pins-and-needles feelings I got when my foot fell asleep.

"Did you feel that?" Quinn asked.

"Feel what?" Asher asked, instantly on high alert.

Oona's eyes darted around. "I didn't feel anything."

I felt it, too, and exchanged a look with Quinn. "It must be because we're Valkyries."

"What was it?" Oona pressed.

"It doesn't matter. Let's just keep going." I held the sunstone on the palm of my hand, with the prism of light pointing directly toward a solid wall in front of us. "The sólarsteinn is pointing straight ahead, but we can only go left or right. Where do you think we should go?"

"The ossuary is supposed to be due north, but to get there, we needed to start going east, I believe," Asher said as he pulled out his tablet.

From where I was standing, I could see the screen as he pulled up the plans, but the image started blinking out and the screen went black. Asher kept tapping it and tried to reopen it, but the tablet remained lifeless.

"Shit. This damn thing is acting up," he growled.

"The city is interfering with your reception?" Oona asked.

"Mine, too." Quinn had pulled out her phone when she saw Asher was having trouble with his tablet. "It's not the reception—it's just not working."

Asher let out a frustrated sigh. "Looks like we'll be working from memory."

"So which way?" Atlas asked.

"I guess we go left," Asher replied.

The outer edge of the Gates was a long corridor, with bare adobe walls towering over it, and the ground a dark crimson-red clay. A putrid odor of sulfur and rotten meat filled the hot air.

Eventually, after a few turns, the hallway widened and opened up into an actual city. Not modernized, like the city outside of the slums or the one we lived in, but more like a bustling Bronze Age civilization.

Small stone shops were set up, with wares hanging from their awnings. They were admittedly disgusting-looking wares, like entrails and bloodied ram's horns, but the setup was similar to that of the street vendors at home.

The shop owners appeared to be entirely demonic, most of them overtly so, with horrific appearances, but some were more humanoid. There did appear to be human tourists here as well, haggling with the demons over the price of their merchandise. A man was shouting that he'd come all the way from Papua New Guinea for some magical elixir, and they were fresh out.

The demon selling the ram's horns had dark crimson skin, reptilian eyes, and cloven hooves. He walked beside us a few steps, narrowing his eyes at us, then he leaned over and actually sniffed Quinn. She didn't protest, because the demons outnumbered us, but the demon recoiled in disgust.

"Move along," he simpered with a forked tongue and shooed us away. He hopped back to his stand and started shouting, "Fresh Cambion horn! Perfect for any dysfunction you might be suffering in your nethers! Make your lovers happy tonight!"

I glanced back at him and realized that those hadn't come from a ram—they had come from Cambions like Jude. They were killing each other here, and then selling their parts in an open market.

"Oh, come on." An Aswang with its gaping mouth of angry teeth was arguing with a woman who looked relatively ordinary, except that she was selling necklaces made of tiny human toes. "Don't pull a fast one on me, Lamia."

"That's the price," Lamia replied, snatching the toe-jewelry from the clutches of the Aswang. "Take them or leave them."

"This way," Asher ordered, touching my arm, and it wasn't until that moment that I realized I'd stopped and had been gaping at Lamia.

"We shouldn't linger here," Atlas suggested, but he didn't need to. The market was not a place I wanted to stay for a moment longer than I had to.

Asher led the way through the crowded bazaar, and I tried to keep my head down. I didn't want to see who was selling what. This whole place was a nightmare come to life.

But by trying to keep my eyes off any of the horrors that surrounded me, I wasn't exactly looking where I was going. I stumbled over my feet and tumbled forward, falling right into the wide-open arms of an iron statue.

The strap to my bag got caught on the statue's hand, and it took a few seconds to pull myself free. But when I finally looked up, I instantly recognized who the statue had been made in honor of—the short curly hair, the high cheekbones, the powerful femininity. Ereshkigal.

"I feel like you're following me everywhere I go," I mumbled, staring up into the dark, cold eyes of the statue.

"Mal?" Oona asked. "Are you okay?"

I shook it off and hurried on ahead, and soon enough we found the exit out the back of the market. Here, there were more narrow hallways, winding toward the ossuary at the center of the Gates. We just had to make sure that we chose the right ones.

FIFTY-ONE

———◆———

As we walked in the stifling heat, I fell in step with Asher, while Atlas, Quinn, and Oona trailed a few steps behind us. The sólarsteinn worked almost like a compass. The light always pointed to the center of the city, and it didn't take walls or buildings into account, so Asher used what he remembered to tell us where to turn.

An olitau flew above, its large red leathery wings blasting hot wind over us, and we all crouched down to avoid getting scraped by its razor-sharp claws. The olitau was essentially a giant demonic bat, and it let out an angry cry as it flew off over the walls.

"This way," Asher directed when we hit a T-intersection, pointing us to the left, and we rounded the corner to bump right into a dead end. "Okay, let's go right, then."

We turned around and walked maybe ten or twenty feet before the corridor turned into another dead end.

"Shit." He ran a hand through his short hair and turned around in circles, as if that would somehow make sense of the dead ends we encountered.

"Maybe we just took a wrong turn," Oona suggested rather unhelpfully.

"Well, obviously, we did," Asher muttered. "I just don't know where." He pulled out his tablet, angrily tapping at it as if that would suddenly make it work.

"There's no one around here." Quinn gestured to the empty space surrounding us. "Why don't you guys see if you can figure something out, and Atlas and I can go back and see if maybe we can find a sign or something?"

Oona was already a step ahead of her. Atlas had set her heavy bag on the ground, and she knelt beside it and pulled out several of her books. "There's gotta be something in one of these."

"Just don't go too far away," I told Quinn. "I don't want you getting lost or separated from us."

She saluted me, then she and Atlas disappeared around the corner in search of some sign of the correct path.

Asher dropped his bag to the ground and began pacing, cursing as he did. Sweat beaded on his temples, and he rubbed the back of his neck. "I can't believe this."

"It's okay. The sólarsteinn says he's still there." I held it flat on the palm of my hand, and the rainbow prism of light still pointed to the same spot it had been aiming at since we got here. "We'll find him."

Asher shook his head. "But we shouldn't be here for nightfall, and it's getting late. I made us waste the whole day."

I stared up at the cloudless sky, and I was surprised by how different it looked here. When we'd reached the entrance to the Gates it had been early afternoon, with a yellow sun shining brightly. But now the sun appeared to be setting, casting everything in dark oranges and reds, and we hadn't been here all that long.

Did time move differently in the Gates?

I squinted up at the sky, trying to make sense of it. "Is it, though?"

"It'll be dark soon," he persisted, and I didn't bother arguing with that. He might be right, and the Gates was definitely someplace I wouldn't want to be after dark.

"We'll find him. It's not your fault." I put my hand on his arm to comfort him, but he shrugged it off and took a few steps away from me.

"How is it not my fault? The task I was assigned was navigation, and I clearly failed." His voice trembled with barely contained anger.

"None of us knew that technology doesn't work here in the Gates. We're almost there, Asher. We're going to find him."

He exhaled deeply and avoided my gaze, the way he had been all day. "I wish I could be so sure."

"Are you okay? You've seemed . . . off all day."

"It's been a weird day."

I moved closer to him. "Is that all?"

Finally, after a long pause, he lifted his head, and his dark eyes were stormy, as he quietly said, "I saw you last night."

"What?"

He licked his lips. "I saw you dancing with Quinn and kissing her."

My jaw dropped. This was not what I was expecting him to say, and I had no idea how to respond. Definitely not now, but probably not ever.

"You were back at the hotel," I managed.

"I left. I found a safe under the bed for the weapons, and I wanted to see how you were doing . . . and then I saw."

"Oh. I . . . I don't know what to say."

"I was just starting to really care about you, and I thought . . ." His mouth twisted into a grimace, and he looked away from me. "I don't know."

"This isn't the time to talk about this, Asher."

"I know. I just . . ." He rubbed the back of his neck, then looked at me again.

"Hey, guys!" Oona shouted, breaking through the tension. She turned her head to yell down the corridor to the others. "Quinn, Atlas, I may have found something!"

"What?" I asked, going back over to where she knelt in the dirt just as Quinn and Atlas came jogging back over to us.

"What'd you find?" Atlas asked, wiping away the sweat on his brow with the back of his arm.

Oona tapped the page in the old book splayed open before her. "It says here that all roads lead from the Merchants of Death, which is the name of that awful market back there, so we just have to go back there and try again."

Asher cursed under his breath again, and Quinn groaned. None of us was looking forward to heading back to the market. The path from there had been wonderfully uneventful—we'd seen hardly a creature or a demon along the way, and that had suited us all just fine.

"Maybe we should just head out and find a place outside of the Gates to camp for the night, and try again tomorrow," Atlas suggested.

"But I don't really think it's that late. I think we—" I began, but the sound of wings flapping and a familiar squawking interrupted me.

There, perched on the edge of the wall, was a huge raven, with the setting sun shimmering off its black feathers. The bird tilted its head at me, and somehow I knew this was the same raven I'd seen before. The one that had been following me around.

"That raven." I pointed up at it. "I know that raven."

"What do you mean, you know that raven? How do you know that raven?" Oona asked, incredulous.

"I just do," I replied as the bird started hopping down the wall away from us. "I think we should follow it."

"What are you talking about?" Quinn asked.

"I'm gonna follow it," I decided just as the bird took flight.

"Malin, that doesn't make sense," Quinn said, trying to reason with me, but there wasn't time to argue before I lost sight of the bird. The raven was flying on ahead, so I took off after it, and I didn't wait to see if anyone else was following.

FIFTY-TWO

— ◆ —

As the raven flew overhead, guiding me through the winding paths, the walls around me grew higher and higher, until I realized that they weren't actually walls at all. They were large pyramidesque structures that soared toward the reddening sky above, and homes were carved into the sides, like cliffside pueblos.

My focus was on the raven and making sure I didn't lose sight of it, but I heard the others running behind me. I quickly looked back over my shoulder and saw that all four of them were behind me.

When I glanced over at the homes built into the towering pyramids, I saw that demons were leering at us from their windows and doorways and narrow balconies. I could almost feel their eyes burrowing into me, and I ran faster, afraid of what would happen if all the inhabitants decided to descend the long staircases after us.

While all of the Gates had a putrid stench, as I neared the end of the stretch of pyramids I noticed the smell growing more intense.

It wasn't just sulfuric anymore—it was moldy and earthy. And beneath that was a pronounced sweetness, sickeningly so, like apples and berries left to rot in the sun.

It was the scent of death and decay.

The raven cawed loudly, soaring ahead of me, and I raced around a corner and stopped in my tracks. I was in front of the Bararu Mutanu Ossuary.

At first glance, it looked like an average chapel built centuries ago, except all the flourishes, every single detail of them, from the archway to the seal of Kurnugia on the wall, were made entirely out of bones. Skulls and femurs—both from mortals and immortals—decorated every inch. The architecture was impeccable, and it would've been rather beautiful if it wasn't so macabre.

"Holy shit," Quinn said breathlessly as she and the others caught up with me. "What is this place?"

"It's the ossuary," Asher explained. "It's the heart of the Gates, and below it is the entrance to Kurnugia."

We were all so enamored with the skeletal edifice that none of us noticed the beautiful woman standing in front of it—not until the hulking albino wolf at her side let out a guttural growl.

"Easy, Surma," she commanded the beast gently, her voice lilting with an unfamiliar accent, and her blue eyes settled on us. "You look lost. Perhaps I can help you?"

Her gown—made of gauzy, half-decayed rags—ruffled in a light breeze, and part of it had slid down off her shoulder. Her pale skin was mottled gray and blue in places, with the dark lines of her veins visible underneath.

As she walked toward us, taking slow steps, she brushed her fine blond hair out of her face, and I realized that scent of death was coming directly from her. Oona and Asher recoiled from her stench.

"You're Kalma," I said to her, remembering what I'd learned

from textbooks. The demigoddess who guarded the passage to the underworld was renowned for her odor.

"I am." She batted her lashes, unfazed. "Why are you here?"

"Are you sure this is the right place?" Oona asked, sounding almost desperately hopeful that we wouldn't have to travel past a goddess of death into a building made of bones.

But the raven had perched on a skull sitting just above the doorway, so I knew this was exactly where we were supposed to be.

"We need to go inside," I said firmly.

"I can't grant you passage in there," Kalma replied, sounding disinterested in the whole affair. "Kurnugia is no place for mortals."

"We're not going to Kurnugia," I explained, hoping to avoid a confrontation if I could. "We only want to go inside the ossuary. There's a draugr inside there that we need to find."

"Those that are inside are allowed in by invitation only, and I am certain that no one invited you."

I stood my ground, holding my head high. "You can let us in, or we will go in by force."

Kalma offered me an amused smile. "I have no fear of you."

The wolf charged first, lunging toward us, and Atlas moved quickly, swinging at it with his mace. The spiked ball collided with Surma, who let out an angry growl as he flew into the building.

Kalma may have looked young and harmless, but when she threw a punch, Quinn went flying backward and landed heavily in the dirt. I barely ducked out of the way of her next attack.

While Atlas dealt with the demon wolf, Oona crouched beside Quinn, making sure she was okay, but Quinn was up in a flash, wiping the blood from her lip and charging in to help Atlas. Oona began rummaging through her knapsack for anything that could help in the fight, leaving me and Asher to handle Kalma.

I didn't want to use the dagger and risk breaking it, not before

I used it on Tamerlane, and I wasn't sure how well Sigrún would work against a goddess of death, so that left me fighting hand-to-hand. When I swung at her, Kalma grabbed my fist and stopped it, grinning at me as she squeezed my hand. She was bending my wrist backward, making me kneel before her. My bones were hard to break, but it wouldn't take much more from her before my arm snapped.

Asher pulled Dyrnwyn from its sheath, the black blade glinting under the crimson sky, and swung at Kalma. He connected with her arm, and I could see he was using all his might, but the blade barely even broke her skin, sending dark gray blood dripping down her flesh.

She let go of my fist and turned her attention to Asher, letting out an ethereal laugh. "You cannot kill me. I am of death."

I wasn't sure if Kalma was telling the truth or not, but in my experience nothing was completely immortal—it was just that some were harder to kill than others.

"Use the power of the weapon!" I shouted at Asher. "Aim for her head or heart!"

He held the sword with both hands. Asher closed his eyes as Kalma approached—presumably channeling the purity of his intentions into the weapon.

Finally, just when she was upon him, the blade burst into white-hot flames, and Asher swung with all his might. Her dress went up in flames immediately, the fire blackening her skin as it burned. Kalma let out an agonized scream that died almost instantly as Asher sliced through her neck.

Her head toppled to the ground, her blue eyes still staring upward and her mouth open in an angry scream as her dark blood poured into the dirt.

Surma—her once-faithful companion—saw his mistress dead

and the sword on fire, and let out a confused yelp before turning tail and running off to hide in the labyrinth.

"You okay?" Asher asked, helping me to my feet.

I nodded. "Let's just get going before somebody else tries to stop us."

FIFTY-THREE

———⋄———

This damned thing won't budge," Quinn grunted as she slammed into the massive arched door that blocked the entrance to the ossuary.

Atlas joined her, and together they hit the door so hard that they knocked a door knocker made of human bones loose and it tumbled to the ground.

"It's enchanted." Oona knelt down in front of the three steps that led up to the door, with her grimoire open. "Like the cabdriver said, the inhabitants are too powerful for anything in the physical world to keep them out, so there has to be magic and spells in place."

"Can you break it and get us in?" Quinn asked, rubbing her shoulder where she'd been crashing into the door.

"Maybe, but you have to shut up and let me read," Oona said.

I stepped back, giving her space, and stared out at the darkening world around me. Kalma's body lay a few feet away, still reeking horribly of death, and I wondered dismally if we'd make it out of here alive. Assuming that we could get into the ossuary, and that we could stop Tamerlane, would the demons that populated the Gates really let us get out unscathed?

"We can do this," Asher said, his voice soft and reassuring beside me, as if reading my thoughts. "We made it this far, we can make it all the way."

I swallowed back my fear. "I hope so."

"How's your wrist?" He gently took my hand in his, as if his touch could heal any broken bones, and the gesture did make me feel a bit better, easing some of my anxiety.

"I can't feel it, really, not now, but I'm sure it'll hurt like hell later," I admitted. The Valkyrie adrenaline had kicked in, so I didn't feel pain the way I usually would.

"I'm sorry about fighting with you earlier. Now's not the time for any of this."

"It's fine," I said hurriedly.

His dark blue eyes met mine. "I just want you to know that, no matter what happens here today, I truly care for you, and everything will be all right."

"Everything will be all right?" I smiled bitterly. "Asher, the world might end."

"It might, but it won't. And you'll be all right."

"How can you say that?" I asked, not understanding where this newfound certainty was coming from.

He shrugged. "It's just something I know."

"How?"

"Remember when I told you about how our ancestors can leave truths in our hearts when we need them most? It's how I knew about you, and as soon as I saw the ossuary, I knew about this. I can feel it, right here." He took my hand, putting it on his chest, right over where his heart pounded steadily. "*You* will be all right, and I need you to remember that."

I shook my head. "Why?" Then the implication of his words hit me. "What about everyone else?"

"I think I got it!" Oona shouted excitedly.

"Malin, Ash, get over here! Let's get this shit done!" Quinn barked.

Asher let go of my hand and jogged back over to them, so I did the same, although I felt more dazed than I had a few moments ago.

When I reached the door, Oona was already pouring vials of a dark liquid around the edge of the door and repeating something in a low voice that I didn't understand.

"What's she saying?" Asher asked.

"I think it's Akkadian, but I don't really know it," Atlas replied, quietly so as not to disturb Oona. "I've just heard Samael speak it around the office from time to time."

"Okay." Oona straightened up and rubbed her hands together. "Let's see if that works."

She took a deep breath and grabbed the door handle—made of bones, just like everything else—and, slowly, the door opened.

FIFTY-FOUR

————————◆————————

Inside, the ossuary smelled like an old root cellar—all earth and must. The doorway opened into a grand front room, replete with several chandeliers made of bones lighting the large space.

The air was cold, strikingly so after the oppressive heat outside, and it was totally silent. I hadn't really expected this to be a bustling hub of activity, given Kalma's warnings about it being invitation-only and the enchantment on the door. But it appeared totally devoid of life in here.

Off the spacious main hall there were six doorways—all arched with bone.

"Which way?" Oona asked.

The raven flew in through the open door, but this time it didn't appear to plan to direct me where to go. Instead, it landed in the center of the main room and picked indifferently at pebbles on the concrete floor.

Fortunately, I still had the sólarsteinn, so I pulled it out of my pocket. The dim candlelight from the chandeliers managed to do the trick, and after a few moments the prism of light shone through the stone, pointing directly toward the fourth door.

I led the way, and while I was surprised when the raven didn't follow, I didn't let that deter me. The sólarsteinn knew who I was looking for, and I wouldn't stop until I found him.

The corridor was narrow but tall, with bones curving over us on the ceiling. Occasionally a skeletal arm would be hanging down, as if reaching out for us.

Softly—almost eerily—the sound of a piano playing began echoing through the hall. The music grew louder, until finally we came upon a large open door that led into what appeared to be a small bar.

At the far end of the room was a piano, and like everything else in the ossuary, it, too, had been created with bones. The pianist himself was a skeleton, with a few bits of flesh still clinging to his bones, and a large pair of dirty white wings sprouting from his back. As he played, feathers would come free and flutter slowly to the floor.

The bartender appeared to be the same kind of creature as the pianist—all bones with just a few bits of flesh, and the decaying wings on his back. He was pouring a glass for the only patron in the place, who sat at the bar with his back to us.

Though I'd only seen him once in real life, I recognized him. The salt-and-pepper hair. The odd bluish tone of his tawny skin. The hunch of his broad shoulders.

"Stay here," I whispered to my friends as we lingered just outside the entrance to the bar.

"What if you need us?" Oona asked, her dark eyes wide and fearful.

"Just stay right here," I insisted. "If I need you, you'll know. But this is my battle to fight."

Asher put his hand on my arm, stopping me just as I was about to enter the bar. "He killed my mother, too. I'm going in there with you."

I nodded. "Let's finish this."

I walked into the bar first, Asher a step behind me. The pianist continued playing, and the bartender wiped the wooden bar with an old rag, either not noticing or not caring about my or Asher's presence.

"Tamerlane Fayette," I said loudly; neither of the angels of death paid us any mind.

Still with his back to us, Tamerlane took a long drink of red wine from a crystal goblet. "I must admit I'm surprised that you haven't given up by now." Slowly, he turned the barstool around so he faced us. "You know this is pointless, don't you?"

My hand hovered above the dagger on my hip. "You don't know what I'm capable of."

He smirked. "You traveled all this way for nothing. You can't kill me."

"Is that why you're hiding out here?" Asher shot back, his voice dripping with venom.

"I'm not hiding—I'm waiting," Tamerlane corrected him.

I raised an eyebrow. "For us?"

Tamerlane let out a low, joyless laugh. "Don't be so arrogant. For *her*."

"Her who?" I asked.

"The only true queen." Tamerlane gestured vaguely around, to the air, to the floor, as if she were everywhere. "The one who I serve. The one who took me under her wing after your mother left me to live in a world that I no longer belonged in."

"The one who killed your family?" I asked sharply, hoping to hit the same nerve my mother had, just before Tamerlane killed her.

It worked. His smile fell away and he stood up, stepping away from the bar and closer to where Asher and I stood in the center of the room.

"Why do you even want to avenge your mother?" he asked, looking at me directly. "You should hate her for what she did. She's the one that brought this all on."

"I do hate her." It was the first time I'd ever said this aloud, but that didn't make it any less true. I hated Marlow, and I loved her. She had good in her, buried beneath so much bad. But in spite of everything, she was my mother and I was grateful to have called her mine. "But it wasn't for you to decide whether she lived or died."

"Just as it isn't for you to decide who lives and dies, and yet you do it all the time," Tamerlane countered.

"No, I am only following my orders," I insisted.

"As was I!" Tamerlane said, almost jovially, and he motioned between himself and me. "The two of us, all of us, really, we're only pawns in the games of the gods."

"Maybe," I allowed. "But I'm not about to let you win."

"It's already too late. Haven't you been listening?" Tamerlane asked.

"It's never too late," Asher replied with more conviction than I felt.

"I can help you," Tamerlane offered, then motioned toward the door, where Oona, Quinn, and Atlas were waiting just around the corner. "And I can help your friends. Let me put you out of your misery before my queen arrives. Humans won't survive long with what she has planned for this earth."

"We won't let her," Asher said.

Tamerlane looked at the two of us. "Do you think that if she could be stopped I would've let her slaughter my entire family?" Then his dark eyes settled on me. "When your mother failed to slay me, I became a draugr, one of the most powerful beings on earth. And yet, I could not stop the queen. I could only fall in line."

"Everything can be stopped," I told him as I pulled Kalfu's dagger from its sheath. "Even death dies."

"That's how you plan to stop me?" Tamerlane chuckled at the sight of it. "With that tiny little knife?"

"We'll see," I said.

"Let's dance, then, shall we?" He motioned for me to come at him. "I'll make it easy for you."

He spread his arms wide, leaving himself exposed, and while I couldn't be certain that it wasn't a trap, I had to take my chance. I walked right up to him, taking careful deliberate steps, and he merely smiled down at me as I drove the dagger straight into his heart.

Tamerlane laughed again, more boisterously this time. "I barely even felt it." He reached down to pull the dagger out, but his expression faltered. "I told you I couldn't . . ." He stumbled back, his skin growing more ashen. "I couldn't . . ."

Then he fell to the floor, slumped back against the bar, and his black eyes met mine, filled with confused indignation. "I can't die," he whispered, and then his head lolled to the side and he fell silent.

The raven suddenly flew into the room, cawing like mad, and Quinn, Oona, and Atlas raced in after it. The entire bar began to rumble. Dirt pushed up from the floor, like giant gophers were pushing their way to the surface, but the reality was much worse.

Skeletal hands broke free, followed by entire bodies. A dozen or more reanimated skeletons came up through the floor, each one of them brandishing a rusty sword.

FIFTY-FIVE

⸻ ◆ ⸻

You really thought you could just waltz in here and kill him, and it would be that easy?" Quinn asked, standing behind me as the skeletons circled around us.

"No," I admitted. "But I had hoped."

The five of us stood with our backs together, and once the skeletons finally stopped pouring out of the earth, they charged at us. Sigrún, my sword, began glowing dull purple, and I felt the surge of Valkyrie rushing through me.

I knocked them back just as quickly as they came at me, slicing through their bones like they were made of ash. For every one I killed, two more rose up in their place, but I kept fighting, moving on instinct, as I dodged and sliced until their numbers finally seemed to be dwindling.

Behind me, I heard Oona cry out in pain, but I couldn't let that distract me—if I wanted her to survive this, I needed to stop the skeletons from overtaking us. From the corner of my eye, I saw

Quinn taking three skeletons down in one fell swoop, and I heard Atlas grunting as he fought.

Finally, the skeletons lay in a pile of bones around us, with mounds of freshly overturned dirt beneath them. And still, the bartender kept wiping down the bar, and the pianist kept on playing, undisturbed by the battle for life and death that had been raging around them.

Oona was crouched down in the skeletal pile with a bloodied arm, so I rushed over to her.

"Are you okay?" I asked.

"What?" She glanced at her arm, as if she hadn't even noticed she was wounded. "Yeah, I'm fine." And then she immediately turned her attention back to the rusted sword she was holding. "There's an inscription on their weapons, and I know I've seen it somewhere."

As Oona studied the blade, I unzipped her bag and pulled out a gauze bandage.

"Well, Tamerlane's dead, so we should probably just get out of here before more terrible things happen," I suggested as I wrapped up her arm.

"Atlas?" Oona asked, too preoccupied to listen to me. "You said you knew some Akkadian?"

"Not really," he said, but he bent over to inspect the sword. "But that definitely looks like the Akkadian writing I've seen."

The room began rumbling again, harder this time, and the bones around us rattled.

"Oona, can we do this later?" I asked, getting to my feet. "We should get out of here."

"I know, I know." She ran her hands over the encryption on the blade. "This just doesn't feel over to me."

"Okay, we need to get out of here," Quinn commanded as the quaking intensified, and the raven squawked again before taking off down the hall in the opposite direction from which we'd come, away from the ossuary. "*Now!*"

I grabbed Oona's good arm and yanked her to her feet. She carried the sword with her as we ran out to the hallway just in time to see the ceiling collapsing. Our path back the way we'd come was blocked, so the only way out now was to keep following the long hallway to wherever it might lead.

"Hurry!" Atlas shouted, not that he needed to. We were already running, and the tremors stopped as soon as the ceiling caved in.

The hallway quickly stopped feeling like any kind of formal structure but rather like a cave. Bones were still scattered about, but less in a decorative way. Complete skeletons lay sprawled, as if someone had lain bodies out for everyone to see—as a sacrifice, maybe—and that's as they had been ever since. They had become calcified, which made them look thicker and glittery, like they were made of crystal.

Opaque stalactites hung from the ceiling, like icy teeth reaching out for us, and still we walked deeper into the cave. Somewhere ahead of us, light was shining, casting light down the tunnel. The cold air—which had gotten frigid—started to warm as we walked.

Finally, we saw the mouth of the cave, opening to a large pond filled with bright aquamarine water. Above it, the cave opened to the sun, which shone brightly on us. Not red or dark the way it had been before we entered the ossuary, but like full daylight.

Quinn walked to the edge of the lake first and stared up. The walls surrounding it weren't that high, and the far wall on the other side of the water even had a mossy staircase carved into the side.

"Well, it looks like we're going for a swim," she said. "Assuming we all want to get out of here."

"Do you have any idea where this will lead?" I asked Asher.

He shook his head, crouching down to inspect water. "I'm not sure. The maps I looked at never showed this place." He cupped some water in his hand, smelling it. "I think this is fresh water."

"We should rest for a moment," Atlas said. "But then we should leave as fast as we can."

Oona sat cross-legged on the ground, still running her fingers over the rusty sword as if it could channel all the answers to her, when she excitedly yelled, "I got it! It's a name!"

"A name?" Quinn asked. "Of who?"

Oona rubbed her forehead, concentrating. "One of the underworld goddesses. It's something. . . . Shush? Or Rash? Something?"

"Ereshkigal?" I whispered, as if saying her name louder would somehow summon her.

Oona snapped her fingers. "Yes! That's it!"

The hair on the back of my neck stood up, and I realized dismally that I should've known sooner. The past few days, I had been seeing her face everywhere—her eyes following me from posters on the street, entrancing me at the hotel, even waiting for me with open arms at the Merchants of Death.

It had all seemed like coincidence, like nothing to pay any mind to, but she'd slowly been raising herself in the consciousness of everyone as she gained power. She was an obscure underworld goddess, banished to Kurnugia centuries ago. Why should her name be on everyone's tongue?

Because she wanted it there. Because her underlings were working to prepare the world for her, to ready us all to bow down and say her name, so they plastered her face everywhere, her name on everything, for us all to see and remember.

The water in the lake began to ripple and quake before us. Everyone moved backward, hurrying away from the edge and into the cave, except for me. Because I knew it was already too late.

The crystal-clear lake, which seemed like an oasis in the harsh world of the Gates, was actually something far more sinister. It was the mouth to Kurnugia, a watery portal through which immortals could pass from one world to the next.

FIFTY-SIX

A man arose slowly, breathing in deeply as his head first broke through the water. He had two massive horns from the sides of his head, but beyond that he was handsome, if not slightly unremarkable, with dark waves of hair dripping down his back. When he shook his head, droplets of water flew around him like a halo.

He smiled as he moved forward, and the dark patch of hair on his chest trailed down his bronze skin . . . and that's when I saw he was no man at all. From his waist down, he was all bull, with four muscular legs covered in thick black fur, and hefty cloven hooves trudging through the water toward us.

"I didn't expect a welcoming party to greet me when I finally arrived," he said, running a hand through his thick hair.

"Who are you?" Quinn demanded from behind me, but I already knew the answer.

I recognized him from paintings and textbooks. Often depicted in the background behind Ereshkigal or sometimes seated at her side, he was her consort, her lover, her partner in crime. Gugalanna, the Bull of Hell.

"I have been called many, many names over the centuries," he admitted. "But the one I am most known by is Gugalanna, and since we are going to be friends . . ."

He paused in his own introduction to give his most winning smile and motion toward us all as he towered over us. In a conspiratorial tone, he leaned down and said, "I can already tell we're going to be bonded together for a long time. I mean, this is a special moment, isn't it?"

Then he straightened up, still grinning, and finished with, "Well, since we'll be friends, you can call me Guga."

"Guga?" Quinn asked with an arched eyebrow.

"I know, I know," he said with a sigh. "It's a terrible name, but my parents were so last millennium, so what are you gonna do?"

"What do you want with us?" I asked.

"Right now I'm just checking out this ragtag group we've got here." With his hands on his hips, Gugalanna looked from one to the other of us. "So what have we got here? Valkyrie, Valkyrie, mortal but . . . powerful? Yes? Sorceress, maybe?"

"Sorceress-in-training," Oona corrected him, standing a bit taller.

"Son of a Valkyrie, son of a Valkyrie," he continued down the line, looking rather impressed. "Wow. We've really got a lot of great blood here. I feel like I won the lottery, I truly do, and I cannot thank you all enough for making this so much easier for me. I was afraid I was going to have to go traipsing off into your world, knocking on everyone's doors and asking if they have any old Valkyries just lying around.

"But see, Resh—that's what I call my wife, Ereshkigal—she got this great idea," he went on. "She said we could just bait a trap for some Valkyries, and it would be far easier than fighting them on their own turf, where it would be nearly impossible for us to take them all on at once, and we just had to wait for one to screw up. All we needed was a little mistake, one tiny crack in the wall of perfect order that surrounds your world—like, say, a Valkyrie creating a draugr."

My mouth felt dry, and a familiar tension grew around my heart. He was talking about Marlow, and Tamerlane. Tamerlane had warned me that we were all pawns, and I had believed him, but I hadn't realized the full extent of it, and I don't think he had, either.

Somehow, they'd gotten Marlow to spare Tamerlane, upsetting the balance so they could get an upper hand and grow more powerful as things began to unravel on earth. And then they had used Tamerlane himself as bait to bring us here.

FIFTY-SEVEN

———— ◆ ————

And you know, I'll be honest," Gugalanna was going on. "It took so long, I started to doubt that it was even going to happen. I was just saying to her, 'Resh, my darling, you are the smartest woman I know, but this just isn't happening.' But then, it did! And boy, do I feel foolish.

"So who was it that screwed up?" he asked, his eyes bouncing over us. "It wasn't any of you, was it? No. It was one of your mothers." Then his gaze settled on me. "Yours, I'm guessing, based on that pissed-off but guilty look on your face."

I could hear my blood pounding in my ears, and my muscles ached to fight, but I kept myself in check. I forced myself to stay calm, to wait, even as Gugalanna admitted that everything terrible, everything that threatened to end the world, was his and Ereshkigal's doing.

"You made my mother do that? How?" I asked, barely keeping my voice even.

"We didn't make her, exactly, but . . ." He waved his hands.

"You know what, I'm already saying too much. I can't give away all the secrets about how Resh works, because her plan is still in action. Don't get me wrong—it's almost done. She's almost ready to come back up here, but not quite. So I better not spoil things just yet."

"What are you doing here?" Oona asked. "What exactly do you want with us?"

"I want nothing with you, actually," he said, gesturing to Oona. "I'm just getting one of the last things on Resh's list. The blood of a child of a Valkyrie."

He let that sink in for a beat before continuing. "It can be from either a son or a daughter, but in our experience, the daughters are harder to control, and I've already had a long day, so I think I'll go with one of you two boys. I don't care which. You can fight among yourselves, if you'd like."

I drew Sigrún and moved, blocking Asher. "You're not taking any of us!"

"Really? You're going to try to fight me on this?" Gugalanna pretended to pout. "I thought we could all be friends."

"You really thought we'd just let you kill one of us without a fight?" Quinn asked, drawing her own sword.

"Whoa, whoa! Who said anything about killing?" He shook his head. "I'm just taking him down to Kurnugia, and, well, we've got some stuff planned for him that I'm really not at liberty to discuss right now."

The cave began to rumble, making the stalactites above us tremble and the water in the lake ripple around Gugalanna's hooves.

"All right, all right," Gugalanna shouted toward the water, as if someone down below could hear him. "The missus says I'm taking too long, so I better get back down there. These portals don't stay open forever, you know."

I charged at him first, but he kicked me back with his powerful legs like I was nothing. He was much larger than us, and too strong—even for a Valkyrie like me. We didn't stand a chance.

As I scrambled to my feet again, he'd already sent Quinn and Atlas flying into the cave walls. Asher was standing his ground, attempting to fight him off with his flaming sword, while Oona pulled a potion out of her bag.

She'd just started reciting an incantation when Gugalanna clicked his tongue at her before turning to kick her with his back legs. I yelled for her to get out of the way, but his massive hoof was already colliding with her chest.

Oona went soaring through the air before crashing down at the edge of the shore, her head lolling to the side in the water.

I wanted to go to her, but Gugalanna had just picked up Asher, and he looked like a rag doll in Guga's massive arms. With Sigrún in my right hand and Rök the shield in my other, I ran at the bull centaur.

I managed to get in one good hit—my blade slid across his leg hard enough to draw blood—and he let out a howl of pain. He knocked me down, and stomped on the shield with all his might. It bent and groaned, but it didn't give.

Then he let out an irritated snort, with Asher held prisoner in his arms, and turned and ran out into the lake.

"*No!*" I screamed, running into the water after them. "Asher!"

The water began swirling, like a whirlpool rising up into a tornado, and Quinn chased after me, grabbing me before I got sucked into it, too.

"Malin, stop!" she shouted. "They're gone! You can't go after them! They're gone!"

FIFTY-EIGHT

———◆———

Oona lay on the lakeshore with water lapping onto her, and her breath came out in loud, shaky rasps. Atlas knelt beside her, rummaging through her giant bag.

"The blue vial," Oona whispered, pointing weakly at her bag.

"Oona!" I rushed to her side. She looked at me through half-closed lids.

"I'm getting her something for the pain." Atlas momentarily glanced up at me from his task. "How are you doing? Can you make it out of here?"

I was bruised and scraped, but otherwise fine. Atlas and Quinn looked about the same—dirty and bloody in a few spots, but they would survive. Oona, on the other hand, wasn't looking good.

Atlas finally found the vial Oona was asking for, and carefully he held it to her lips. As she drank it down eagerly, he looked at me with worried eyes.

"We need to get out of here, fast, if we want her to make it," Atlas said in a hushed voice.

Quinn was already loading up her gear and adding Atlas's smaller knapsack on top of hers. "We'll have to swim across and use those stairs over there." She nodded toward the mossy staircase on the other side of the lake. "Atlas, will you be able to carry Oona?"

He got to his feet, holding Oona's limp body in his arms. Her head lolled against his chest as she let out another painful breath. He waded out into the lake, and when it became too deep for him to walk, he floated on his back, with Oona lying on his chest, and swam backward toward the stairs.

Quinn went after them, but I waited at the edge, staring down at the water where Asher had disappeared with Gugalanna. Only moments ago the water had been swirling and rising upward in a supernatural tornado, but now the water was still, aside from the ripples Atlas caused as he made his escape.

"Malin, we have to go." Quinn stopped, with the water up to her waist, and looked back at me. "Oona needs medical attention, and you can't go to Kurnugia. Gugalanna said the portal doesn't stay open forever, and even if it did, there's no way you would survive down there on your own."

I swallowed back my sadness and followed Quinn out into the water. I hated that she was right, that there was nothing I could do for Asher right now, but my only chance at rescuing him was getting out of here and finding help.

The trek up the stairs was more arduous than I had expected because the moss made them slippery, but we all managed to make it. At the top was an amazing view of the Gates of Kurnugia—we could see how the maze stretched out around us, bending and winding around pyramids and dead ends.

Quinn ripped a page from one of Oona's books and hurriedly drew a map, sketching what we could see around us with a stick of charcoal Oona had in her bag. From where we were, we could see the fastest route to the plaza, and from the plaza it was a relatively straight shot to the entrance.

It was a rather sheer descent down the outside of the cavern to the land below, but sliding down on our backs made for quick travel. Once we were all on level ground, Quinn got her map ready, and we raced toward the exit with the sun slowly setting behind us.

FIFTY-NINE

———— ◆ ————

As I sat on the bench outside the hospital in nearby Caana City, I watched as a steady stream of patients came in. Somehow, even with head wounds and cardiac arrests ambling in past me, the night air felt strangely still. Above me the stars twinkled, shining brighter here than they did back home in the city.

"Mind if I join you?" Quinn asked quietly.

She was backlit by the bright fluorescent glow from the hospital doors, giving her an ethereal glow as she stared down uncertainly at me. She had a few stitches above her left eye and a bandage around her forearm, but otherwise she'd made it out of the Gates okay.

I motioned to the bench beside me. "Go ahead."

"It sounds like Oona is going to pull through," she said once she sat down, close enough to me that our thighs were brushing up against each other.

"Yeah, the doctors said she needed to rest now, but I should be able to see her soon. So that's good news, at least."

"You don't look happy about it."

I breathed in deeply. "I'm happy about Oona. I really am."

"But you're thinking about him."

The lump in my throat grew, and the tears I'd been fighting off since we had left the Gates stung my eyes. "I feel like I let him down. I should've fought harder or done more."

"Gugalanna was too powerful."

"Then I shouldn't have let him come with us," I insisted.

"He had every right to be there, same as you."

"No, I should've—"

"Malin, stop," Quinn said sharply, so I looked up at her. "You couldn't have saved him, okay?"

Part of me knew that was true, but I just kept replaying all the moments over and over again. How when he kissed me, he made everything feel better, and when he put my hand to his chest, promising me I would be all right but knowing that he wouldn't.

I hadn't realized it right away, but that's what he was doing. He'd been given the horrific truth that he wasn't going to make it out, maybe so he could prepare himself or leave, but instead of worrying about himself, he only tried to make sure I would be okay with it.

"He knew I couldn't save him, and he went anyway," I said in a shaky voice.

"What are you talking about?"

"Something he said. . . ." I trailed off as tears spilled down my cheeks.

"Wow." Quinn sounded awestruck. "I didn't realize. . . . Were you in love with him?"

"No." I wiped roughly at my tears with the palm of my hand. "Don't be ridiculous. Valkyries can't fall in love."

"What are you talking about? Of course they can."

I shook my head. "No, we can care about stuff, yeah, and we can love things, but we can't be *in love*. It's not possible."

"Are you serious?" Quinn asked, and I looked over to see her gaping at me.

"Yeah. That's what Marlow always told me, and I've never known of any Valkyries in any kind of serious relationship, so . . . it makes sense."

She leaned back on the bench, looking in shock. "Damn, Malin. Is this why you broke up with me?"

"No. I mean . . . I guess, maybe, it was part of it. I just didn't see the point if we . . ."

"Malin, I loved you." A pained smile had spread across her face. "I was absolutely completely in love with you. So I *know* that Valkyries can fall in love."

I lowered my eyes and swallowed hard. "I . . . I don't know what to say to that."

Quinn sighed and then stood. "You don't have to say anything. I'm gonna go see how Atlas is doing."

SIXTY

———— ◆ ————

I stayed out on the bench a few minutes longer, planning to get myself under control before going back inside to check on Oona.

All night patients had been heading into the hospital, but for a few minutes there was a lapse. The entrance was quiet. But quickly I realized it was too silent. I couldn't hear any cars or anyone talking.

Far off in the distance I heard crickets and howler monkeys, but that was it. Everything had gone away.

I stood, preparing to go see if the hospital was the hive of activity I knew it should be, or see if perhaps I had head trauma that was blocking out sounds. Then I heard a bird—the flapping of wings and a loud caw.

The raven appeared out of the night sky and landed on a light post in front of me.

"What do you want with me?" I shouted up at it. "Why are you following me? I thought you were helping me, but you disappeared when I needed you back there! Why are you doing this to me?"

"I'm sorry I couldn't be of more help," a deep voice, thick with a British accent, came from the left of me, and I jumped back in surprise.

While I had been focused on the raven, I hadn't noticed a man materializing outside with me. He was tall and broad-shouldered, larger than Atlas, even, with dark skin, and his left eyelid was withered shut. He wore an impeccably tailored suit with a charcoal-gray duster over it, and he stepped slowly toward me.

"That's my raven, Muninn." He gestured to the bird. "I sent him to watch over you and help you, but unfortunately there was only so much I could do to intervene. My hands are tied in a lot of this."

"Who are you?" I asked, taking a step back from him. "And what do you want?"

"I'm your boss," he said with a smile. "Odin."

I gasped. "Holy hell." I ran my hand through my hair and tried to figure out if I should bow or kneel or what was the proper protocol when meeting with a god of his caliber. I'd never met a Vanir god, and from everything I had learned, they almost never came to earth anymore.

"I can help you get your friend back," he said, drawing me out of my panic to look up at him. "All is not lost for him, not yet. But I need you to do something for me."

Even though I knew I would do whatever it took to get Asher back, I waited a beat before asking, "What?"

"I need you to help me take on Ereshkigal. We must stop her before the entire world belongs to Kurnugia."

Since there didn't seem to be much of a choice—I couldn't exactly let the world end, and I wanted to save Asher—I nodded once. "What do you need from me?"

NEW YORK TIMES BESTSELLING AUTHOR
AMANDA HOCKING
BETWEEN the BLADE AND THE HEART
VALKYRIE BOOK ONE

NEW YORK TIMES BESTSELLING AUTHOR
AMANDA HOCKING
FROM the EARTH TO THE SHADOWS
VALKYRIE BOOK TWO